The jet had grown taller ...

... from ankle to waist height, and the bright parts of its flame were much brighter now, almost blinding, though somehow still deep red in hue. The dark parts remained absolutely dark, darker than anything Shighius had seen outside of his blackest beetledream. As they stood frozen, momentarily dazzled by the display, the rock around the jet began to bulge and fail, as if pushed up by a force from below. One of the faults began to lengthen in their direction. It forked in two as they backed away from it, and another pair of cracks branched off just a handsbreadth or two below the flames.

"A person," Shigius said before he had finished thinking it. The faultlines were quickly growing to resemble arms, legs, a trunk, like a child's scribble of a man with the mouth of the jet as its tiny head ...

The Dust of Rhll

by J. F. Meskimen

BONGO BOOKS

This is a work of fiction. Names, characters, places, and incidents are the products of the author's imagination, and any resemblance to an actual person, living or dead, business, company, event, or locale is entirely coincidental.

Cover art: Erol Otus
Production design: Richard Lange

Bongo Books
P.O. Box 162096
Sacramento, CA 95816
www.bongo-books.com
info@bongo-books.com

ISBN: 978-1-7375065-3-9

A pronunciation guide can be found on pages 230-31.

I

Standing beside one of the empire's most powerful men, across the desk from the chancellor, Tutor Garong was almost pleased with himself.

He had, after all, much to be proud of. He was, as far as he knew, the only man who had ever worn both a surgeon's bronze and the secret black silk of a serviceman. In service he had taken twelve lives, each a memory most exquisite, though the sum in total, if that was going to be it for him, felt spare and paltry. He owned four slaves he had never seen, who refilled his coffers week by week dredging lizardfeed from the distant Slimes of Megala. All this from a legionary's whore-borne bastard, a poxed son of beans who had risen to Dominance on his own merits.

But he had also fallen to schoolmaster, teaching Blood to snotty rich boys while only dreaming of the real thing spilled in anger. He told himself every day that he was not used up, that they'd put him here to tame him, to cage him, because he frightened them. Yet he didn't feel himself getting any deadlier, and certainly no younger, training future surgeons at the Imperial War and Mining College.

So the chancellor's invitation was interesting, and Senator Taz being there even more so. On the desk there were three crystal flutes of wine and a platter of pickled fingers. Garong understood the meat and drink weren't provided out of kindness, but rather to maintain the pretext of a social call. Since they were just having a friendly talk, no record of what was said needed keeping. Garong was used to working this way, at least when he was doing what he really did.

"Have a seat, Garong," the chancellor said. He looked more like a cartlizard every year. It was the sagging folds at his throat in particular, but also his yellowish eyes and steady, mirthless grin.

Senator Herrin Taz, already seated, was himself nothing lovely to behold, with his sharpened teeth and the dark discoloration around his irises. Garong had encountered him more than once in his former life, which the chancellor apparently knew, since he saw no need for introductions.

"Take a finger, my friends," he beckoned.

Garong had no palate for human flesh, especially not when it was pickled. But he selected a delicate specimen—he imagined a girl, about twelve years old—and plucked the bone clean with a well-aimed nip. The flavor was vile but he savored the cruelty, the unfairness, as if he were tasting the essence of the victim's indignation. It also made his wine taste sweeter.

The chancellor and the senator tossed their bones on the floor for the slaves to clean up, and Garong did the same. Taz took another, the biggest piece, which looked like a man's thumb. He flensed it sloppily with his side teeth, the juice dribbling down his cheek. The chancellor sipped his wine and looked pensive for a moment, his mouth still grinning but his eyes far off and full of concern. He opened a drawer and produced two clay tablets.

"Well, here it is. Two things I can't stop putting together in my mind. You're going to be the first to know about either. One is a secret I've kept for a long time. The other, well, it just came in last week. Allow me to explain.

"We're an imperial college. We'd have no land and no gold in our coffers if it weren't for Senator Taz here and a few of his friends, but we still exist under the emperor's authority. When a new vicar takes the throne, it's customary for the chancellor to send a clay asking His wishes of the college. His ministers draft a bland response, something about making the empire ever richer and her engines of war ever mightier. His Dominance stamps it, they bake it, send it back, and we're left in peace to do our scholarship for as long as He shall reign. That's been the custom.

"But this is what our latest Asb Aq sent."

The chancellor set the newer-looking of the two clays on the desk. It read:

Make me live forever and give me rule over all men.

Beneath was the seal of the emperor and a date ten days past. A full three years had gone by since His coronation. Garong wondered over the long delay. Had it taken His Dominance so long to craft such a brutally simple request? It surely warranted a discussion between the chancellor and the senator, though what part Garong might have was still a mystery—a delicious mystery that tasted of promise and salt and fear. He took an impolitely big drink and didn't regret it.

"Add that to the evidence," Taz said, "that we have another Yirin on our hands."

In Garong's lifetime it had never really mattered who was emperor, cloistered as His Dominance was on His isle. He did control the military, tithing a small contingent to the senate for necessary policing duties. The rest He sent into endless, inconclusive wars of expansion at the empire's far and barbaric frontiers. But only a few civilians saw much evidence of that beyond high taxes, a robust trade in arms, and maimed men sent home to rot in the streets and squares.

A normal emperor's tablets and inscriptions would exhort the Society of Za to be more Zalike; the senate more senatorial; the legions bolder and more persevering; the people more obedient, less concupiscent, harder-working. None of this really touched the lives of the empire's cities and towns or even the men who ran them. Only when a madman took the throne would His

Dominance's directives begin to intrude on everyday affairs, and Yirin, the last emperor like that, had been slain by His own guards right after the Fist, twenty-some years before Garong was born.

The chancellor seemed to want to ask what other evidence there was that such a creature had returned to the palace, but changed the course of his tongue. "So that's half of it. The other half is a little more complicated."

He set down the second clay. This one was apparently decades old and densely packed with glyphs—an inventory, it seemed. Garong couldn't take it all in, but he noted nothing but rare items, the feathers of birds long extinct and gemstones from wilderland veins. What stood out above the rest was a hatchery stocked with living beetles of the highest grade.

"I'm sure you know I was the only scholar who lived through the Fist."

Everyone knew this. Azag, the future chancellor, had been a young tutor in the Maritime Department when the Fist fell. He had been one of the few people, and perhaps the only one still living, who had witnessed the city's destruction from the decks of ships offshore.

"Chancellor Zata, my predecessor, also lived through it. His father was dying then, and he was down here arranging his affairs."

Like the chancellor's House of Azag, the House of Zata was an enormous fish-paste concern as well as one of the empire's oldest and greatest families. Garong had often wondered why the chancellery always seemed to stay in the hands of this particular industry. The one before Zata had been a Lul, from yet another noble family whose fermenteries stunk up half the East End.

"I was groomed for the chancellery because he wanted someone who remembered," Chancellor Azag continued, probably lying or twisting the truth. "Someone who remembered Sasp and the way things were done at the old college. He spent the rest of his life rebuilding the faculty with scholars from around the empire. It's how we ended up with so damned many foreign tutors—no offense, Garong."

"I'm Saspian and nothing else," Garong replied, "despite my features."

"Of course," Taz said, in a tone not exactly agreeing with the words.

"In the end," Chancellor Azag continued, "Zata entrusted me with all his secrets, including this inventory of the old college's crypts."

Garong struggled to contain his excitement. Tutor Lom had mentioned once that his own beetles could survive a hundred years without his help, though they would not increase in number. So it was possible these beetles were still alive if the Fist had not crushed them along with the rest of the old capital. There was no reason the senator or the chancellor, being neither bestiarists nor surgeons, would know this. They'd assume the brood was all dead and gone, and want nothing to do with it anyway unless they were secret fiends. There was plenty else on that clay to interest them.

"A real treasure trove, I'm sure," said Taz. "But what are you suggesting?"

"Well, the way I read it, one order comes before the other. His Dominance didn't tell us to conquer the world first, He told us to make Him immortal first."

"True," the senator conceded. "And I take it there's something in the crypts that you think would do that?"

"Not in the least!" the chancellor chuckled. "But it's perhaps the only item in the world with such a legend surrounding it that its retrieval might count as an effort in good faith to fulfill His

Dominance's requirement."

"The Dust of Rhll?" Garong blurted out. He was out of turn, having not been addressed directly by either of his betters, but he couldn't help himself. The idea was maddening. "You mean to tell me that all this time, it's been under the old college? How did it get there?"

The chancellor paused a while, his eyes boring into Garong. It was quite a feat to bore into eyes that were so accustomed to boring into eyes. It felt like their gazes were wrestling.

"I don't know. No one knows. I don't even know if it's really the Dust of Rhll, or just some old dust they put in a vial and marked as such. But this inventory bears the chancellor's stamp. I'd say that puts us in the right in claiming to believe it."

"Are we also claiming to believe," Garong went on, assuming he couldn't make the repercussions for his impudence any worse, "that the Uthu physicians raised the dead, that the lich was put to holy fire by Walth before he became a sun god and cursed the necromancers to fall up into the night sky forever?"

"Why not?" the chancellor said. "Who's to say what did or didn't happen thousands of years ago? Most importantly, what does it matter?"

"The way I see it," the senator said, "it's the closest thing you have to deliver. My best men would pull together and bring it in if His command were mine. That's how I see it."

"As a surgeon, I can tell you it's medically impossible to raise the dead," Garong put in.

"Then don't tell us," the chancellor laughed.

If this reputedly magical powder was the topic, and his medical expertise wasn't wanted, Garong wondered what he was meant to be doing here. But this time he held his tongue.

"It's a sound concept," the Taz said, "but every account of a survivor—including you, Cim—says the Fist struck the college directly. Everything near it, save the bottom third of the Great Pyramid of Za, was flattened at once. How could such force fail to collapse the crypt, leaving your dust as nothing but a bit more dust amid the rubble?"

It was jarring to Garong to hear the chancellor called by his first name, which he had known once and forgotten. He was simply Chancellor Azag to everyone in Za'ar.

"Zata was convinced otherwise," he said. "I was never allowed down there, obviously, as a junior member of the faculty. But when he passed this clay to me, he told me he was sure it was still there, seventy-eight steps deep under the solid bedrock. Or so he said. But does it really matter?"

Taz smiled. "Of course not. If you simply mount the expedition, you'll have done everything in your power to meet His Dominance's charge."

It began to dawn on Garong what role he was meant to play in this little pantomime. A return to his old ways of sorts, but he didn't like it one bit.

"Rumors of treasure beneath the ruins of Sasp are nothing new," he put in. "There have been parties going up there for decades. The first ones embarked just a week after, when the news reached Glind. None have returned. Why would you expect this one to?"

"It doesn't need to," the chancellor smiled.

"Obviously," Taz said.

"Oh, my dear Garong," the chancellor added, "don't look so stricken. You'll have a much better chance than all the others. You'll have gold, men, lizards, and guides. Isn't that right, Senator?"

Taz looked cornered for a moment, his expression verging on rage. But then he composed himself and broke into a grin to match the chancellor's.

"Indeed," he said. "You'll have everything you could possibly need to make this expedition a success. In return, of course, if you do return, I'll have first pick of whatever you bring back."

"Except the dust, of course," the chancellor put in.

"Yes, not the dust," the senator said, "I've no use for it anyway."

"Of course," Garong said, barely hiding the bitterness in his voice, "unto His Dominance alone be that old, dead Dust of Rhll."

When he was finally released, Garong rushed out into the streets of Za'ar, picking up his pace as soon as his footfall could no longer be heard in the chancellor's office. He paused only briefly in his chambers to swap scholar's robes for an old army tunic, once white, now a moldy-looking beige with a stripe of piss and cinders to decorate the hem. At times like this his low birth served him well. Even without a glance in the mirror, he was sure he was the picture of a dockside ruffian with many years of skulduggery behind him.

The West End, where the college stood, was nice enough if one loved nice things. Garong was not a nice man, but he loved the capital as much as any common aficionado of West End pleasures. By his lights, any fool with coin in his purse could have a fancy meal or a fancy courtesan. Most didn't see that the really interesting opportunities lay east of the pyramids, around that warren of shit-strewn runnels, off streets barely fit for their traffic in rats, in those hells that passed for neighborhoods, inside the tenements of baked mud, aboard their seething desperation. There, everywhere one looked the city had brought a person low, and most of those people could be squeezed for something of worth.

On this occasion, however, Garong had only one thing in

mind, so the young waifs with expressions as grim as any hag's, the terrified newcomers fresh from some village, the old ones weakened by drink or injury, he let pass with nothing more than a leering glance. The avenues were crowded at this time of day, and he was proud of how well he knew the rice-noodle tangle of the East Side's back streets, those deceptively quiet byways where the vilest of the city's trade proceeded. Things only grew more sordid as he approached the Gheevi Docks, the whorehouses giving way to open-air brothels, the unlicensed wine-sinks to brazen beetle dens.

Garong knew where he was going, whom he was looking to meet, and what he was going to propose, but only as he made his way through the stinking alleys did he begin to recognize why. The idea that he might be going to his death didn't bother him nearly as much as the idea that someone could send him off to die. He was, after all, himself a master of schemes, a taker of lives. The truly maddening thing was that he had made himself what he was, and these men who held him in their clutches were born to it.

Too agitated to feel fear, he saw his life as something of his, like a fine wig or a piece of good food, that others were trying to put their hands on. The only thing for it, then, was to make the mission his, to do more for himself than he'd be doing for them. The thought of risking skin for his own ends was always delightful, and the more he thought about what he was planning on doing, his anger at being used as chit in some rich boys' game washed away like a tide.

As the ordure of the slums gave way to the overbearing stench of the fish-paste factories, he knew he was nearing his destination. The Prow was the lowest tavern the docks had to offer, which stood as an accomplishment of sorts. Garong knew Shigius, the master smuggler accountable for half the fiends in Za'ar, would show up if he sat there long enough. So he took a stool at the end of the bar, ordered a bowl of wine, and kept his head low as he nursed it.

He was sitting with his back to a table where men who did nothing ashore but drink were getting into an argument. He felt it verging on a brawl, but he knew how to fight a man behind him. He'd often fought men he couldn't see.

Nonetheless, the smuggler got the drop on him.

"What're you looking for this time?"

A matter-of-fact, side-mouthed mutter from the next stool over. Shigius was there, since when, Garong had no idea.

"Not buying today," Garong said.

He liked a dab of firebeetle now and then, and always bought enough to cover his own use by peddling it to his fellow tutors at the college. Their own master of beetles, Tutor Lom, was far too prim to let his stock go that way. Garong liked going to Shigius just to be able to say, to himself at least, that he got his supply direct from the most notorious smuggler in the empire. He was no man to do things halfway, Garong.

"So, this be a social call?" Shigius said, masking his annoyance with mock amusement. "How's your—camprat? Did you have a pet camprat? I know you aren't married. You've got that feral look of an aging single man. Was it a camprat or a bastard you had? I can't keep track of people, let alone their families." The smuggler spoke fluent Saspian with a slight Nydhian accent, betraying his birth across the Crimson Sea.

"No," said Garong, "I don't have a camprat. I'd like one, but we're not allowed them at the college. Too many things that could go wrong, with all the experiments going on. Can't have pets muzzling around the place."

Shigius only snorted in reply. He was pale for a Nydhian, a northman most likely, with reddish-black hair and eyes so small and nostrils so big that it was impossible to look at him without comparing their sizes. The barmaid came over and Garong bought him a bowl, which made him seem less irritated.

"I have a strange opportunity in front of me, and it could mean a lot for both of us."

Now Shigius laughed in earnest, displaying a mouth in ruins. "Hard to fathom what could mean much to two men so unlike, unless it be gold."

"Gold aplenty, yes. But it will take daring."

"Guts of bronze is all a smuggler needs, and I'm the finest of smugglers." His face darkened. "But you don't mean to raid that Lom fellow's hatchery! I'll have nothing to do with his—Min Khunen weird stuff. Had my fill of that in the jungle."

"Well, what I'm proposing might be weirder, but it isn't that." He paused, he had to admit, for dramatic effect. "I've been tasked with leading an expedition to the ruins of Sasp."

"Then you've been tasked with dying," Shigius said, his expression turning to disgust. "No one has ever come back from such an adventure."

"No one has ever been on such an adventure. We're pledged gold enough to equip, pay, and ration three hundred light courserymen and a hundred foresters as guides. A full train of cartlizards and wagons will be lent us. Bolt throwers and a catapult in case we encounter such foes as must be fought with such. It's not to be another misfit handful of thieves and sword-swingers following some self-styled wizard to their doom amid the burnt stones."

Shigius seemed to consider this carefully. You had to believe in some supernatural evil to think such a party as Garong described could find itself in any great danger. What the Min Khunen beetle sages did was weird indeed, but as Tutor Lom would be quick to point out, it wasn't magic. Garong didn't believe in it, and he trusted that no one who had mastered an art, even the art of smuggling, could be so gullible.

"Who's paying for all that?" Shigius asked.

"Never mind who," Garong said. "You're not stupid or ignorant. You know there are but a few men in the empire with such a fortune to wager with."

"All right. How about this, then. Sure, there's treasure down there. If you flattened Za'ar today, there'd be plenty of treasure under it. But I know what things cost, and treasure alone won't pay for what you describe. So, either you're lying to me, or the expedition is looking for something other than gold."

Garong smiled. It was a calculated smile, designed to draw him in. It would be fine, he decided, to let him in on the stupid, secret reason he was being sent to the ruins of Sasp. The whole being of Shigius was founded on keeping his mouth shut, after all.

"Some things are worth more than gold to those with a glut of it," he said, lowering his voice to signal his confidence. "Under the old college, there's a vault, seventy-eight steps down through solid bedrock. They kept relics down there, items collected since the time of the Beheader. Things purported to contain great power."

"So it's sorcerous material they seek."

The smuggler's face filled with the disdain of sorcery that everyone claimed to hold. The power of sorcery was phony; it was a fraud, a sham; it was outlawed; it was ridiculed as the belief of simpletons and bumpkins. It was frequently sought by all classes of people from the highest to the lowest, keeping an entire underworld, separate from but connected to the one Shigius ran, in business. Whole towns in the Outland were devoted to it.

"More than sorcerous," Garong replied. "They think the Dust of Rhll is down there, sealed with gold in the crystal tube Walth made for it."

Shigius seemed to rack his brains for a moment to recall the myth.

"Prince Rhll? Old geezer that rose from his grave and set everyone on fire? Turned 'em into flaming wraiths and flew off to the stars with 'em?"

Garong nodded. "It's the rise-from-the-grave part that interests our benefactor."

There was nothing to say to that. Even within the illicit world of sorcery, nothing was more forbidden than the necromantic arts.

"So, in sum, there's a person with more money than sense that wants to talk to the dead. He, or she, is sending you somewhere no one comes back from and you want me along. Why? What's in it for me?"

"The old broodstock. I got a peek at the tablets that show what's in the vault. There's a hatchery down there. Strains that don't exist anymore. I like beetle as much as the next man, but I wouldn't know what I'm looking at. I need your nose for the good stuff."

At this Garong knew he had him; Shigius looked at once possessed by the notion.

"It's not impossible they're still alive down there," Shigius said with studied indifference. "They eat their own dead and it's enough to sustain the colony at mass, without population growth, for at least a century. And that's just what's been recorded."

It was jarring to hear such a lowlife speak in the terms of natural philosophy, but Garong supposed he himself made a similar impression on men like the chancellor and Senator Taz. Of course Shigius knew beetles. A man who didn't know his product would never have come to supply half an empire.

"Can I count you in?"

"I'd need some time to think about it. When do you set sail? From Glind, will it be?"

"Sail? We go by land, by the Witchroad."

At this Shigius darkened a little, but the glow of secret riches didn't leave him altogether. It wasn't the thought of witches that was bothering him.

"The long way, is it?" he sniffed. "That's a lot of time to spend with folk. Folk who'll talk, and notice who's out of place, and ask questions. What am I meant to be in all this?"

"Up the Witchroad about four coursings north of the highway, in the Wailing Wood, there's an encampment where the dark foresters gather. They've already sent heralds to spread the word we'll be recruiting our scouts from there. You'll show up with the rest in the guise of an Outlander."

"Seems reasonable, I guess, if you're not Nydhian," Shigius sniffed. "But I'm a coasterner from the Chiggol, east of the hills. Sandies, they call us, learned in handling dugouts and rafts, not antelopes. The northmen will know at once I'm not one of them."

"I thought of that, too," Garong lied. He stalled by sipping his wine before explaining, "The Outlanders come from all parts. Most are just young men from the cities with a price on their heads."

"It's true those Dhularite boys wouldn't know the front of a buck from the rear. Liable to get a horn up their ass first time they try to ride."

Garong snickered. "I take it that's not true of you."

"Nay," Shigius agreed, "in getting away from things, and folk, I suppose I've mounted every species men use for riding and then some. I rode a sealizard once from a wrecked ship to a sound one."

This wasn't true, no truer than Garong's own tale about the typical backgrounds of outland men. He had been deep in the Outland, that much was true, but he'd never bothered to inquire about anyone's past while he was there. Similarly, the sealizard ride was at best something Shigius had heard about happening to somebody else, someone who presumably did not live to tell the tale himself. But it was a good one. It made Garong consider how the sealizard swam, and he liked the way its movements would bring the passenger close to drowning over and over again.

The argument behind them suddenly resolved itself into a round of maudlin sea shanty, making further conversation impossible for the moment. He thought about ordering another bowl, but that would be the start of getting drunk, and he had no time to get drunk. He was no man to do things halfway, Garong.

II

Shigius leaned forward on the bench and cursed as the wheels, the axles, the very frame of his cart groaned at too sharp a tug on the brake-chain. His impatience was earnest but also in keeping with his disguise, as men all around him were acting the same. Just for runs like this, he'd learned enough about driving to pass himself off as a rated lizardman. Whenever he had to, he was always thankful it wasn't his job every day.

The cartlizard was a smelly brute no matter how much you paid for one, and if you were driving, the smellier end was pointed at you. Now, at the busiest hour of a warm Spineday afternoon, with the Avenue of the Most Dominant blocked by some unseen disturbance at the Street of the Gods, Shigius was sharing his air with dozens beyond the two he was driving. He might as well have been bathing in dung.

He had at least a thousand carts to his name (though not in his name), three times as many lizards, and lieutenants to hire contractors to hire men to drive them. But no matter how many fiends he enslaved or how much gold he piled up, there were still certain things he had to do by himself. Supplying the House of Taz with firebeetle was one of those things, and pretending to deliver a cartload of vegetables from the Great Market to the West End was how it got done. Sometimes it amused him, but this was not one of those times.

"Who cares who they are, just run 'em over and keep it moving!" he shouted up the line, prompting angry notes of agreement from the carters around him. There was a feeling of brotherhood among these men, and as long as they saw him as one of their own, he could leave his goods for a moment without fear of pilfering.

It wasn't that he cared about a pile of cabbages and melons—the real goods were under his robe—but appearing not to care would reveal him. So he dismounted in classic lizardman style, vaulting off the bench using his prod to break the fall and landing crouched against the meaty side of his lead brute.

On a two-lizard yoke, he had learned, the right-hand one was always the lead and the carter's favorite. So he feigned affection for the creature, smoothing its leathery wrinkles and imploring it to stay calm during his absence. The drivers nearby looked on approvingly.

"When you get back, you can tell us what the fuck's going on," one said, and the others growled their concurrence.

For a moment after laying his prod in its rack, Shigius paused to search the dull, yellow eye and fixed, corpse-like grin of the lizard—features level with his own, though it went on all fours—for any sign of a response. As always, there was none. The only way he knew to get anything out of a cartlizard was to poke its nerve-endings. The commerce of the empire ran on those pokes, but as a basis for mutual sentiment they felt rather tenuous.

At least the cartlizard's teeth were rounded, and its appetites ran more to swamp slime and ricecake than the parts and guts of people. Shigius couldn't say as much for the courser, the smaller, four-legged lizard that the Saspiards had tamed, sort of, and bred for riding. As he drew near the front of the crowd, he could see a column of men on courserback headed from the Senatorial Plaza to the Street of the Gods.

The coursers looked fearsome, the riders much more so. To a smuggler, they represented the worst possible combination of authorities, two parties all dressed in black and white: robed vicars from the Society of Za, and a troop of senatorial sergeants in their government livery. One force was charged with keeping the populace moral, and the other with maintaining order around the public buildings of the central city. Seeing them together was almost enough to make Shigius abort his run. When he realized the sergeants were carrying not their usual arms but slave-catching equipment—weighted nets, bronze shackles, rope tethers, and pole-snares—every nerve in his body commanded him to flee.

Instead, he boldly threw back his cowl, aping the rest of the crowd's determination to get a better look, as he elbowed his way to the front. It was strange to see so many ranks of Saspiard and foreigner sharing the same predicament. While most of the frustrated were people like the man he was pretending to be— humble but free, poorly clad but covered, paid in coin rather than scraps—there were also a number of slaves, naked except for bronze collars. Halted in transit with no one to whip them, they'd set down their burdens and were gawking along with the rest.

There were fancy Saspiards, too. Whatever the obstruction was, it wasn't parting for anyone. The West End crowd sat atop fine saddlery or unseen behind the silken drapes of their palanquins, bearers holding them aloft for a better view as they peeped through the cracks. Shigius found his place at the front of the crowd by getting a touch closer to one of their coursers than anyone else was willing to stand.

It was a big Red Racer, a male with deep ruby scales and a perfect smile, obviously tended at one of the capital's finest stables. The man sitting on the courser was too short to have mounted it without using the stirrup, and he wore a brief robe of pink silk over bicolored leggings. Nonetheless, Shigius could see he had perfect control over his lizard. Unless he angered the man, he had nothing to fear from it.

The crowd was being held back by a line of sergeants on foot bearing ordinary polearms and tower shields. Their weapons were raised, not leveled at the crowd, and their expressions were more bored than hostile. Behind them, appearing considerably fiercer, their mounted comrades and the holy vicars were advancing on a separate crowd that was gathered between the two colossal statues of Za flanking the Street of the Gods.

"Behold *the* apostate!" boomed a man's voice from above them.

With ears made keen by years of guilty vigilance, Shigius quickly pinpointed the voice to the phallus of the farther colossus, a carved pillar of limestone jutting out above the roofline of the temples beyond. The carving was blocky and crude like the rest of the lizard-headed humanoid form it belonged to, with a line of foreskin roughly etched around its tip. Such sculptural features, ubiquitous along the empire's highways and around its public squares, had a well-known habit of slipping out of their notches and crushing passers-by, and Shigius, who'd never seen a person stand on one before, wondered how long it could bear the speaker's weight.

He was an elderly man in a Master's robe that he surely had no right to be wearing. He was perched atop the stone member flailing his skinny arms in the air, whether for emphasis or to keep his balance, Shigius couldn't say. No matter how ridiculous he looked, it was impressive that such a frail-looking person had climbed to such heights.

"Our way is *the* Way of Za! The *silver* swords will cast *out* the purple apostasy! Lo!"

One of them, *then.* Shigius allowed a wave of genuine disgust to cross his face. It was fine to show his feelings toward the Silver Prophets, the most annoying breed of street preacher currently plaguing the city, spouting gibberish about men in silver armor coming across the ocean to punish the Saspians for not being Saspian enough. Though the prophets themselves had been banned long ago, he hadn't heard anything about merely listening to the Prophecy being outlawed. Apparently, it had been.

Too bad for the onlookers. As the first screams of terror broke loose from the crowd, Shigius fixed his attention on the coursers. They were all of the brown Shadaghi strain, the least expensive and most common variety, standard for common soldiers, smallholders, taxmen, and "property wardens," as the Saspians called their slave-catching contractors. Compared to the Red Racer, the Shadaghi lizards were dull, lean, and bony, and most of them had a few missing fangs. But they were a landrace of the Crescent, not an import from Old Saspia, and closer to the wild by centuries of breeding. They were the kind of courser you put your men on if you cared less about losing a few to mishap than you did about reducing the enemy to a pile of bloody tags.

But that wasn't always desirable, even to a Saspian, and in this case not only were the coursers' gizzards swollen with meat; their lids were also drooping, a sign that sandbeetle had been applied to their gums. Shigius suppressed a chortle at the thought of his second-most popular product in the hands of his avowed archenemies. How many sergeants, how many of the holy vicars themselves had taken a secret taste while preparing for their mission? How many would end up fiends at *his* command? *How's that for your Way of Za, eh?* The Saspians were a funny breed, outlawing the beetle while prescribing it indiscriminately to man and lizard alike. Half his fiends came to him by way of their surgeons.

As for the congregants, it was all the worse for them that the coursers were drugged: better to be devoured in the street than taken alive by the Society or the Senate. The Senate would send their catch to the slimes, or chain them to the oars, two places few people survived a full year and fewer still would want to. As for the

Society, in the worship of Za, God of Dominance, the humiliation and punishment of slaves was a sacrament, and the Masters' hunger for flesh was boundless. The difference was between great pain and certain death on the one hand, greater pain and certain death on the other.

"Nay! *Do* not run, my brethren! Let righteousness *be* your shield! Hold fast, for Za *is* your lord and none but *Za* can be your master!"

Shigius idly wondered what they were going to do about him—bring ladders, or just knock him down with an arrow? It seemed that getting slaves was a higher priority than removing the preacher. One neatly-dressed woman, caught around the shoulders in a snare, started wailing loudly enough to drown out the rest of the commotion until a sergeant rode past and knocked her out with his fist. Free citizens of the empire had a few rights, but for all except the rich these were wholly rescinded at the slightest infraction. It seemed a high price to pay for listening to a silly sermon.

"Hold *fast* your lines!" the old man was still screaming from his penile perch. His voice had grown more shrill against the din. "If ye *be* cowards, the sons of silver *will* take ye *with* the apostate! Stay!"

A number of those who were not heeding his words had by then run close enough to make the sergeants blocking the street turn to face them. Some stopped short when they saw the points, the blades, the bronze-bossed shields in their path. Others attempted to run between them. A tall man with a long, pointed beard got through and found himself running directly at Shigius. Shaking off an urge to pull his knife, Shigius stepped aside, jostling a portly Walthorian in a tattered cape of grey wool. The Walthorian swore. The fleeing man shrieked.

Turning back, Shigius saw that the little senator on the big Red

Racer had swiftly and silently wheeled his lizard around to take him from the flank. Where Shigius had been standing a moment before, the courser had clamped his right side, fangs impaling his liver in half a dozen places. The spurts of blood were so many and so fierce it was more of a storm than a wound.

The man went silent, eyes wide as moons, the flesh of his face turning chalky. The Walthorian, cursing him a moment ago, was now holding Shigius like a frightened child clutching at his mother. The scene grew progressively more hideous as the lizard went about its work, dissecting the man with the grace of a surgeon, pulling out the best parts first.

If this little pink-robed fucker has any sandbeetle around the house, or any meat for that matter, I guess he decided not to share it with his lizard this morning. Of all the laws the Senate passed, he thought it might be useful to have one against riding hungry coursers on the common thoroughfares. But they'd never allow any law they passed to get in the way of one of their own.

In front of him, the sergeants were cursing their luck at having lost a good-looking prospect. One of them was yelling that they should've been armed with snares like the coursery, another shouting back that they didn't want to start a panic up and down the whole fucking avenue. A third argued that if they didn't shut the fuck up before the centurion heard them, he'd have them skinned and packed in salt. They looked ridiculous bickering under their shiny, crested helmets, and Shigius held back a grin, the carnage forgotten as quickly as it had occurred.

Most longtime residents of Za'ar had seen more than one mishap with a courser, not to mention a neverending round of public flayings, beheadings, burnings, disembowelings, and dismemberments. Though their faces showed fear and revulsion, the crowd behind the line of sergeants was not backing away from the mess the Red Racer was making. They had places to go, and they weren't going to break stride over something so mundane as a courser eating a person.

The centurion's inquiry into the death would not hold them up for long.

"He was a fugitive from justice, obviously," the pink-robed rider said. "I had no choice."

"Of course, Senator. I hope none of this has been too great an inconvenience."

The senator scowled and nodded ambiguously. There were two kinds of "senator" in the empire: every rich man held the title, but only a few sat and voted in the palace. Such deference from a centurion of the sergeants meant this was one of the latter. The centurion was Nydhian, a big, dark-skinned man with a beard half-grown over half a day, and eyebrows like black hedges. He was mounted on a courser called a Blue, another fine lineage from the lost Saspiard homeland. There were only three centuries of sergeants in total, which made the commander of one of them a high-ranking figure around the capital.

The package under Shigius' robe burned against his skin. It might have been fear, the sensation of being noticed, or it might have been that the flour he'd smoked that morning was growing thin in his blood. By this time, he'd been planning to be done with his errand and well on his way back to the Great Market, to Yaay, to the best smoke he'd have all week, driving an empty cart with nothing but gold on his person. Instead, he'd have to tamp down the early rumblings of withdrawal at the House of Taz, a grim prospect considering most of the people in that house were themselves secret users of the beetle.

Shigius was no fiend. He used with discipline. Nonetheless, the most disciplined user felt at least a little like a fiend when he was coming down. The dispersal of the congregants was proceeding too sluggishly against his raw nerves. He closed his eyes and chased the fading shapes and colors of the morning's beetledream. *Not for too long, not so they'll notice. Gods, it is hard to be a smuggler.*

When he opened his eyes, he saw the faces of the new-made slaves being led away. A few looked indignant or defiant, many wept, and occasionally one would scream, eliciting a punch or whiplash from the nearest of their captors. They weren't acting like criminals, like people who'd known they were doing something wrong before they were caught. It was just like the Saspiards to announce a new law this way, letting terror and rumor do the work of a hundred heralds. They were an efficient race.

Soon enough, the intersection was clear, and Shigius made his way back to his cart. The good will of his fellow drivers would only last until he held them up further by remaining absent after the sergeants stood down. So he made sure he was back in his seat well before the cart ahead began rolling, ready to prod his team in the haunches and get their big stumps of legs off the ground again.

Cart traffic was still thick as he passed the colossi at the Street of the Gods, but, between the spokes of the wheels and through gaps in the stacks of freight, he caught glimpses of the broken body of the preacher lying on the cobbles. It seemed they'd knocked him out with a slingstone and let him drop. *Efficient.* He was bent up wrong in every way, like a crushed bug. A Blue Service man, gaunt and dull-looking in his dirty white tunic, was directing a slave to set straw around the corpse to prevent the pool of blood from becoming yet another obstruction on the avenue.

West of that intersection was where the city turned sweet-smelling and gentle, the tenements of the east side and the brutal palaces of the central district giving way to Nydhian-style pleasure villas and expensive taverns designed to look like charming, rustic inns. The avenue was lined with flower-beds instead of running slops. More of the residents traveled by palanquin than on foot, filling the avenue with flowing silk and eunuchs in brightly-colored livery.

At Khlokhli Square, the exotic-animal market was in full bloom, with all the furriers, saddlers, and perfumers of the West End shops picking over the offerings of pelts and glands. The plain, white buildings of the Imperial War and Mining College peeked over the gaudy rooftops. It reminded Shigius of Garong and his offer.

He'd never felt more like getting out of town for a while. If they were trying to round up all the Silver Sillies, the sergeants and vicars would be out in force for weeks. It would be far too easy for a man just moving around the city, going about his private business, not meaning to bother anyone, to get caught up in something like that. Besides, he was sure the centurion had noted him as a fellow countryman, and a rogue-looking one at that. It seemed prudent to give him time to forget such a face as his.

But then he checked himself. *Prudent?* The word for running from phantom fear into known danger was *daft.* The beetle, or rather lack of it, must have been doing the talking in his head. He had a good thing going in Za'ar, and with his lieutenants in place around the empire and across the sea, he hadn't needed to leave the city in years. Things were flowing smoothly at last, in every direction, and he wasn't about to let a little trouble in the streets make him stumble.

Still, he continued to mull the tutor's offer as he executed the painfully wide turn into the nameless alley behind the Way of the Taz. This was a narrow lane of crushed rock running along an open swale that carried the filth and trash from the great houses above to the city sewer. Along the slope leading up to the houses, the use of the land was plain and practical, courser cages and grassfowl coops between the stone-lined ditches that carried off the drainage, and cartwheel-ruts for the comings and goings of men like the one he was pretending to be. The gardens and statuary were reserved for the fronts of great houses, whose rear ends were rather plain. The House of Taz was plainest of all, a chunk of black granite amid cakes of pink and yellow plaster.

He pulled his team up at the turnaround. This was a place to dismount respectfully, and so he did, setting his prod on the rack first and using the step. Aphynhis, the head cook, was waiting with her arms crossed, looking most displeased. She was another free Nydhian, around fifty years old, built as square as the house she served, with a face like the knuckle of a thumb.

"You're late, Naiman," she snarled, but not without affection.

This was just the sort of woman "Naiman" would naturally pair with, so Shigius had to flirt to maintain his façade. He would've taken it all the way if it came down to that. She wasn't bad, really. With enough wine and a good reason, no woman was.

"Fondest regrets, m'lady," he said with an ostentatious bow.

"Convey them to the Senator," she replied, "it's him whose soup's to be late now."

"Well, if he complains, you can let him know it's his own boys to blame. Sarges had the Most Dominant blocked, both ways, all over some silly preacher."

The kitchen slaves, dressed in nothing but collars and aprons, were already hauling the vegetables into the house. Aphynhis walked over to give her order a perfunctory examination. As always, the produce was excellent. There was no need for Shigius to cut corners when the profit lay elsewhere. There was no need for the cook to ask questions when she was getting good ingredients at a good price.

"Well, late or not, I can't complain about these cabbages," she smiled, giving one a squeeze with her huge, meaty hand. "You'd think it was grown in the market square and cut this morning."

"Only the best for you, my dear," he said, aware that his ugliness and generally sour look made his smile more charming when it cracked. "Forgive me, I've been much delayed. Might I trouble you for use of the servant's garderobe?"

"Every time!" Aphynhis laughed loudly. "By Jurgar, Naiman, you've got a woman's bladder. Makes me wonder about the size of the spigot."

"Perhaps one of these days," he winked over his shoulder, heading for the outhouse, "your curiosity will get the better of you!"

The garderobe, designed for servants' use, was nothing fancy: a mud-brick structure just big enough to surround a wooden bench with four ass-sized holes, drilled uncomfortably close together. Someone had dragged in a leafy branch to clean with, but the leaves had grown too dry to be useful. The stench was as you would expect. It wasn't the kind of place you'd expect to find a young man like Irrian Taz, but there he stood.

At sixteen, the boy already towered over Shigius. His years at the Zaist academy had built up his muscles, now proudly adorned with a fresh crop of body hair. He had the pale skin and menacing courser grin of a purebred Saspian aristocrat, and a nose as thirsty as any gutter fiend's. As a youth under instruction, he wore nothing but a plain white tunic, but he somehow managed to wear it with fashionable arrogance.

"I've been breathing slave-shit in here for an hour. How do you do?"

"I do as I do. There was trouble in the streets that delayed me."

The slap seemed to hang in the air forever on the way to his face. Shigius had ample time to consider whether or not to block it and perhaps show the boy just a little of what a man who knew how to fight could do to him. There was so much meat behind that sailing palm, the blow was sure to be more than trivial. But getting hurt was only the smallest consideration.

Irrian Taz was a wily young fellow who had found Shigius by working his way up the chain, using bribes and threats to find the supplier of each supplier. In the end, it had been Shigius' own choice to meet the boy and start serving him. Like any Black Service or Society man attempting the same approach, of which there was always at least one, Irrian could have been stopped well before reaching Shigius. But an invitation to the House of Taz didn't seem like a bad thing to have, nor did information about the peccadilloes of its favorite son.

So he let the slap land on his cheek. His vision went red and he felt his brain splashing against the inside of his skull. The boy hit hard.

"You'll speak to me with respect in my house, Nydhian."

Even as he tasted blood where cheek had come to grips with tooth, Shigius had to stop himself from laughing out loud. My house. Of course, he'd meant the property in general, but it came out sounding like the stinking garderobe was his home. *The perfect home for a budding young fiend like yourself.*

"My apologies, sire," he said, rubbing his face. "I was delayed so long I forgot my manners."

Irrian snickered. "You amuse me. Keep it up. It might save your skin someday."

Shigius reached under his robe for the package: four talons of top-grade overseas flour, wrapped in parchment. It was enough to keep the whole college up for a moon. Irrian's childish glee at the sight made Shigius shudder. The boy was overgrown, cruel, rich, strong, fiending, perhaps, but still a boy. He wasn't a fiend, really. He wanted something to brag about, something to show his friends how grown-up and suave and unrestricted he was. With the Society running rampant, it was only a matter of time before he found himself under questioning, at which point he would piss himself like the little boy he was, and tell all.

It took all the effort Shigius had to keep from shaking as he handed off the package. *Remember, he knows faces, not places.* Shigius viewed it as a matter of hygiene that his customers never saw any place where he stayed, nor any hatchery, flour mill, or storehouse he was using. His face was known to many, but minus a place, it was just another face in the sea of faces called Za'ar. If he absented himself from the city, he'd leave nothing but a tale and, by all appearances, a foolish boy tricked into believing some ordinary rogue was an infamous smuggler.

The coins that Irrian put in his hand were a comfort. They glowed with warmth from being hidden next to the boy's skin, and, even without looking at them, Shigius could tell they were freshly minted. In his experience, there had been no bump in any road that the right amount of gold couldn't smooth. Roads were for traffic, but also for fleeing. And Tutor Garong supposedly had gold by the cartload for the little jaunt he was planning.

With these thoughts turning over in his head, Shigius left Irrian in the outhouse and walked back to his cart. The slaves, moving at the speed of a whip, had already unloaded it down to the last melon and disappeared into the house. Aphynhis was pressing a Taz seal into the damp clay at the bottom of his invoice, making it redeemable at any counting-house in the city.

"As much as I'd like to stay and chat a bit, Naiman," she smiled, "I've got a soup to boil. See you next time."

She turned and walked back into the house with a wiggle in her wide, wide hips.

Shigius climbed onto the bench and raised his prod, not sure when or if next time was to be.

Spineday, the last of ten in a Saspian week, was a day of rest for most free people in the empire. At The Water Lily Peak Academy for the Strengthening of Morals and Physique in Young Ladies of Appropriate Breeding, the upperclass girls would be released to the custody of their fathers at sunset every Lungday, presumably to spend the day of rest in courtship, receiving young gentlemen of appropriate breeding. But no one was courting Aga Taz at the moment, so she spent her Spinedays gazing out the tiny window of her childhood bedchamber onto the bleak back lot of the House of Taz.

She noticed things. It distracted her from brooding over why no one was courting her at the moment. She noticed which of the kitchen slaves were freshly marked by the whip, and how it seemed to be the same ones every week. She noticed that a new lizardman started bringing in the vegetable cart. She noticed how ugly he was, and how he flirted with the cook, who flirted back like she didn't have eyes. She noticed Irrian spending long stretches in the servants' garderobe every Spineday, but somehow she never caught a glimpse of the servant or slave whose company he was presumably enjoying in there.

They were close, Aga and Irrian. People often thought they were twins, though she was older by a year, and they had once been close like twins. But in the past year he had reached the Age of Dominance and commenced from the West End Township School to the Imperial War and Mining College, and their lives had grown apart. The township school kept boys through the week like her academy, and she'd grown used to spending lazy Spinedays getting into mischief with Irrian around the great house. But now he lived at home all week, coming and going as he pleased, mostly going. He spent more of his Spineday hours in the servants' garderobe than he did with his favorite sister.

The first couple of times the lizardman walked in on whatever he was up to in there, Aga thought nothing of it. Surely men in his trade were used to encountering that sort of thing where they went about their less aristocratic business. But the third time, though again the ugly carter stayed no longer than a man would need to empty his bladder, she knew it was no coincidence. Irrian was getting something from this ugly little foreigner, and it surely wasn't the tender comfort of his loving embrace.

So when he left the garderobe that Spineday, adjusting his tunic as if he'd done what might be expected of him in there, Aga followed her brother to his chambers and stood outside his door. She thought to burst in right then, but instead, she waited and listened. There was an angry, rhythmic scraping sound she couldn't place at first, and Irrian quietly cursing. He was, she realized, striking flint against bronze without success. *What kind of Taz lights his own lamp, anyway?* Of course he had no idea what he was doing. He did succeed at last, the sound of his struggle replaced by the familiar smells of a lit wick and oil igniting. It was such an absurd little thing for him to accomplish. *Did we lose all our slaves in some fiscal debacle while he was out in the garderobe?* Perhaps it was one of the frivolous arts they'd been teaching him at the college, the ones their father complained about.

Then the smell changed. It was like peppercorns burning in a pan, but with a disturbing, alien undertone of something that should not be in food. *Cooking, now, is he?* She nearly laughed aloud at the thought. But the quiet that followed was too quiet. Irrian made noise when he was by himself, pacing and thinking out loud and pushing things out of his way. Aga had been picturing herself flinging open the door, catching him at something, but instead she cracked it just enough to fit her slender body through, and latched it silently behind her.

The room was dark, curtains drawn across the expanse of windows overlooking the garden, distilled-oil fixtures stoppered down to the faintest glow. By the only source of light, the little lamp she'd heard him working at so laboriously, she found her brother sprawled on his bed as if someone had dropped him there from a height. He was dressed in his student garb of a white ripreed tunic, much like Aga's shift, but with short sleeves instead of none at all. It left his lower legs and forearms bare. His flesh looked rougher and darker than the last time she'd taken notice, but perhaps it was just the contrast with his fine white Walthorian goatswool bedspread, as well as the white of his tunic and the dimness of the room, that made it seem so.

We're more different than we've ever been, she thought as her eyes followed the bulging veins of his arm down to a big, well-fleeced, and grasping hand. But what was it grasping? It looked like a tiny flute. She nearly tittered again at the thought of her brother cooking and practicing the flute and learning how to light lamps like a chambermaid. But really, what was the thing in his hand? Not a flute, certainly. She leaned in to examine it and the peppery smell grew stronger, as if it emanated from this mysterious instrument.

The oil lamp flickered on a shelf beside the bed, and as the light shifted Aga could see a wisp of smoke rising from the end of the thing. *A pipe—for smoking?* The details of all she had just heard, smelled, and seen fell at once into place and made sense.

Irrian was smoking something. He had to light the lamp himself because no one else could know why he needed the flame. *Was that—could it be—the firebeetle?* They said it smelled spicy, and the stronger strains would lay a user out like this. Visions of toothless, noseless, eyeless fiends washed over her, memories from times she'd made the mistake of cracking the drapes as her palanquin passed through the wrong neighborhood.

He can't, he won't. That doesn't happen to us. We're better. We've proven we're better, age after age since the dawn of time. Gingerly she withdrew the pipe from his strong but flaccid fingers. It was made of clay, and too hot to touch at the burning end. She sniffed it. The smell seemed familiar now, from long ago, from infancy. *Did Father? Rubbish.* The august Senator Taz led the yearly campaign for more troops to stamp out the scourge of beetle-smuggling. If she'd smelled it as a babe, the odor must have drifted in from the slaves' quarters, or up to her palanquin from some fiend lighting his pipe in the gutter.

"Aga," his voice came croaking, strange, not his at all. "Aga, my love."

She looked up from the thing she was holding and saw that he was smiling. His eyes still appeared to be shut, making her wonder how he knew it was her. He could've been in so much trouble if it were anyone else. He didn't show the least sign of caring.

"Irrian, what do you think you're doing?"

"I think?" He laughed, a high, almost girlish laugh she'd never heard from him before. *Is that how I laugh?* "I think. I think. I think I'm doing, doing, just, just great, and it's so very kind of you to ask."

"If Mother or Father saw you like this—"

"Like what, Aga?" He suddenly sounded like himself again, and lucid. "Like what am I?"

"I'm not stupid. I know what this is," she said, brandishing the warm end of the pipe at him like a dagger.

"And what do you think it makes people like?"

"It turns them fiend. They sink to the gutter and rot from the inside out."

"But what does it do to a Taz? The same as anyone else? Could it bring one of *us* low? Is it stronger than Za Himself?"

He had a point. The family did follow different rules from the rest of humanity, and she'd already been thinking along these lines. Even if the beetle was stronger than most men, a Taz could be stronger than it, as they were stronger than most men in all other matters. Perhaps people like them, or at least men like Irrian, were allowed to have their hobbies, their private passions— their freedom, as others had their masters.

"What does it feel like?"

"You'll never know," he snarled, shooting upright and snatching the pipe from her hand with a lunge. No sooner did he have it than he fell back on the bed, reverting at once to a state of drugged lassitude. His eyes were hooded; his expression, pompous. "I'll not be responsible for setting you on this path. I'm going to be a surgeon. You're going to be a great man's wife. Imagine what he would think if he found out you'd smoked the beetle. Imagine what my patients would think if they found out I never had."

Irrian had been talking about joining the medical course at the college for the past few weeks, and now it was clear to her why. He was going to be one of *those* surgeons. They were everywhere; their mother took an occasional dab of sandbeetle paste in her wine, courtesy of a local one, when her nerves got the better of her.

Aga was honestly quite squeamish about putting any part of an insect into her body in any manner. She'd had copperbeetle once, for a bad attack of the flux, and had to think about other things to make herself swallow it. But she absolutely hated what Irrian had said. If he could have something, she could have it too, and that was that. No matter what the Grandmaster had proclaimed at his commencement exercises, he was no man yet, any more than she was already a woman. They were still brother and sister, living as children in their parents' house, as they had since he was born. What he'd said was unfair and he knew it. She knew he knew by the nasty little grin he was wearing.

"I'll tell," she pronounced. "You have to share with me, or I'll tell."

"And then what?" Irrian chuckled. "They'll make me go live in the dormitory with the poor and foreign students. What do you think happens there? I'd never lack for good flour in my pipe, nor a mouth to feed my meat."

"You're hideous. Put more of that stuff in it for me or I'll go tell right now."

Right now were the important words for him. There was no long-term consequence that could bother him, but he was having his fun at the moment and didn't want it spoiled by the interruption.

"All right. But you have to promise to do something for me."

Aga shuddered. *Surely he doesn't mean* that. *He couldn't.*

"What."

"Hhule Capaz. I want some time alone with her. Make it happen."

Hhule Capaz. She was sick of hearing that name on the tongues of boys. The girl was cheap, that was all. Her father was a provincial senator who'd squandered his family fortune to keep a lavish house in the capital. To hear Aga's father speak of him, Wan Capaz would sooner or later have to sell himself into slavery to pay his debts, and he'd be lucky to end in the slimes instead of being torn to pieces on stage for the amusement of all the people he'd annoyed. Though Aga didn't know Hhule well—no one did—she felt she could safely assume the child of such a man to be equally degenerate. That was why they were all saying her name. She was cheap. They wanted a cheap and undemanding place to stop off on the way to marrying someone like Aga.

Still, she was uneasy that it might be something more. Among the Water Lily Peak girls, Hhule was a follower, never starting anything, just going along, never the first to open her mouth, really only speaking when it was required of her. Her features were soft and rounded, as if touched by native, servile, Crescentine blood. Aga had the pure lines of a classical Saspian beauty, hard and angular, and where it was her place—among girls, for instance— she carried herself with the Dominance of a senator, of her father and his forefathers. She was supposed to be the bride that all the boys aspired to, and not just because there were countries smaller than her dowry.

But what if they didn't aspire to her, or the closest thing to her they could get? What if they truly wished for something lesser? Irrian himself, who could have anyone but Aga, just as she ought to be able to have anyone but him—for him to want a crack at Hhule Capaz was unsettling. She couldn't understand what the boys saw in such a halfway kind of person, when they had such a selection of slaves and whores around the capital, and so many proper girls needing a husband. *Well, at least if it's Irrian going at her, it won't be one of the ones I have to choose from.*

"Done," she said. His leer in response was enough to make her regret the bargain, as if the mere thought of smoking the beetle weren't daunting enough on its own. But she had to admit she was curious. Anyone would be, growing up around so much talk of something, hearing every day how it's the worst thing in the world. If she were being entirely honest with herself, Aga would have to admit she'd always known she'd try it the first time it was offered. She hadn't foreseen orchestrating the opportunity this way, but so be it. This was a matter of principle.

The stuff was wrapped in parchment, concealed at the waist of Irrian's tunic. She was surprised she hadn't noticed the bulge as she studied him in his stupor. He unfolded it twice—the packet was folded a certain way, and his confidence in going about opening it made her certain he'd done this before. Inside was a pile of powder that looked black to her at first, like the peppercorns she'd thought she smelled. But then the lamplight changed and the powder glowed red. It was both colors, like a burning coal, shifting between the two as the light and her eyes moved around it. Aga idly considered how elegant a gown like that would be. Squinting, she thought she saw legs, antennas, and bits of shell ground up in it, so she quit squinting right away.

"I can't fill the pipe for you if you don't give it back to me," Irrian snickered.

Feeling as foolish as he intended her to, she handed the pipe to him and watched as he dipped the end in the flour. After examining it and brushing a little excess back into the packet, he beckoned her.

"Come sit on the bed. You're going to want it to fall back on."

She sat down stiffly next to him, wondering what kind of pranks he might get up to once he got her at a disadvantage. But she was doing this. Pranks or no pranks, he wouldn't trick her into backing out. Instead of handing her the pipe, he placed it gently against her mouth and raised the oil lamp. The mouthpiece had a thin coating of sticky resin that burned where it touched her lips. Her misgivings and her determination to go forward both soared to new heights at the moment the flame touched the powder.

"Suck," Irrian commanded, and, without looking up at him, she could feel how much he savored her compliance. The smoke felt cool at first, the same way a scalding bath could confuse a testing finger. But then her whole mouth was ablaze, like she'd just had an enormous bite of the hottest Shadaghi-style dish she'd ever regretted tasting. It was the same down her windpipe, but not quite so unpleasant, just a warmth entering places inside her where she'd never felt a temperature before. She felt something rattling and crashing that was either the contents of her skull or else the whole House of Taz falling down around her. She wanted to turn back; it didn't seem fair that she couldn't now.

Even more unfairly, it killed her. She'd never heard of someone dying just from trying firebeetle once, but Aga Taz was apparently the first. She found herself in total silence and absolute darkness. She was dead. The darkness had been there forever, would be there forever, went on forever in every direction. It was how she'd always pictured death, except that she was there, as quiet and still as a corpse in a tomb, but there. And all because of her stupid brother.

But then she realized the darkness was not death, but the shadow of something. She could feel it looming over her, blocking out everything else, not just a thing but the only Thing. It might have been the moon in its dark phase. It might have been Irrian getting between her and the light of the lamp.

Whatever it was, the world she had lost began to reassemble in its shadow. First, the shadow split into sea and sky, equally dark but palpably different in substance. Her own body spanned them, floating on both, as if up and down had yet to be invented. In the water she could feel the first stirrings of life, and then a great upheaval—was she vomiting?—as earth was thrown up from the ocean's bottom, and the lands of the world were formed.

Aga found herself where she'd been before, but at the dawn of time, on the patch of mud that would someday be Za'ar. Her true homeland, the stormy isle whose songs the Maids of the Way would lead the Peak girls in droning every day at dawn, Old Saspia was but a distant speck on the far horizon, if she could see it at all. Of history, she witnessed only Crescentine foolishness. The dead turned lich and rose from their graves. Their breath turned men and women and beasts into fiery wraiths, spreading the fire across the land until Walth, while he was still a man, banished the liches and their spawn to the night sky. Nonsense, but she watched it all and hated herself for admiring its beauty.

After Walth ascended and became the noonday sun, pyramids rose and towns began to sprawl around them. In the west, they piled up temples to the sunset; in the east, mounds honoring the dawn. Armies met in fields and made each other smaller; walls rose around towns; the first sieges were laid. When her people finally appeared on the scene, they were tiny at first in the midst of what had already been built, but the path of their destruction was great, soon surpassing all that had ever been destroyed before.

She was heartened by this until she realized the world she was seeing was not her own. It was Hhule's. It was the first Capaz, not the first Taz, that Aga saw jeering at the defeated Crescentines as they felt his cold bronze at their necks and begged for enslavement. A generation, two, three passed with the newmade thralls toiling and breeding under their masters' roof. Aga watched in horror as one took his revenge atop a Capaz woman, and not by force. No, the slut invited him behind her and howled like a rutting beast as he left his mark, creating a line of purple-blooded monsters that, hundreds of years later, would still mingle in respectable society. Aga saw North Nydhia sundered from the empire, watched the Fist strike Old Sasp, and still the Capaz abided, just as they had since the crime of that woman, soft and weak, pretending to be real Saspians, getting away with it.

This made Aga so angry that Hhule's world began to burn, as the liches and wraiths had once set it afire, but thoroughly this time. Even after all she could see was consumed, her rage found yet more fuel in her brother's laughter, a faraway echo at first, drawing nearer as the fire burned brighter. She squinted into the glare, and as her eyes grew accustomed to it, she could see she was lying flat on his bed, just as he had predicted. The fire was still around her, but so were the familiar contours of the room, and so was her brother, his hands on her shoulders, a strong arm crossing her collarbones, hot puffs of his laughter on her cheek.

"You know," he said as his mirth subsided, "most people try it up their nose before they smoke it, Princess Pass-the-Pipe."

"Princess Pass-the-Pipe indeed."

At first Aga wasn't sure if her mother's voice was another figment of the dream or whatever she'd just had, or if the sound was coming out of her own mouth. But Gihha Taz was in the room, and Irrian seemed to have no better idea than Aga did as to when she'd entered, or what she'd seen. She was smoldering around the edges with the lingering flames of the dream, but it was her in the flesh, without a doubt. Her face was slathered with putty and shiny paint wherever it showed itself a day older than Aga's, and the gloss catching the lamplight assured her the apparition was real.

"It reeks like a brothel in here. Open the window, and don't ever let your father catch you like this."

Behind the cosmetics, her expression was grim with disappointment, not anger. What they'd been doing, the face said, was simply too exhausting to be dealt with.

"I expect better of you, Aga," she added, pointedly leaving out

Irrian.

She then turned and exited the room, latching the door behind her with the caution of an accomplice.

Once, and only once, Shigius had gotten up the nerve to ask Yaay where her beetle came from.

"You. Silly."

When they were alone, they spoke her native tongue. Few outsiders could crack Min Khunen, and he attributed much of his success to his hard-earned mastery of it. The forest fever still soaked him some nights, and that was the smallest part of what the learning had cost him.

"You know what I mean!" he said, inflecting the words with humorous impatience. It was a language of few syllables and many nuances.

"My beetle." A tiny upturn crossed her mouth, Yaay's version of a smile, rarely seen. "The beetle *I* use. That uses me. That I give you. That gives itself to you."

"Yes. That beetle. I know where mine's from."

"I am sage." The smile grew wider than he'd ever seen it before, though still among the narrowest of smiles. "The beetle flies to me."

At the time, he didn't want to look like a fool by asking, and he'd never found out if she meant this literally. Beetles *could* fly; it was a damnable nuisance when breeding or moving them. But the idea of them hopping out of their nests in Deep Forest Province, winging their way across the Copper Sea, and landing on or near some particular person in Za'ar was the stuff of fable. She couldn't have meant that. He assumed she referred to some network of Min Khunen smugglers, or "sages" if they wanted to call it that, who had a line on sacred strains direct from the homeland.

But there were times when his doubt itself fell into doubt, and this would be one of them. As always, on his return from the West End run, he found himself sitting next to her in the small, neat office she kept, overlooking the lizard stalls at the edge of the Great Market, where she provided the transport and vegetables in return for a discount on her package. Her partner, Lubris, the Nydhian slave trader that traded beetles under the table and often helped Shigius with his shipping needs, may or may not have known about this arrangement. Knowing Lubris, a neat and tidy man, he probably wouldn't have wanted to.

Yaay was fair-skinned, slight, and completely unadorned. Her shock of black hair, cut in the severely straight lines of bangs and a bob, matched a square-cut shirt and trousers so dark they might've been dyed in ink. People would look at her and see nothing but another plain Min Khunen lady of indeterminate age, most likely engaged in peddling grassfowl eggs or keeping books for some petty merchant. Shigius had come to understand that her beauty lay in offering very little to see.

The beetle was perched on the web of her open hand, making his spit taste coppery and turning his bowels into a ball of mating serpents. He couldn't believe she'd let such a rare beetle just sit on her like that without securing it. If she'd handed it to him, his fist would've closed around it so fast that he probably would have crushed the thing to death. The sheen of its shell, the red and black together, reminded him of the eruption of Mount Olias, which he'd watched from the beach as a boy, the brilliant flares of liquid rock against the smoke-blotted night. But that wasn't the incredible part.

The incredible part was when the beetle opened and flew into the glowing bowl of her water-pipe. Shigius barely got his lips to the mouthpiece in time before the precious thing incinerated itself. *Easier than tongs!* he heard her joking, far away, as the peppery fumes filled his lungs and carried him off.

There were three kinds of firebeetle for sale in Za'ar, and Shigius held the corner of each market. The flour from his hatcheries and mills around town kept the gutter fiends cringing for more but wouldn't be of interest to a connoisseur. He never touched it. The flour he shipped from overseas was the same stuff the surgeons used, potent enough for a nice dream and a lasting glow—the flour he used every day. But a person couldn't use it every day without wanting to get better, go higher, feel more, and that's where the living beetles came in.

He could pull them out of his own hatcheries, but his beetles weren't much better alive than an overseas flour, and besides, cutting into broodstock for personal use was a bad approach to life, one he had tried in the past. Shipping beetle live from Min Khune was an ordeal fraught with hazard, but there were people in town who would pay a premium commensurate with the effort. That made it even harder to look at a buzzing cage full of beauties he'd prefer to smoke himself. The live beetle from the Vale would take a person away, all the way away. And there were times when a person really needed that.

But even the live beetles he shipped and occasionally indulged in were weak compared to the ones Yaay smoked. The ones he got were broodstock from the commercial hatcheries over there, operations like his own but with the benefit of native soil and sun and moonlight. Hers were sacred beetles from Deep Forest Province. However they came to her, he was sure they weren't for sale in town, or even in the Vale. Shigius would have been first to hear about that.

He hadn't even blown out the last of the smoke when the room,

Yaay, and everything else around him vanished. The red and the black flooded in, the colors of carapace, of the molten heart of the earth, of death itself, more substantial-seeming than the forms revealed by daylight, thicker somehow, as if colors had mass and light had weight. Shifting, turning, the shade wove itself into figures, faceless at first, arms linked, legs dancing, placing him at the center of a spiral that stretched as deep into the surrounding dark as time was long.

It was like this every time. The faces came next. At first they all looked the same, hairless, bloodless, asleep or dead. But swiftly the sameness evolved into features, the pallor into colors, the silence into a hundred thousand heartbeats. All of their eyes opened at once.

Before him then were his people, the ones he had tossed. Some betrayed and double-crossed, some turned from innocents to slaves of the beetle, so many simply gotten out of the way. All gone. He couldn't remember a single name at the moment, but he knew all of them, knew them all so well. There was an intimacy greater than any other he had known in sending a person from the world. The strange sorrow he felt for them was as close as he had ever come to love.

And they smiled at him. They smiled as if he were their god, and the things he had done to them, His grace. They smiled as little children smile at their mothers. They smiled as the vain smile into mirrors. They smiled at themselves and all that had befallen them, and Shigius, who was all of them, smiled back. He smiled their smile. This was the peak of the dream, the illusion, to feel for a fleeting moment that the way he had set the world was right.

Then, pleasure. He would never have any idea what she was doing, whether she had taken him in her sex or her hand or her mouth, if she was even touching him at all. The audience of lost souls faded into a brighter and whiter glare until nothing was left but light and the circle of ecstasy that engulfed him, moving up and down, faster and faster, until finally it, too, became part of the light. And Shigius went away.

When he came back, he was lying naked on the floor of the office. Yaay was facing him, also nude, on her side, with one tiny hand pressed under his shoulder. Even though the disintegration of his beetledream had left the room full of bobbing, glaring, circus-colored nonsense, he could see from the tiny cues on her face that she was amused and a little bit angry. Suddenly he could feel the bruise on his cheek again, and taste the cut.

"You called it *drug*," she said, the last word in Saspian.

He didn't recall referring to the firebeetle as a *drug*, but it seemed reasonable enough. The surgeons used it as a drug, after all, to stop bleeding and infection. It seemed a strange and offhand thing to bring up right after making him spend so hard that his spirit departed his flesh. *Women are women,* he supposed, *all the world over.*

"Beetle is no *drug.* Your bluecaps: *drug.* Your hempwine: *drug.* Your grapewine: *drug.* Kota leaf: *drug.* Shadaghi cactus: *drug.* Beetle: no *drug.*"

Shigius began to prepare a lengthy argument that mushrooms, leaf, cactus, and the various wines were each somewhat like one beetle or another, but he was too tired to think so abstractly.

"What then?" he asked instead. "What is the beetle?"

"What you saw. What you see. Life and death and the places in between."

"And other *drugs* aren't?"

"The power of the *drug* is in the *drug.* Beetle power is from elsewhere. Not inside the beetle. Everywhere."

"Everywhere," he grinned, thinking he'd caught her, "including inside the beetle."

"Yes. There too."

As Shigius laughed, he felt himself growing lighter, like he was floating away from himself again, but without losing his sight. Then he realized she was lifting him. Her childlike hand was lifting the whole weight of his body, by the shoulder, from below. He kept rising until her forearm was perpendicular to her biceps, holding him a bit less than a cubit—since her arm was smaller than the average arm—above the floor. The rest of her showed no signs of strain.

"Where does that come from?" she asked. "You think I'm this strong?"

Wildly confused now, Shigius couldn't come up with an answer. Her eyes were fixed on his but gave no clue as to why she was doing this.

"Sage," she said, the second time he'd heard her use the word, and the little smile, her biggest ever, came back to her lips. She eased him down gently, and the floor felt like a soft bed. For a while they lay in silence.

"Death and life," she repeated, her voice barely above a whisper. "Life makes death. Death gives life shape. Without the other, each is just a color of fire. White fire, black fire. Both burn."

"Sage," he said, thickly, the word strange in his mouth. He'd never said it before except in jest. "What do you know of Tutor Lom's beetles?"

"He knows where they are. Always. If that's what you're thinking."

"No. I mean, how strong are they? Like yours?"

"No. Stronger. Long ago, the Saspians stole the sacred beetle. They enslaved sages to breed it at their college." Even rarer than her smiles, a hint of horror clouded her face. "Tutor Lom has the legacy. He is no sage. Traitor, but he has the legacy. Mine are restored. His, most ancient lineage."

"And what about before?"

"Before what?"

"The Fire. The Fist. Whatever you call what happened to Old Sasp."

"At the old college, true sages kept the beetles. They were stronger still than what Lom breeds today."

The words sent a thrill and a flutter through his veins. Stronger than this? He had nothing to worry about, beetle-wise, until the Hour of Nisi or so, the morning of the next day. For now, the sacred fire had cooled to a warm embrace, and he wallowed in it, vaguely wondering how a person dressed for the Witchroad at this time of year. *Woolens or linens?* It seemed a toss-up, the way the weather had been lately.

III

Life in the outland was never easy, and anyone who told you otherwise was planning to rob you or worse. That had been Yharalon's experience growing up bored on a farm outside Vydhmia, where a tramp full of charming tales had come through one day and, once he'd led him up the Witchroad past the reach of crown and kin, proceeded to take from him everything a boy had to offer a man. At night and sometimes during the day, the tramp would get drunk and chain the starving child to a tree while he slept it off. The boy used these times to knap a knife out of a long piece of flint, using the edge of the cuff around his ankle as a striker.

He killed the tramp in broad daylight, in front of everyone in the tiny market square of an outland hamlet called Yharalon, and its people had looked to him for protection ever since. A young boy in chains killing his master, looking him right in the eyes as he stabbed and stabbed and finally sawed through his vitals, was the greatest thing any of them had ever seen. He became Lord Yharalon in their eyes and, soon enough, in his own. He couldn't even remember the name he'd used as farmboy and with the tramp, who'd mostly just called him the dirtiest words for a woman in various tongues. In the eyes of the king he was an outlaw and a murderer, but there was no king where he lived. None, that was, unless one counted Lord Yharalon.

But life in the outland was never easy, and the past year had been harder still with spider mites taking down half the seed-hemp crop and his people swallowing mashes of bitter leaves to keep their stomachs from wrapping around their backbones. Yharalon had taken the best of his men to the heart of the great slothstone wood east of Muzmuf Hill, but they had not seen, let alone killed, even one giant sloth. So when word reached Yharalon that there was high pay and promise of even greater plunder for a job no one in his right mind would take, he answered not the lure of shining riches but the hungry cries of the babies in the village that had given him his name.

He saddled up his best antelope and outfitted himself for the warpath, looking more like a noble stag than a meager outlaw. There was as much bronze as hide about him, the metal patinated to a brilliant green as befit a northern forest fighter, and his helmet bore the long, curved horns of a warbuck he'd buried in his youth. Some might have seen wearing the horns of his battle-killed mount as a noble air he was putting on, but that wasn't why he did it. He had loved the beast that now lay where he meant to have his own mound someday, and his grief had made him understand why a man must strive to claim and keep land for his mound.

Before setting out he kissed the three of his five wives he was then on speaking terms with, and held his newest child in his arms for a while. It was good for a boy, he thought, to be held in mailed arms, to feel protected by what protection truly meant. Especially if the boy was to stay in these parts. Half of him wished his children would wander south as soon they got big enough to fend for themselves.

The last visit he made was to the corner of his lodge where he kept his scrolls. It put him in agony that he really had no idea how to care for them. He tried to keep them cool and dry, as he would with stored hides, and it seemed to be working so far. There were nine scrolls now; he counted them as always before replacing them carefully in their sack. For years he'd acquired all he came across, often paying dearly for them, seldom knowing what they were even purported to contain.

One thing he was certain of: he would someday, somehow, from someone, learn to read. It befit a lord to have letters. The people of Yharalon, poor though they were, deserved one who could fix his words to clay and parchment, or even have them carved in stone. He wondered if any of the city people on the job he was going to would be kind enough to teach him some of the rudiments while they camped.

The rendezvous was in the Wailing Wood, in the place called First Clearing, since it was the first clearing north of the law's reach where a substantial body of men could make camp. Hundreds were already there by the time he arrived, and the whole forest stank. The nearby trees had been stripped of limbs and the ground of vegetation to make a village of the roughest, rudest huts Yharalon had seen in his life, most of which he'd spent in a world of rude, rough huts. On the northern end of the clearing, a pasture for hundreds of beasts had been fenced with knotty sticks, and when the north wind wafted in, the grassy antelope-shit smell came as a relief from the pervasive human and camprat waste.

The bosses were already a few days late by the time Yharalon arrived. He'd taken a long time deciding to go through with this, knowing the mission was likely to leave his people with neither gold nor a warrior to defend them. He might have missed it entirely if the commander had been on time. Indeed, that might have been his deeper intent in setting forth, yes, but a little bit late, so as not to go without openly deciding not to go.

There weren't many dark foresters who got themselves up as much as he did, and as he rode into camp, he sparked a wave of hope that he was one of the commander's forward scouts. Without anyone telling him anything, he knew the men had been feasting and now their rations were running low. The air crackled with blame and everywhere he could see men's eyes on each other's purses and gourds and packs. In a land defined by its roguery, shared scarcity and discomfort always came to the same bloody ending.

The first person to come talk to him as he set up his own camp was an ugly little lout. Yharalon guessed he'd run three different ways from as many crimes or more before ending up here. By his garb—a floppy hat and homespun, undyed hempen shirt and trousers—he looked like a woodsman from a fairy tale. By his face—misshapen, all nostril—he could be nothing but a rogue.

"Hail countryman, what news d'ye bring?" he said as he approached, repeating a standard formula for Nydhians approaching each other abroad or in the wilderness.

"Hail," Yharalon said with no enthusiasm and turned back to brushing Tooth-Head, the nickname he used for his buck so the spirits wouldn't know his true name. "No news. Just come for the job."

"And quite a job it'll be. My name's Naihard Shig. There's three men here for every one they're taking. What makes you think they'll pick you?"

At this Yharalon turned. He looked down at his well-repaired armor and the fine saber he wore, then up and down "Naihard Shig," who had a dull-looking knife stuck unsheathed through his greasy leathern waist-sash and an unstrung longbow that he held like a broomstick.

"Wouldn't it make more sense for me to be asking you the same question?"

"Would it?" the rogue smiled. "If you need anything, just ask for me by name. I was one of the first ones here and I know the whole camp. There's a lot more here than anyone's letting on. Anything to suit your fancy. One fellow's even got girls in his hut, brought 'em in real quiet like."

"I don't go in for that. I'm here because my people are poor."

The rogue seemed to be dumbfounded for a moment, perhaps by the mere concept of feeling responsible for other people.

"You didn't tell me your name."

"I'm the Lord of Yharalon. I go by Yharalon." He said what he said next without thinking it first. "I'm going to lead the foresters on this expedition because I am surely the most honorable among us."

"Well," Naihard said, his face straining to fight back a gale of laughter, his voice dripping with mock grandeur, "Lord Yharalon! Your honorableness! It's an honor to stand in your presence, sire! Pray tell me about this Yharalon where you lord."

"Just a poor outland village, probably much like the last one you robbed, sir. But the people are mine and I protect them, mostly from villains like you that pass through our countryside."

"You really do talk like one of them." The rogue actually looked impressed. "Well, good luck. A lot of men here'd like to be chief. I'm not even sure how they're going to pick one. Probably a vote to send a few fellows forward and then the Saspiards pick which of those they want."

"You know them."

"Who, me? No, not at all. I heard about this just like anyone else. What gave you that idea?"

"No, I mean you know the Saspiards. You've lived in the empire."

The rogue looked relieved for a moment and asked, "Is it that obvious?"

At this Yharalon grinned. "Not at all. I'm a Vydhmian. It's a border town and we see all kinds. I learned from an early age how to pick out an Empire Nydhian from us stay-at-homes."

"You've never been there yourself?"

"No. Just the North and the outland all my life. I've never even seen Dhular or any part of the South."

"Well," Naihard said, his eyes visibly calculating, "it's the toss of a chit whether they're going to want someone who puts on airs the way they do, or someone just as nasty as they are. If you're both you're in good shape, but all I know of you is you put on airs."

"What would they consider nasty?"

"It's not what they'd consider nasty, it's the stuff they do that we consider nasty. Like punishing slaves for insolence by chewing the flesh from their living bodies. That kind of nasty. They really respect someone who has a taste for flaying, impaling, disembowelling, slow-roasting, that kind of thing. Remember their whole thing started with a brute called the Beheader."

Of course Yharalon remembered Zoba the Beheader. No Nydhian was allowed to forget the name of the vicious conqueror who had taken half their country and much of the freedom of the rest seven centuries before. For a northman, the terror of direct imperial rule was but a few generations past.

"I've never been a cruel man," Yharalon conceded, "though I have known cruelty. How would I prove myself to them, anyway?"

"Who knows? But if there's a test, you can be sure it'll be something nasty."

Three days later they showed up in a small batch, just the commander and the captain with a few lizard-riders in escort. Yharalon had seen Saspian soldiers once before, when during a desperate season, his father had gone up Far Mountain for skins and taken them to sell at the Saspian border fort. They cheated him ruthlessly, and he was silent on the wagon home. The boy had thought he himself must have been to blame somehow for the bad weather and the bad behavior of the soldiers at the fort.

The captain and his escort were exactly as he remembered them, and he wondered if it was actually the Saspian military that was hiring. They wore bronze breastplates over white ripreed tunics, helmets with an ugly decoration that was meant to be a lizard's crest, black studded loinguards, and bronze greaves. The commander wore no armor and carried no longarm but was otherwise outfitted exactly like his men. The captain distinguished himself by wearing a white feathered shortcloak about his shoulders. In armament, the escort were a mix of lancers and javelineers, but each scabbarded a shortsword at his waist. They mounted mostly fine coursers, Red Racers and Blues and Reticulates, which made Yharalon think these must all be officers or hand-picked men.

There were a dozen in all, and the nations they came from numbered nearly as many. The commander was a pockmarked, greasy-haired mongrel who clearly had a lot of Nydhian blood in him. The captain was Salt Folk, pale for a Crescentine and probably ruddy-haired when his head wasn't shaved. Several of the men were Cucuthi, who came from far away, but Yharalon was familiar with their broad frames and sandy complexions because they could be found wherever on earth there was banditry to be done. There were two or three whose races he didn't recognize, either because they were so exotic or because their parentage was so mixed as to blot out any sense of nationality. There were even a couple of Saspians.

Yharalon had made enough friends since coming to the camp that his name was likely to be among those considered for chief. His fine armor alone was enough to start conversations. For all the repute of the dark forester being a selfish man who'd gone off on his own, most of the ones he talked to were in the same situation as he was. They had places much like Yharalon to protect and the bad harvest had brought them down to First Clearing. Yharalon had made the wise though painful choice to bring extra dried meat and fodder, and these had turned out to be handy for making friends on the third day in particular, by which time most of the camp was beginning to starve.

"I am Commander Garong!" the pockmarked leader announced as he rode into camp at the head of his little column.

His voice was pure viciousness buttered with layers of pomposity and lies. As soon as he heard it, Yharalon was sure he'd been nearby spying on the camp and waiting for everyone there to be very hungry before coming in to negotiate contracts with them. The antelopes in the makeshift corral began thrashing and screaming at the smell of the coursers.

"Know ye this!" The commander spoke in Nydhian, though everyone also spoke Saspian, and he was using some of the archaic flourishes that Nydhians were used to hearing in poems and political speeches. "You shall each of you that ride with me be a rich man when ye return to your lodges and your wives."

He waited for a cheer that came unenthusiastically, in pockets, from around the camp. The foresters were beginning to line his path. Yharalon hustled to position himself near where he expected the Saspians to come to a halt. He could tell it was hard for them to figure out where to go in a place that had no government. But there was a big avenue between the huts that more or less bisected the clearing from its southern end to the corral, and it seemed most likely to Yharalon that they would stop around its halfway point. He got to the likely spot and wormed his way to the front of the gathering crowd.

"Know ye this!" the commander continued. "If ye ride with me I shall be your lawgiver. And my law is to take the hand that steals from me, the tongue that defies me, the eyes that spy on me, the head that plots against me, the heart that betrays me, the manhood that touches a woman of mine, and the skin that covers a fraud."

The speech was standard fare. He'd ridden as a guide with royal expeditions before and their commanders sounded about the same. The message was always that they knew outlanders weren't good folk and they'd be keeping their eyes on them.

Of course, anyone truly rogue would assume as much of the authorities without being told, making Yharalon wonder whom the speech was meant for. If a rogue didn't need to be told, all that was left were the supposedly non-existent foresters of good character. But they didn't need to be warned that they were being watched, since they'd act the same if they weren't being watched. Most people, he supposed, didn't think so much. Most people would just hear the commander saying he was prone to cut off parts of anyone that crossed him.

"Can any among ye make letters or glyphs?"

"Aye," said a familiar voice from the crowd. The commander had halted by now, and Naihard Shig stepped into the road in front of him. "I can make both, and would be pleased to offer my services."

"Good," the commander said. He was either a fool or a crafty bugger for trusting this Shig or pretending to. He produced a ball of clay from his saddle bag and tossed it to the rogue. "Make me the names of each man who would lead ye in Saspian glyphs, and by each the number who support him. In two hours, the candidates will be summoned to me. When a leader has been chosen, he will choose who among ye rides with us."

He looked around at the crowd, his face twisted with disgust at the sight and stench of the men he addressed, yet also seeming to want some sort of reaction from them. When none came, since he'd said nothing unexpected or happy or sad from their perspective, he turned his courser in a broad loop, causing a few men lining the path to back up and others to laugh at them.

Yharalon was the first person Naihard approached, still pressing the clay between his palms into the form of a tablet. Surprisingly, he had a bone stylus with him as if he'd anticipated this duty.

"Your name at the top of the clay, your lordship, and one mark of support from me!" he said in a sing-song voice as he deftly marked the soft surface.

The look on Yharalon's face made it unnecessary for him to ask why.

"Why, because you're the most honorable among us! Just like you said." The rogue grinned widely, showing a mouth that looked like it had failed to withstand a siege. "We'll have to get some other names down, for appearances' sake, you see, but you've nothing to worry about, I'm sure." At that Naihard winked and moved on to the next man.

Yharalon had a strong sense that something he didn't understand was going on, but it was overwhelmed by his desire for letters. He decided to play along with whatever Shig was trying to set up, since it seemed unlikely he'd agree to teach him if he tried to foil it. Besides, if the plan would make him chief, he wasn't overly concerned about what the rogue might gain from it.

Two hours later, he stood with half a dozen other well-outfitted foresters in front of the commander and the captain. The way they were being eyed up and down—by the captain appraisingly and the commander leeringly—Yharalon thought they were about to be made to disrobe. He swallowed hard and resolved to do whatever he needed to do to take command. Even if it came to dueling, he'd commend himself to Nydh and throw himself into it.

The other candidates were older than him, scarred and grizzled fighters who had probably piled up five enemy corpses for every one Yharalon had tossed on his own lifetime stack. Other than his claim to be honorable and righteous, which at the moment seemed pretentious even to him, there was no conceivable reason to choose him over one of them. So he was surprised when the commander addressed him first.

"You, Yharalon?"

"That is me, sire." The words sounded awkward coming out but he had no idea how else to put it.

"You have seventy marks supporting you as chief of foresters. The next best has forty-six. What did you do to get so many of your brethren behind you?"

"Sire, all I can say is that I am a man of honor. Men see that if they follow me, they follow me straight, not askance."

"Fine words for a rogue." The commander grinned hideously. "But don't these fellows want to ride, as you say, askance?"

The other candidates were glancing nervously over at Yharalon, as if he was about to reveal things about them that they didn't want known.

"Not this time, sire. The treasure at the end of the straight road is too great for us to be drawn off to the side. These men know the temptation will be there. Unknown country always has unknown lures as well as unknown dangers. They understand they need a man with bronze in his backbone and eyes dead ahead to get them where we're going and back."

"You tell a fine tale."

"I tell no tales, sire. I only speak of what I see and know to be true."

"You defy me?"

By this time, the commander was standing directly in front of him, close enough for Yharalon to smell his rotten breath.

"No, sire. If you call my truth a tale, so be it. As you said, you are the lawgiver, the law here is yours. Tale or truth, sire, my words be the same."

For a few moments, almost touching noses with him, the commander put on a show with his face. He started out angrily suspicious, then looked amused, then pensive, then devious. And then he stepped away.

"Bring out the girl!" he called to the treeline. Turning back to Yharalon, he said, "It's all good and well what you say, but we need dark foresters on this mission for a reason. My employers have leverage with the king and I could've hired a company of his on excellent terms. The problem is—and I share this observation with you because I can see you're an intelligent man—loyalty is, as they say, a Trasporian axe, with bits on each side of the haft. Straightness, indeed, backbone, yes—but if we're to work together, I need to be sure you're also rogue enough not to entertain any foolish notions or squeamish compunctions."

Everyone was turning their heads now, and Yharalon followed their gaze to two dismounted courserymen dragging a little girl into the clearing. She was black with dirt, her roughspun dress torn almost in half, and she was bleeding from every fingernail. She looked like she barely outweighed a grassfowl, but she'd left marks on more than one of her subduers. They dragged her in front of Yharalon and held her by each arm.

"Kill her," the commander said. "Here. Herald!"

A herald came running up, a watery-eyed and scrawny young lad, with the mace of his office in duty position on his shoulder.

"Herald, your mace. Give it to this man," the commander said, pointing to Yharalon. "I don't expect you to take pleasure in cruelty, though I would far from hold it against you if you did.

Therefore, I offer you this mace to take her life without pain or suffering to the child, if you so choose."

Yharalon trembled as the herald pressed the weapon into his hand. The herald noticed and gave him a grim, searing, hateful smile while the others could only see the back of his head. The child looked merely sullen. Yharalon could feel, behind her scratched and filthy face, the determination to give her murderers no pleasure in the form of tears or screams. He knew the feeling precisely, right down to the filth and scratches.

He lifted the mace. Though he had wielded much heavier weapons in the past, this felt like the heaviest. He held it up long enough to make his arm burn, as if the pain would give him either the strength to do what was needed or the cunning to get around it. He knew he didn't have much time before he started to look squeamish about murdering the girl.

It rang like a chord of gongs when he bounced the macehead off two helmets in rapid succession. He hadn't hit hard enough to injure the wearers, just enough to stun them with the sound and impact. They stumbled, dropping the girl, who took off for the woods as fast as a young camprat. Everyone was too shocked to give chase. A few whelps from the huts she passed did go barking after her, but they wanted to play, not bring her back to be murdered.

"Seize him. Kill him," the captain said sternly to the nearby guards who were still standing.

"No!" the commander said. "Leave him. You. Why did you do that? By my law, what should I take from you for what you have done?"

"Nothing, sire," Yharalon answered, surprised at how little fear he was feeling at the moment. "You should do nothing because I've just saved our mission. Your test was a riddle, and I gave the answer you didn't know yourself."

"Explain." The commander looked grim now, but the expression was almost reassuring next to the captain's growing fury.

"Sire, where did you get that girl? Playing in the woods nearby, I wager." The commander winced, almost imperceptibly, but it let Yharalon know he was right. He continued, "And where do you suppose she came from? The loins of one here, most likely. If not, his kin, or a family he protects. And how many friends does that one have here? Dozens, if he's from nearby. And how many new friends would they suddenly make if a Saspiard—no offense intended, sire—were to murder a local girl in cold blood? Never mind it's me holding the mace, the crime would be yours by our law, such as it is. Did you come with enough men to fight this whole forest and still win your prize without any of us as guides?"

Yharalon could see that the commander was a man who was accustomed to using his face as a tool or a weapon to break people down, but for the moment he had lost control of it. His little plan to test his candidates had indeed been poorly thought through. The dawning of this fact on him was visible to Yharalon well before he finished speaking. It seemed the commander was used to places full of discarded children that he was accustomed to grabbing and using as he pleased.

"Commander," the captain said, "this man has to pay for striking my guards."

"I'll pay them for it," Garong said, raising a dismissive hand between himself and the captain. "This is the man I choose for chief of foresters."

He was given free choice of the men in the clearing, but for one. Naihard Shig was to be chosen, even though—minus the promise of learning some letters or glyphs—he was the last one Yharalon would've picked. This was the commander's order and it was final.

No matter: a company of a hundred could carry a weakling or two.

As to the rest, he had a tough time making his picks. He couldn't reject his neighbors back home unless there was something obviously wrong with them, like the open tumor on Humius Phyggum's knee. But the better fighters hailed from richer and more contested lands to the south and west of Yharalon. Among them a choice between two often came down to some tiny detail like a saber hilt that didn't show wear commensurate with the wearer's tales of battle, or a poorly kept bronze pauldron. Each time he chose one over another, he felt like he had made an enemy but not necessarily a friend. The rejects walked away with hot eyes as if their very manhood had been injured by his decision.

But, with thoughts in mind of what the Law of Garong might prescribe for dawdlers, he got the work done quickly. Once a hundred men were assembled, they set fire to the huts, knocked down the corral, and rode through the Wailing Wood to the Witchroad. A small train of lizard-drawn carts awaited them there, tended by lizardmen of a foreign race Yharalon wasn't used to seeing and couldn't place.

The captain informed him that his main column was a quarter coursing behind them, where it would remain throughout their northward movements. The foresters would arrive at each night's stopping point in the late afternoon and build two camps and two corrals, one for themselves and the other for the legion, far enough apart that the coursers and antelopes wouldn't bother each other. Captain, commander, and escort then departed amid the sounds of the near-riot the last order incited.

"Build their camps for them?" asked a young Dhularite lad who'd been run out of the city for working off the books of the Thieves Guild. "What comes next, wiping their asses?"

Yharalon was actually pleased with the comment because it

shifted some of the angry noises to laughter.

"No," he said, trying to keep it going, "they'll have us chewing their food for them, as their little Saspiard teeth are too small and dainty for a northman's field rations!"

There was a bit more laughter, but it was soon cut off by a roar from one of the biggest and wildest among them:

"They're women! I say we jump 'em, fuck 'em, cut off their balls, string 'em up to bleed out, and ride off with all their gear!"

"There's plenty on the train they left with us," said Yharalon's neighbor Mynch when the howls of approval finally abated. "Why not just vanish with all that and chalk it up to a profit?"

"Mynch, everyone!" Yharalon cried, raising his voice as high as it would go over the hubbub. "The Saspiards number three to our one, and they have coursers, catapults, and bolt throwers. We can't just melt into the woods. Especially not for a haul that's going to be mostly canvas tents."

"How *dare* you! We are *foresters!* We *live,*" the big one screamed, "in the woods!"

Another voice called from the back of the crowd, "And canvas tents are expensive! I wish I'd had one these last two weeks!"

"And I," Yharalon said, "just sent two hundred of us who were looking to work for the Saspiards into the nearby woods, disappointed. A lot of them are fine trackers and seasoned fighters. What's the first thing the commander's going to do after he finds out we robbed him?"

"Round up the rejects and use them to hunt us down," said Mynch. He'd always been a reasonable fellow.

"We're stuck with these cunts for now, I'm afraid," Yharalon concluded, "so let's just ride on and make sure we make their beds nice and lumpy."

At that there was a great round of laughter that lasted through much of the twisting and maneuvering involved in getting every pair of horns pointed north.

That day, they reached the edge of the great bog below Muzmuf Hill and built their camps on the last reach of dry land. The clearing was rough against the sun and swordgrass and tules with skins like oxhide, and Yharalon made sure he poured out as much sweat as the lowliest of his men. By the time both camps were made, the sun was low in the sky and the advance picquets of the coursery column had begun to arrive. The foresters, Yharalon included, were all quite naked by then and stank to the very House of Walth at the roof of the sky. When he heard the first conch call, he wobbled back to where he'd stacked his clothing, arms, and armor.

Naihard Shig was there, as if watching over his possessions for him. He had somehow acquired a clean towel and a bundle of fresh herbs. Yharalon found he was too thankful for these offerings and their timeliness, just ahead of having to don his furs and his bronze, to chastise the rogue for being presumptuous. As Yharalon cleansed himself, Shigius lifted a gourd to his lips, and the water within was cold, as if drawn from a deep well.

He was glad to be fully dressed and accoutered, just buckling his swordbelt, when the main column came into view across the floodplain. Yharalon wondered what the Saspiards would think about their first sight of Muzmuf Hill. A giant sculptor of talent as prodigious as his size could not have made its crestline more like the knuckles of a fist. Legend held that *muzmuf* was the word for *fist* in a tongue long dead.

Once the Saspiards had staked their coursers to the ground and fed them live rats and drugged them goodnight, the herald came to Yharalon's tent to summon him to the commander's. He followed him to the lizardry camp in the gathering dusk, all the while looking at the brutal, flanged head of the mace jutting over his escort's shoulder and thinking about how he'd been expected to bury it in the skull of an innocent child. He thought about its owner, too, how readily he'd participated. It seemed Garong vetted all his men for the same set of traits.

When they arrived, Smatt, a fat, hairy Walthorian who'd signed on as the expedition's chief engineer, was leaving the commander's tent with a disgusted look on his face. As Yharalon entered, a slave girl, little more than a child herself, slipped out from under the commander's desk and went to stand by his bed to await her next order. She was naked except for a bronze collar, and the shadows of an oil lamp heightened the fear and revulsion on her face. Yharalon remembered the tramp who had stolen his own boyhood, and he wanted to draw his saber so badly it made him retch in the back of his throat. He was surprised the commander's guards hadn't taken his weapons before letting him into the tent.

Garong, half-drunk and dishevelled, smiled lewdly.

"Good timing, my friend," he said, "I was just finishing up this round."

Yharalon made a knuckle-crackling fist with his right hand and caught the commander noticing it, which made his smile grow bigger and more lascivious.

"So, Yharalon. Tomorrow. What's the plan?"

His change in tone was jarring, but it made sense. Garong was paying for guides, after all. Of course he'd be asking for guidance. His tyrannical posturing back in the clearing had mostly been for the benefit of the common foresters—and, of course, his own men. There was no need to keep it up with his chief. Besides, he was probably now too deep in his cups to add any intentional flourishes to his speech.

"Well, sire," Yharalon began, provoking a dismissive headshake from Garong, who apparently liked to pretend he didn't go in for *sire* and such. "The first stretch is the causeway, and that's a straight shot, but we'll have to string out. At most you can fit three coursers abreast, and the wagons'll have to go single-file."

The commander frowned appropriately over the time that would be lost to this.

Yharalon continued: "As you can see for yourself, I'm sure, you can't get a wagon train over the knuckles of Muzmuf. The road goes around, but that means going up the Sunsets a piece. It's a pretty steep cut, and though the road's as wide there as it is here, it'll be slow going for your cartlizards in particular. And it does narrow to one track as you get near the top, to make some sharp turns. At the end of all that, you'll reach the Fools Meadow."

"What's foolish ugh! about this meadow?" Garong asked while expelling something between a hiccup and a belch. The stink that wafted over his desk to Yharalon had the two distinct flowerinesses of liquor and corpse.

"The meadow's not foolish," Yharalon replied, trying not to grimace, "it makes men fools. It's a round meadow hemmed in by the mountains on every side. Six passes lead out, including the one you came in on. After all the switchbacks on the grade, the road from the south enters the meadow from the west. The right one to take, to rejoin the Witchroad heading north, is in the southeast. And the mountains hide the sun except at noonday, so you can even argue over which way is east.

"That's how most of your past expeditions to Old Sasp have failed, you see. Even the big ones. They get into the Fools Meadow and can't agree which road to take out of it. So they split up into small bands that get swallowed up by the usual outland hazards. Often with none of them going the right way. I can't recommend none of the other roads, not to anyone who likes to hold onto his gold and his parts."

Indeed, because the last thing Yharalon needs is for these fuckers to know about us. The road home was one of the wrong ways to leave the Fools Meadow. If his warning put the Saspiards off that road for a generation or more, even if he died on this mission, he felt he would have done plenty with his life.

"So how will the main column proceed?" Garong slurred.

"I'll leave a dozen of my best trackers in the meadow to wait for you and help get the column across."

"No," the commander said, "I want you to stay. Put Naihard Shig in charge of your column and wait for us in the meadow."

As much as he wanted to protest it, this was clearly an order, not a suggestion. It made him wonder what on earth the rogue was doing to gain so many advantages so quickly, and how the commander could possibly not be onto him.

"Very well," he said. "Shig won't know the road, but I'll appoint a lieutenant who does."

"Do whatever you need to do," Garong concluded, "just be there for me when I arrive at this hic!—pasture of distraction."

He clapped his hands once, and the slave girl scurried back to her position at his feet. Yharalon left the tent trembling, his mind full of things to forget, his hands aching to hurt someone. That night he had to drink most of the wine he carried with him to get to sleep.

The next day at noon, the Hour of Walth to people who bowed down to sky-gods and kept time by the hour, Yharalon found himself standing in the Fools Meadow and feeling himself a bit of a fool. He'd given Tooth-Head over to Mynch to tether to his own antelope, and planned to ride on a wagon once the Saspiards arrived. This was something he hadn't considered when he received his orders the night before, but it was the only way he'd be able to accompany the main column. Mixing antelopes with lizardry was never a good idea.

Every moment he stood without a mount he grew more anxious. For a man who'd led the life he'd led in the places he'd lived, he might as well have been naked or barefoot. What if the column never showed up? It would be a steep and treacherous walk home for Yharalon.

For a long time, he fought the temptation to sit, telling himself the commander would be here at any moment and he didn't want to be seen sitting down on the job. But moments stretched into hours as the sun disappeared behind the Sunset Range, named after this very trick they did each afternoon. Some called this the Outlaw's Hour, when the outlands were shaded by the mountains from the eyes of the Sun God, and misdeeds would go unpunished. On the west side of the peaks, in the glare of the setting sun, the King's Law prevailed even in the Far Far North, where the other parts of Nydhian civilization did not.

Yharalon thought little of the Outlaw's Hour, since right was right and wrong was wrong whether some mythical man in the sun was watching you or not. But it certainly meant the column was late. He sat down in the soft grass of Fools Meadow to preserve his strength. If you forgot its dread repute it wasn't a terrible place, this gently sloping bowl of green sprinkled with wildflowers of every color he could name and then some. He remembered deeper tales that told of other follies, a root or flower that would make men who ate of it linger in the meadow forever, growing roots, becoming flowers. The light from above turned golden and the skylizards on the crags above began to sing.

It was getting too late. If a courser's head didn't poke out soon around the bend he was watching, it meant half or more of the column, and presumably all the wagons, would be picking their way around the switchbacks in the dark. They'd almost be better off making camp in the middle of the road until dawn. He thought about heading back up the road on foot to help guide them, but whoever was at the front of the column probably wouldn't know who he was, his courser surely wouldn't, and Yharalon could guess Captain Kyrik's rules of engagement for armed strangers on an outland highway.

So he waited anxiously as the gold turned to pink and the skylizards began their evening hunt, diving for some small prey whose movements only they could see among the grass and the flowers. It was always a pleasure to watch skylizards hunt, so he distracted himself by observing their spearlike plunges, almost perpendicular to the ground, and the graceful way their wings would arch to break the fall at the very last moment.

They made him feel like, if worst came to worst, he could hunt and trap and forage his way home. A man's mind, after all, was to him what beak and wings were to a skylizard. He remembered the large part of him that hadn't wanted to join this expedition at all. But he also remembered the hungry children of Yharalon, and prayed in his manner that the commander would come through.

When he finally did, the meadow was wearing the eerie blue cloak of an outland dusk. It wasn't until nightfall, usually, that newcomers really felt the farness of the things that comforted them, their laws and nations and kings and kin, and the closeness of fears they thought they'd left in infancy. As the first courserymen descended the pass, he wondered what they thought about it all. Their faces were downcast, but that wasn't surprising seeing how hard the day's ride had apparently been for them.

As soon as the command detail came into view, Yharalon hailed them. In return, they sent out a conch call which he hoped was a signal for the troops not to attack him. As they drew nearer, he could see that the men in the advance ranks were not just tired and forlorn but also fearful. What had appeared as a dejected look from further off was actually them keeping a close and terrified eye on their own lizards.

"We lost the cart with the rats," Commander Garong explained when he reached Yharalon. He rode bareheaded, and his hair was so wet and his cloak so dampened with sweat that he looked like he'd been rained on. "She rolled right off one of those curves and into a canyon. The cages got smashed up along with the rest of her, and by the time my men reached bottom the ones that lived had all scurried off somewhere."

At first, coming from a lacklizard country, Yharalon couldn't understand why the loss of a wagonload of rats would cause general fear among the courserymen. It dawned on him as the commander kept talking that the rats had been the coursers' live food, and without them they would resort to other sources.

"Is there anything here for them?" Garong asked.

"I don't know. It's not considered wise to spend a long time in this meadow, or go hunting here. Just a local custom." He flinched inwardly at having used the word local to describe something from a place that was in fact near Yharalon. "The skylizards were hunting something earlier, something I couldn't see, but since they've stopped, I reckon the prey is, as you said, all scurried off somewhere."

"Then I suppose we press on," the commander remarked, offhandedly, his words madness.

"No, that we can't," Yharalon replied firmly. "Only a madman travels any part of the Witchroad at night. Not even a madman takes the Sunset Bypass in the dark."

"But I thought you said it was unwise to stay here in Foolish Meadow."

"There's a difference between a warning from ancient legends and the certainty of ambush and slaughter."

Garong laughed. "Who could slaughter this army? Coursers can see at night, and lizardmen can light torches. We're no more vulnerable than we'd be in the daytime."

"It's the mountain men. I picked a couple of them for our band of foresters with this part of the road in mind. If I'd known you'd be so late, I'd have kept them here with me, or better, posted them with you in the morning to help get the carts across."

Now the commander looked displeased, almost enough so to assert his position to quell his hireling's commentary. But he did not.

"And what makes these mountain goats such a threat to us?"

"They go up and down as easily as we go across open country. Goats, indeed. No amount of arms, armor, lizardry, or even engines of war are going to amount to much against a rock as big as ten men rolling down from a place you can't see."

"Can't they just as easily take us like that in the daytime?"

"Perhaps," Yharalon said, "but it's not their way. They probably know that if they started taking daytime traffic the rest of us outlanders would band together against them. But no one misses the kind of fool that travels at night. It's usually because they've crossed someone and have to leave in a hurry."

"Once again, you tell fine tales," Garong said, "but I still detect a bit of outlander superstition creeping in around the edges. How long has it been since these—mountain men—attacked anyone?"

"No one knows. We keep no records up here, especially not of those that travel at night."

The commander smiled. "Then I'm going to say we have nothing to worry about. We move on. Can you ride a courser?"

"I never have, and don't much want to learn."

"Very well. You can take the back of my saddle. We'll get to know each other very well tonight."

Yharalon had never felt stranger or more out of place than he did sitting on the back of a courser. The darkness and his constant urge to clutch the waist of one of the vilest men he'd ever met made it even stranger. It felt better having Garong's back to him than his front to him, but they were closer than Yharalon liked to be to any man. Still, he had no stirrups of his own, and the temptation to grab the rider instead of the saddle when the courser dipped or wobbled was always there, without regard to who he was. He was there, in the saddle, after all, and not on the ground in a pack of starving carnivores. At the moment that made Commander Garong seem like a good thing to hold onto.

Only six men rode ahead of them, two abreast for the moment, half of them having relinquished their longarms in favor of torches. Now and again Yharalon would lean to one side or another to catch a glimpse of them, but he could never lean for very long without getting scared he'd fall off, and in those moments, he'd see little more than an orange glow on the black stone. The road here, a streambed before it was widened and graded by some long-forgotten clan of builders, was cut so deep in the rock it felt like a roofless tunnel.

He could feel the mountain men, almost hear them snickering in the towering darkness above, but the greatest terror was just beneath him. Garong was a confident rider—it was easier than ever not to slit his throat, knowing he was the one thing between Yharalon and the lizard's fangs. But his own silence bespoke at least a greater concentration than usual. The ride seemed rougher than the road warranted and the courser's hunger could be felt in its unpredictable jerks and lurches.

But then it suddenly slowed, Garong's knees digging sharply into its sides to give the command. He grasped the loose hide at the lizard's scruff with both hands as it reared up slightly before halting. For his part, Yharalon did catch Garong around the waist, so alarmed he was at the sudden backward jolt.

"I didn't know you cared," the commander laughed as Yharalon hurriedly pulled away, like a man who'd accidentally plunged his arms in dung.

Over Garong's shoulder, he could see through the gloom that they'd reached a rise in the road, which the advance courserymen were mounting at a steady pace. As they rose higher and his eyes adjusted to the light, Yharalon saw, first, that they were desperately and without success trying to halt their own coursers, and second, that an enormous oblong stone was lying across the road, blocking it completely.

For all their vaunted night vision, it seemed to Yharalon that these fearsome lizards were going to crash into the obstacle at full speed and brain themselves. The notion would've been comical were it not for the string of hundreds of famished coursers behind them and the thought of where he would be when they began to pile up.

Instead, the first courser went over the rock. It barely broke its gait getting vertical. Meanwhile, its rider had dropped his torch, casting light on the scene from below, drawn his shortsword, and tried to get off the lizard. But one of his feet was caught in a stirrup, so he dangled uselessly, out of reach of his mount as it hauled him up. He was trying to cut himself loose with his sword when the second courser arrived.

It no longer saw a rider, a master, but instead a struggling, immobilized animal. Its own rider did manage to jump free of his saddle just before the courser leapt into the air and came down with most of the front-rank man's left arm in its crop. To his credit, the man kept hacking away at his stirrup strap with his other arm even as the blood spurted out.

The smell caused his lizard to turn, though, and soon he was being whipped through the air and landed back on the road so that two coursers now could feed on what was left of his body. The second-rank man, crouching with sword in hand, let them eat until the neck of one was exposed and within his reach. In a flash, the shortsword was deep in the lizard's neck, and it began to expire at once.

The other courser looked up calmly from its meal, which had become much less interesting since it stopped writhing. The second-rank man was struggling to pull his sword free of the gushing wound he had made. Yharalon guessed he'd got it stuck between two vertebrae. Tough break, but he should've let the weapon go. The other courser proceeded to open up his cuirass as easily as a child splitting a pistachio shell with his first set of teeth.

By then, the third-rank man had arrived at the scene. He didn't try to break free of the saddle. Instead, he let his courser eat of his comrade the same way he would with any disadvantaged enemy on a battlefield. The roadway just before the stone was by this time quite crowded, and the fourth- and fifth-rank coursers seemed chary to jostle their brethren during a meal. So they were successfully halted.

The third-rank man waited and watched with either great patience or extreme depravity while the lizards ate the corpses. When they were finished, there was almost nothing left, just a few broken, twisted scraps of bronze armor. Their tongues had even cleaned the blood from the road. The riderless courser promptly mounted the face of the rock again and vanished over the top of it. But the third-rank man now had his mount at a calm and dignified halt before the rock, and its attitude seemed to be spreading backwards down the ranks.

"Isn't it marvelous how efficient they are?" Garong remarked, bringing up the furthest thing from Yharalon's mind at the moment.

"If my antelopes could climb walls like that," he said, "I wouldn't have a single antelope to my name."

"Are there any trees around here?"

"No. The closest ones are either back at the edge of the Wailing Wood, or else up above us in the house of the mountain men."

Yharalon knew what the commander was thinking. He wanted to fashion an enormous lever to roll the rock out of his way. This might have been a good plan if the rock hadn't been on a hill, with his army downhill from it. There was little question in Yharalon's mind what the rock was doing there.

"You do understand this is an ambush, right?" he asked. That sarcastic tone again—he somehow couldn't help it with this particular commander. Garong's own know-it-all tone invited it.

"Your mountain goats?"

"Indeed. Once we're nicely backed up on the road, they'll drop another one on our rearguard. I assume you've placed rearguards?"

"I don't know. That's Kyrik's department, not mine."

"At any rate, whoever or whatever is at the back of the column is about to take a rock that size or bigger to their heads. And there's nothing to be done about it because we don't have any room to turn around."

"So then what?"

"A rain of smaller stones and arrows from places above we can't see. Then, once every man and every lizard in the column is dead, they come down and pick through the wreckage and take whatever of yours they choose."

"That sounds unfortunate. It also sounds like there's not much we can do about it."

"Not that I can think of."

"But I'm not one to sit and wait to die. Herald!"

"Sire?" said a voice from behind him.

"Stake down your lizard. Go back to the train and return with ten men—soldiers, lizardmen, slaves, it doesn't matter, just get strong ones, and each of them with a bronze pick."

"Sire!" the herald said in acknowledgment.

But even with its neck chained and the stake ready in his hand, the lizard got out of his grasp as soon as he dismounted and darted forward among the ranks. Its tail brushed against Yharalon's leg, sending spears of ice through his veins. He could feel the urge in the courser under him to go after it, like an earthquake centered in the creature's heart. Garong was squeezing fiercely to keep it still. Two of the advance men, not so resolute, perhaps, at least managed to jump free as their lizards went over the rock. Where the men landed there was only the glutted courser of the trooper who was now in the first rank, and it had no interest in them.

"Since they're already there, bring two extra picks!" the commander called down the line to the herald, who, ignoring the loss of his mount, was already making his way back to the wagon train on foot.

"Sire!" the herald shouted back, seeming happy to be back on his own two feet.

Yharalon braced for the assault and told his dead he'd be seeing them soon, but the assault never came. The pickaxes rang out as the torches burned down and the night grew darker and darker. No giant boulder was heard tumbling down behind them, and no hail of slingstones and fire arrows came raining from above. Surely it had been the mountain men, though. Rocks did fall on mountain roads, but it was too much of a coincidence that one should fall here between the passing of the foresters and the arrival of the main column.

Yharalon figured the mountain men had made a calculation. Their projectiles would be none too accurate, sent down from a great height in the dark. Their tactic was just to pour death down onto the road, not really picking targets, until most of the screaming stopped. The problem, in this case, was that a volley like that would take out the men first, and then their coursers would be free—and able, presumably, to go right up to where the mountain men were lying in wait, or to where they hid their own animals and families and stocks of dried meat.

He was less interested in considering that his own men had set the trap. The possible reasons why they'd do such a thing were many, from simple practical joking, to buying more time to rest in camp after a hard day's ride, to much more sinister concepts: someone bent on undermining the entire mission, or one of the men who'd wanted to be chief trying to wreck Yharalon's reputation as a guide.

Whatever the cause of the rock being there, it was a lot of work to break through it. The men began spelling each other in shifts and eventually a turn for Yharalon came. His homeland, Vydhmia, was a rocky country, and he'd grown old enough there to become handy with a hard-rock pick. Swing by swing, ring by ring, the obstacle was reduced to a rough cobble path.

The sky was already turning back to blue by the time they had the stone level enough for coursers to cross without throwing their riders. The commander ordered all coursery forward before work resumed on clearing enough of a path for the wagons. He was still strapping his armor back on when he had to rejoin Garong in the saddle.

They rode into the grey of dawn on a steadily dropping grade that promised a near end to the mountain stretch. Yharalon himself hadn't gone this way many times, though plenty of his men had. He knew that as soon as they exited the pass they would see and hear the falls of the mighty Baloc thundering down from its highland source. This side of the river was called "Nydhia" among outlanders, even though it wasn't the king's land. The people were mostly northmen who'd left for one reason or another, and Nydhian was the tongue of such taverns and markets as there were.

On the other side was "Walthor," a different sort of place because its people were drawn from the empire. In fact, it had only a few Walthorians, but many of every other nation under the Saspiard thumb, including Saspia itself. The majority of the people living in "Walthor" were runaway slaves, a type that Nydhia did not breed, having outlawed slavery thousands of years ago. The Walthorians there were mostly men who loved other men. Two of their villages were called Inirriu, after the shrine where they'd been commanded by Walth to cleanse themselves, but which no one had ever found.

It was a confusing place, "Walthor," and not just because it had more than one village of the same name. There was usually a war going on there, but that wasn't it either. The northern end of the region butted up on the places south of Witches Valley, unvisited by the wise. The farther you went in that direction, the more witchery could be felt in the land itself, by the roadside, in ordinary places the realm of weeds, bugs, trash, and other negligible things. Opaque mists spread along the ground at ankle height and, when they cleared, would make you swear the road had shifted under you. There were grabbing roots under the mist that seemed to be looking for your feet, and shimmering berries that made your mouth water even after you'd seen them drop a comrade dead the moment he tasted them.

In short, north of the Baloc along the Witchroad was the sort of place Yharalon would normally avoid. He'd never been in a mood to dabble in any kind of sorcery; he wasn't even curious to see it in action. Two or three times he'd been up into "Walthor" with a cartload of something he couldn't sell south of the river. That was all.

Yharalon had instructed Shig to set up the camps on the banks, so that all water supplies could be replenished and the animals given a long, cool drink. Now that the main column was a whole night delayed, haggard beyond repair, and mounted on dangerously famished lizards, his decision not to push on across the river seemed more than prudent. It was noon by the time they descended into the lightly wooded valley of the Far Upper Baloc. After conferring with the captain, who still hated Yharalon, Garong ordered the coursery to forage for wild prey for an hour and, once they'd fed their lizards, get back on the road and have their own midday meal in the saddle.

The commander left Yharalon sitting by the roadside while he went off to hunt. By the time they returned, he was hungry and resigned himself to a heinous offering of the smoked lizardmeat that imperial soldiers mostly lived on. He got back in his seat behind Garong as reluctantly as he chewed the courser's grass-eating cousin. His own rations were still in Tooth-Head's saddlebags, and he hoped they hadn't been pilfered in his absence. Mynch was a good man, and it was a comfort to have him watching over his belongings.

"No one had much luck out there," Garong remarked. "We

caught a little groundling bird but this girl is still hungry."

"Unfortunate," Yharalon said. "Wrong time of day for a hunt."

He thought he was beginning to smell the smoke of the foresters' camp, though it might have been a forest fire.

"Indeed. What are they going to eat when we get to camp?"

"I'm sure my boys could go up the hill and round up a few beasts—rock rats, rock lizards, that sort of thing. Your coursers eat anything that moves, right?"

"Indeed. But that sounds like a lengthy prospect. I'm afraid their jaws will be on us before your boys get back."

"Could be, sir. I don't know much about lizardry. It's live food they need, right? Would they eat a flopping fish? Plenty of fish in the Baloc. I'm sure some of my boys are rivermen with nets and basket-catchers in their packs."

"It still sounds like it'd be a long while before our coursers feast. What about your camprats?"

It was a horrible thought. The camprats were rodents, big versions of the rats the Saspiards fed their lizards, but to the foresters they were family, and their keen ears and noses and alarming voices were essential for survival in the outland. They had names and personalities, and not a single man in the camp would sooner feed his camprat to a courser than feed Commander Garong to his own courser.

"If you take a man's camprat, it's like taking his child. Just because we have two armies in two camps is no reason to start a war between them."

"You barbarians are so sentimental," Garong sighed. "If that's the way you're going to be, I suppose we can spare a couple dozen slaves."

Yharalon shuddered at the fate of the slaves, but it was nothing as grisly as what would ensue from the commander's original proposition.

"So, what's tomorrow look like?"

"We might think of resting, foraging, that sort of thing. The banks of the Baloc are as good as it's going to get for a while. Or really, at all, until we get back here."

"That might sound good to you, but you don't have senators and chancellors breathing down your neck. You probably don't even know what those words mean."

They were Saspiard words, and Yharalon affirmed that he didn't. It was all the same to him. The lizards were the ones that could run short of food. Antelopes never really did. You only needed to bring along fodder if you wanted to be sure they could run whenever you needed them to, but that was true most places you'd ride in the outland.

"If you want to press on, we'll be going through runaway slave country for a spell. A small risk there; since you look so much like the army, someone might think you're a slave-catching detail. But the most they're going to do is throw rocks at you."

"I've had worse thrown at me."

"I'm sure. Further along, it gets more settled. There are towns of a sort, but I don't recommend stopping there."

"Inirriu. I know it well. I had some senatorial business to conclude in the court of King Sdubb. I found him an excellent fellow."

Garong spoke of one of two towns of the same name, both of which had "Kings" who also went by the same name, styling themselves heirs to the ancient, fallen kingdom of Walthor. In fact, they were rivals in the business of sorcery, a trade that both towns plied based on their nearness to the so-called witch lands. The commander surely referred to the larger and more southerly of the two, which lay at the end of the road connecting this part of the outland to the empire.

It was strange to be employed as guide to a man who had been places he himself had never dared to go, and to guide him through those very places. Yharalon reminded himself that each had his own area: Garong, without him, would be lost in the woods and swamps, just as he would be lost in a world of slingspells, charlatans, and whatever these *senators* and *chancellors* were.

"North of Inirriu is where it starts to get weird," he went on. "We'll have need to rest well because there'll be no camping in Witches Valley or the places south of there."

"*Places south of there?* That's rather specific."

"It's as specific as you want to get with places like that."

Garong was silent, his face calculating. He was probably resolving that some local superstition wasn't going to stop him from finding something valuable. Many before him had had that same thought, and none had ever been seen again. Actually, it wouldn't have been a bad thing if the commander were to follow his urges down a witch-country side road, as long as he left his paymaster's chest with the column.

"It's best we go through at speed," Yharalon continued. "Eat and drink in the saddle and don't dawdle anywhere. There's not a thing in those lands, not a tree, a pool, a stone, the moss on the stone, the flea in the moss, that might not have been put there to trick a traveler. And gods preserve us if we come across a hut or a cottage."

"What harm could a cottage bring us?"

"There's not supposed to be anyone living out there, even by the laws of the outland, such as they are. Picture the person who does."

"A witch?"

"Or something."

By then, he could tell that the smoke came from campfires, and even detect a hint of antelope dung. The homey smells heightened the strangeness of the topic at hand: the places where a whiff of chimney smoke might carry you off to the land of the imps, the places where stepping in a dung-flop might pull your foot through to the dark side of the world.

"When's the last time you were up that way?" the commander asked.

"Never."

"Then what kind of guide are you?"

"The kind that's alive today. Because no one who's been up that way is."

The shadows were lengthening by the time they arrived. As they came down through the valley the two camps on the riverbank had been visible from a long way off; the neat, townlike arrangement of the Saspian bivouac and the spiraling rows of the foresters' tents. The lightly-wooded land gave the road a pleasant dappling of sun and shade, and above, graceful spade-tailed skylizards were gathering for their evening fish hunt.

The coursers were moving slowly, half-drugged now to keep them docile at the peak of their hunger. It had been the captain, not the commander, who insisted on a stop for this treatment. Yharalon was in no hurry, and he was glad to have the mass of coiled-up, angry sinews he'd been riding reduced to a slow river of jelly. Then again, he'd heard that coursers, even well-fed ones, would sometimes attack their riders or each other because they were too tired to march on.

Everything the Saspiards did, it seemed, depended on this kind of balance; a tiny, tippy toehold with death lying in wait whichever direction you might fall. A man might own a thousand slaves, most of whom would kill his whole family given the slightest opportunity, yet he'd keep them on his land and even in his house. For his part, Yharalon preferred to stake his life on things more dependable than gold or the loyalty of hireling guards.

Around a bend in the road, the falls of the Baloc came into view. They'd been able to hear them faintly since coming out of the mountains, and now that there were no trees or hills to block it, the noise rose to a deafening roar. The falls looked like a giant's staircase, half a dozen enormous cascades leading upward into the mysterious heights of the Sunsets. An outland legend held that the giant's wife had tipped over her pail to wash the steps at the beginning of time, and she'd be coming down with her mop when the bucket finally drained at the end of time.

Yharalon smiled slyly when he realized he'd set the camps in a place where the men wouldn't be able to converse normally. That was good—the usual drinking fights might not break out if men had to shout themselves hoarse just to get their insults heard. But as he rode into camp, he wished he were able to hear what the men were saying. Whatever they were doing, they stopped as soon as they saw him. Games of chits, antelope grooming, drinking, and sword sharpening paused. Even one man who was pissing turned to gawk at Yharalon, without bothering to stop or put himself away.

Once their eyes were on him, there was no mistaking the look on their faces. They suspected him. It wasn't anger, yet. It was more like someone had made sure the question *Who is this Yharalon, really?* was on all of their minds at once.

He was used to being suspected. The outland was not a trusting place and its people were both suspicious and suspect. Suspicion had pushed them there or drawn them there, or perhaps they'd been born there, which made their whole lives suspect. But it wasn't the same thing when you were supposed to be a leader of men. It was almost as if Yharalon the town had turned against Yharalon the man, its own embodiment.

So he walked on to his tent, fixing his gaze dead ahead and carrying himself as nobly as he was able. It was at times like these that the airs he put on, if that's truly what they were, turned out to be useful. Mynch was outside his tent waiting with Tooth-Head on a hempen tether.

"Lord Yharalon," he said, not intending, it seemed, to be funny or caustic, but using the title to create distance between himself and his longtime neighbor. "He's in good spirits. I gave him some of your redcorn fodder earlier and he took a long drink from the Baloc."

"Thanks, Mynch."

Mynch handed him the tether and walked off without saying goodbye or looking back once. Yharalon set about unpacking Tooth-Head then led him to the corral. The sun was behind the mountains by then. With his buck all squared away, he decided the best thing to do was retire to his tent. It was already quite dim inside, so he lit a sloth-fat lamp of boiled hide. The stink of the burning oil reminded him again of home, of his lodge. How he wished he could read and had something to read, some words from long ago and far away to distract him from everything outside the tent.

Instead, the only distraction that night came in the form of Naihard Shig, who strolled right through the canvas flaps without so much as a *By your leave, sir.*

"Good evening, chief," the rogue said pleasantly, his face betraying none of the suspicion he'd seen in the others.

In truth, he should have checked in with Shig immediately upon returning to the camp, but he'd been too shaken by the men's reaction to think of it. He'd actually left the rogue in charge, technically, by not seeking him out and letting him know he was relieved.

"Good evening. I trust your ride here was less eventful than ours?"

"Nothing untoward. Just a bit of panting over the steep rises."

"We ran into a bit of trouble, as you might've guessed from the late hour."

"More than guessed. Been through it all with the commander. Tough break, losing the rats and then running into that rock."

"Tough indeed."

He peered into the rogue's eyes hoping to catch a glimmer of guilty knowledge, but the rogue was much better at this game than he was. Even if there was something there, it would have taken someone much more devious than Yharalon to find it.

"We've had a lot of time in camp," Shig went on, "and you know how men get bored. I sent out hunting details and scouting details but that couldn't be all of them, all the time. Once the tents were all set up and the corral staked out, they took to gossiping."

"As men do."

"Indeed. But the rumor that's spreading, well—it's unfortunate. For you, that is. A very unfortunate thing to have people saying about you."

The multiple references to *fortune* or lack thereof made Yharalon wonder if luck had anything at all to do with the start of this rumor.

"Well, what is it?" The mystery had been gnawing at him long enough that he was in no mood to hear some delicate version.

"I mean, with all your talk of honor and such. Who talks like that out here? It was only a matter of time before people started smelling silver on you."

Shig referred to the Silver Prophets, a banned cult in the empire that believed the ancestors of the Saspiards were returning from across the ocean to seek their vengeance on a nation grown soft and weak. It was a preposterous tale, but it did proliferate in the outland, since the Prophets all had a hefty price on their heads and often took to the Witchroad as a last resort. Yharalon almost laughed at the notion he'd be part of such a thing, when he struggled sometimes to believe in even the Nydhian gods.

"And then this weird Saspiard shows up dripping with arms and gold," the rogue continued, "and he picks you as chief above, I'm sorry, but I think you know, better men. Older, steadier, more blooded fighters. What do you think that looks like to people?

"I'm sorry to be the bearer of this rumor, since it's the last thing I'd ever believe myself. But if I look at it through their eyes, not knowing you as I know you, I mean, it does make a lot of sense."

Yharalon fell into deep thought, ignoring his company for a moment. There was no way he could lead the foresters, especially not in battle, if they believed he was out to betray them. And the idea of a plot was quite plausible. In a land that swallowed armies, there would be many opportunities for two devious persons to walk away from this expedition with gold enough, just from the pay chest, to set themselves up for life.

The gold being the only thing that held a mercenary army together, the loss of it would probably spell the end of all of them. They'd go off alone or in small bands, trying to make their way to here or there, and most wouldn't. So it was in everyone's interest to keep the army together—everyone except the supposed conspirators. Among campfire rumors, this was one of the more credible he'd heard. The silver cult was one of the few places two men as oddly matched as the commander and Yharalon might have forged a secret connection.

"What can I do to prove myself to them?" he asked after a long silence.

"Short of cutting the commander's throat, I can't think of what," Shig replied. "Oh, and this is from him," he added, detaching a skin of wine from the back of his belt and tossing it onto Yharalon's desk.

It was funny to have a desk in unmapped country, a surface for rolling out scrolls that he didn't have and couldn't read anyway, but this was a Saspian officer's tent and equipped as such. He thought about broaching the topic of a writing lesson, but it seemed too much to add to this conversation. So he conveyed his thanks for the wine and gave Shig permission to take his leave.

Army ricewine was not to Yharalon's taste, but he needed it that night, and it did the job.

IV

"Inirriu!" The commander smirked. "You can't fault a place for announcing itself boldly."

For his part, Smatt could barely look at the fresco. Of the religion he was raised in, the only tenet he'd faithfully kept was the prohibition of the act depicted, if only because he found it the opposite of tempting. Seeing such a thing at such a scale—the figures eightfold their natural size, in vivid color—was worse than repulsive. It made him want to turn his courser and flee, abandon the whole venture with no regard for anything, not his contract nor even his precious engines of war.

"This is a bad place," he pronounced. "We should put it to the torch while we're here with an army."

"Nonsense." The grin spread wider across Garong's pockmarked face. "These are your own people, brother." He said the last word in Walthorian, ridiculously. "Tonight, we dine with the king. He's an old associate of mine."

It was more surprising to Smatt that this place had a king than that the commander had done business with such a person. A feast was not a terrible prospect after a week of field rations. He just hoped the enormous painting didn't foreshadow the evening's entertainment.

"Burn a town for nothing? I don't know what sort of slingspear you call yourself," Oo'ogrin, the expedition's master waggoneer, remarked, "but I'm not doing any fighting I'm not paid for."

"Calling yourself a fighter now, are you?" Smatt chortled. Oo'ogrin was a lizardman, not a soldier. His habit of attaching himself to mercenary columns didn't raise him above a carter in Smatt's eyes.

"I think we can all find it in our hearts to do a little good now and again," said Kyrik, the coursery captain. He, too, was sneering at the hideous painting. Smatt wondered if this lackship Mirsatic had made his career on land out of an aversion to his own race's reputed practices on the high seas.

"If you think torching a town is good, even a town full of buggers," Oo'ogrin replied, "I think you might be a stretch farther down the road to evil than I am. And I'm a few coursings east of good, myself."

"The town's not full of buggers, no more so than any other town," Garong laughed. "The painting is just a joke on the name."

In Walthic scripture, Inirriu was the name of a spring where the god instructed His sons to cleanse themselves should they ever have intimate contact with each other. It was said to be to the north and west, but no one had ever found it. Smatt had long known there were at least two towns of this name in the outland, hearkening back to some pious bugger who'd gone off looking for the spring. He'd never given it much thought before, but now Smatt wondered what Garong was referring to that could possibly be more vile.

"Whatever you say," Smatt concluded, "but if the order of the day is trifling with fancy-boys, I'll just set up camp right here and sup on gruel and dried meat, like the foresters. You can have your bugger king and his bugger feast to yourself."

"Gods, you'd think I was trying to fuck *you,* the way you go on. I'd rather fuck an actual he-goat, and I'd pick a skinnier one."

At that the whole company burst into laughter, and even Smatt grinned in spite of himself. The word *goatman,* to which Garong referred, was undoubtedly a slur, but the Walthorians matched the Saspians one for one on this count by slandering their forefathers as having lain with snakes. The commander wasn't all that Saspian himself, so what did he really have to say about whose grandpa fucked which species of animal?

The four of them were riding abreast at the head of the column. Of the expedition's officers, only Yharalon, the scout, was absent, since the beast he rode wouldn't mix with coursery. They were out ahead somewhere, his antelope riders. Better them than Smatt to be first to meet whatever came at them. Smatt's job was to knock things down from a distance, and he preferred to do it without getting blood on his nice white goatswool kilt.

"Besides, if you knew what business this place was really in, you'd probably make a waddling run for the nearest den of fancy-boys, and hide behind their skirts," Garong added with a sinister chuckle.

"Sorcery," Oo'ogrin said softly. "I heard about it. The people here sling spell the way we sling spear. And have they not done well for themselves."

The lizardman had a point. Gross as it was, the fresco was as brightly colored and finely detailed as it was enormous, and must have cost a fortune to produce. As they drew closer to the center of the town, the buildings were proving to be fine, built mostly of sandstone like old Walthorian temples. The stone must have been dragged or carted in, since there were no such formations or quarries nearby. For all its evident vice, the place didn't look like it belonged in the outland at all. Squinting, Smatt could have believed it was any number of open market towns in the province of his birth.

"I can't argue with any of what you say," the commander said in a tone of mock disappointment, "but I'm sure this place has a few surprises left that you haven't spoiled yet."

For Smatt, the first of these was seeing a warrior monk, or at least a man dressed up as one. The caste had been banned in

Walthor at the time of the conquest, so it was like seeing a figure that had come to life and stepped down off some ancient frieze. His tonsure, the drape of his robe, the way he slung his quoits and fighting-stick all suggested slavish reproduction of a very old model—seven centuries old, at least, and probably older.

Smatt felt an urge to address the man, but thought better of it as they rode by. Whether this was the adherent of some mad cult or an orthodox man of god, conversing with him was likely to lead to trouble. Smatt, after all, was not exactly a pious son of Walth. For his part, the throwback monk observed the newcomers carefully but with neither surprise nor suspicion, as if columns of armed riders were an everyday sight on the main street of this town.

Anything went, Smatt supposed, in a town where the main street was the Witchroad. He took one last glance at the fresco and shuddered. Between the buggery and the sorcery, this "Inirriu" was no place he wanted to mingle with. Yet his companions seemed ready to dive in, and without them he'd be as good as fucked. Three fine field-pieces and one fat man without guards would count for nothing but easy pickings in the outland.

They entered a plaza set around a pyramid constructed in the image of the Great Pile at Kwalt. Though it must have been smaller, it looked as big as the original after so many coursings through empty countryside. The structures around the square were stately, built like shrines and meeting-halls and monasteries even if none of them were any such things. Some appeared to be functioning as shops, but it was hard to tell since they had no signboards or barkers hawking their goods. At the pit of his stomach, Smatt knew these must be the businesses Garong had mentioned. Their facades were bright with red ocher paint and blue faience tile, and the few people milling around the plaza wore fine attire.

"Who pays for it all?" Smatt asked of no one in particular,

assuming Garong would be the one to answer no matter whom he addressed.

"Who indeed? Haven't you ever been tempted to cast a spell, or have one cast on your behalf? I pity you if you haven't. For what is it, after all, to live, to lust, to yearn and strive, if not to reach for the impossible? Show me the man who's never heard the necromancer's call, and I'll show you the man who's had little to lose and small hope of gaining much more."

"I suppose I'm that man," Smatt said. "I've always been content with the world as it is. I like the dead to stay dead, thank you very much to the gods or whatever keeps them that way. But I wasn't looking for a philosophical answer. These people are up to their brows in gold. Where is it all coming from?"

"For some reason, I've never been invited to peruse their account-books," the commander said wryly, "but I'm sure our host will be able to shed more light on the subject if you inquire politely."

They had arrived before the finest building of all, set behind a portico of towering columns at the top of a flight of steep stone steps. Some heavy-set guards in a strange, gold-trimmed livery were waiting at the bottom to take their coursers. Smatt hadn't seen the commander send anyone ahead, but it was obvious they were expected. He chased from his mind a banal and foolish notion of wizards gazing into crystals. *What would've been magic is if anyone managed to miss us coming up the Witchroad.*

"But none of it is real," Smatt went on, half in the tone of a question. "Sorcery and necromancy and such. It's all bunk. How could there be so much gold in it if it never really works?"

"Are you really quite sure of that?" The commander smiled as he dismounted.

"Half the time, there's no saying if it worked or not," Oo'ogrin chimed in as two of the guards led them up the steps. "Because the caster got what they asked for. Was it the spell or was it chance. No one can say. When they don't get what they want, they just say someone else had a stronger spell. That's the magic of magic." *Not surprising the little freak knows about this sort of thing.*

"Yes, what he said," Garong said, "but also—well, let's leave that for tomorrow. By the end of tomorrow, if we live, we'll each have a much better-informed opinion as to what is real, and what is not."

The words were something worse than ominous.

10 talons of gold, above all costs. That's what they were paying Smatt. *10 talons of gold, above all costs.* He silently repeated the sum in time with the slap of his sandals on the steps, pushing terror down into the soundless depths of his gut, where it would soon turn to a hunger so profound as to overwhelm any sense of disgust at his food, surroundings, or company. A fat man did have some advantages in war and adventure.

"I hear they can only get to you if you believe in witchcraft," said Captain Kyrik.

"Haven't you also heard they can turn you into a lizard just by showing you their naked bellies?"

The commander seemed to be enjoying this so much that Smatt almost wondered if he were trying to increase his profits by thinning the ranks of his officers through desertion. It made no sense, though. Oo'ogrin's departure, in particular, would have rendered the whole venture useless. Without carts and lizards, they'd be able to carry back little more than a good night's take by the thieves guild of any small city. It seemed Garong just couldn't resist an opportunity to sow dread.

They passed between columns as girthy as the eldest trees in the Forest of Oobh. The sandstone had been laboriously weathered with adzes to look much older than it was. Beyond, the facade of the palace loomed, showing scenes in bas-relief from the life of Walth. When the Noon God was still a mortal priest and His kingdom was still known as the land of Uthu, Walth had fought a war against the lich prince Rhll and his followers.

The subject had been a favorite in Walthorian art since before there was a Walthor. Smatt paused to study the scene where He cast the liches into the sky, the last time they were seen on earth. Instead of the usual anguish, the sculptor had carved a look of sadness in their hollow eyes, as if one was meant to be sad to see them banished.

Smatt shuddered again as Garong's words—*the necromancer's call*—echoed in his mind. His trepidation worsened when he realized that the statues flanking the palace gates were also meant to be liches. From a distance, they had looked like the statues of warriors that stood by the entrance to nearly every old, important building in Walthor. Up close, he could see that their faces were fleshless, their eyes mere sockets, their gaping mouths painted black with rose-gold flecks. They warned him not to enter, yet he followed the others in.

Past the gates, the building presented no grand antechamber nor inner atrium. It seemed so dark after the sunlit portico that for a moment Smatt thought he'd been served some blinding poison in his canteen water, or by a needle so fine he hadn't felt its punch. But as his eyes adjusted, he could see they were standing in a corridor no wider than the gates, its ceiling completely obscured by the gloom. The walls, set with burning torches none too close together, appeared rough-hewn at first, but in fact they were scored with Walthic verses in old-fashioned chisel-point hieroglyphics. Smatt was thankful he could barely read the symbols and whatever distorted blasphemies they surely contained.

The corridor seemed longer than the depth of the building's

exterior had appeared. No sorcery—a familiar pain in his shins informed him that the floor must be sloping upward, adding the square of the elevation to the square of its horizontal extent. As an engineer, he prided himself in making such calculations without the aids that others used, wax tablets and compasses and counting-frames, but indoors he found his skill quite useless. All he could be sure of was that they were headed for the upper rear part of the building, as far as one could get from the only exit he knew of, and he didn't like it.

At the end of the passage, the guards pulled back a massive drape of crimson silk to admit the guests to a large and elegant dining hall. There was nothing morbid or eerie to speak of here: no liches adorned the walls, which instead were hung with tapestries of hunting scenes in the Nydhian style, all soft shades of russet and green. A long marble table carved with mercifully abstract designs was pushed to one side of the room, leaving most of the floor open as if for dancing at a feast. Smatt was still trying to decide whether all this made him more or less uneasy when an unseen gong sounded so suddenly and thunderously as to drive all thought from his head.

Wild music erupted from the same hidden place, the traditional instruments of Walthor—shrill bone whistles, ringing frame drums, barley grains hissing and swishing against the walls of gourd rattles—at a pitch and tempo never heard in the solemn rites of his homeland. From a side-door he hadn't noticed before, a troupe of dwarves burst into the room. They were clad in bright silk, and the way they all came out dancing in a line would have been rather comical if he weren't so afraid of what was coming next. Indeed, his fears seemed close to realization when the dwarves began stripping off their clothes, which turned out to be long scarves cleverly draped around their otherwise nude bodies. Once reduced to tiny loincloths, they began to perform acrobatic feats with the scarves, swinging each other in circles like slingstones, whipping the cloth in the air and pretending to climb it like stairs before it settled, all in time to the frantic playing of the orchestra.

The performance ended with the dwarves stacked up in the shape of a pyramid as the music slowed. When the acrobats went out, they were replaced by a troupe of dancers, all comely young women wearing skirts and gorgets of strung beads and little else. A bass flute, absent from the last arrangement, set a hoarsely erotic tone, and the rhythm mimicked the build of passionate lovemaking. As the song went on, Smatt realized there was a different musical theme for each of the dancers' feminine characteristics, which the choreography would emphasize each time the theme returned. He lost himself in the music and the spectacle, forgetting all his premonitions of wrongness.

When the music reached its crescendo, the one he'd had his eye on—a dark-eyed, purebred Walthorian girl with a boyish build and thick body hair that flashed darkly with every flip of her skirt— danced up to Smatt, rousing him from his stupor. To his further surprise, she took his fleshy hand in her small, delicate one as best she could and led him to one of the seats at the table. Most shocking, she seated herself in his lap, arms draped around his neck. Smatt wondered nervously if he was going to be expected to pay for all this.

Once he and all the other guests were similarly situated, a conch-blast blew and two guards walked in. They were followed, none too closely, by a man Smatt assumed must be the self-styled "Sdubb, King of Inirriu." The name he had taken was that of Walth's only son, a mortal, whose line had ruled Walthor until the day Orthox bent his knee to the Beheader. In keeping with his moniker, this so-called Sdubb was dressed in yellow-embroidered robes of snowy goatswool, with a circlet of gold on his head. His bearing too, was credibly regal, compensating for both his unusual height and the large gut that most Walthorian men carried once youth had left them. The only things out of keeping with the image were his shaven head and face, but even the greatest kings of Walthor had worn this look at times as a penance.

"Welcome, friends," he said, smiling graciously. His voice was as deep as his appearance and manner would have suggested. "I hope you enjoyed the entertainment."

"Still enjoying it," Garong leered as he tugged at the sullen girl on his lap. "Of course, you know my taste in entertainment."

"Indeed, doctor," Sdubb leered back, "though for the sake of your men, I have arranged for something more to general tastes, at least while we dine."

"Reasonable," the commander replied. Smatt felt sick that he already knew how this man behaved when he was aroused, the way he'd clip his sentences. Garong repositioned the girl as if she were an inconveniently situated piece of saddlery.

"Have I said welcome to Inirriu, my friends? Well, let me say it again, for the welcome of my court is the most generous to be found." As he spoke, a trio of servants in the same strange livery as the guards put silver goblets in front of each guest and filled them with beer from a gourd. Sdubb had his own special cup—the gourd, and its remaining contents—which he raised with both hands upon receiving it.

"To the success of your journey!" he roared. The whole company drank. Smatt found the beer quite to his taste, thin and sour like the stuff his mother used to brew at home.

"Our journey will make us wealthy men," Garong replied, his composure regained. "Kings in our own right. Someday, we shall return the favor of Your Highness' hospitality."

"I do not doubt you are stalwart in your mission, and sure to succeed where others have failed," said the "King," his smile becoming faint as he spoke. "But how can you be a king when you live beneath an emperor? No matter how much gold and land you claim in his house, you still live in his house, and he can send you again to the edge of the world and even more dangerous places. The Volcano, perhaps, or the isle of his forebears, where they say man is his own meat."

Smatt could feel the commander bristling. He had long suspected that, while Garong didn't mind being on this mission, he hated the fact that someone had been able to send him on it. Smatt and the others had this over him, being freely contracted, rather than coerced by some greater power, to go on a journey from which none had ever returned.

"For some of us, the outland isn't enough," Garong said after regaining his composure. "Your house is fine, but your people are few, and your law doesn't stretch a coursing from here in any direction. I get gold every week from slaves I've never seen in a place I'll never visit. Does your kingdom give you that?"

A crash of the gong saved Sdubb from having to answer this impudent question. What followed was the arrival of nothing less than a full Walthorian feast: goat haunches rubbed with herbed salt and roasted over a fire, whole grassfowl cooked under the goat in its drippings, an enormous lobefin steamed with turmeric butter, and stacks of puffed barley-breads that would burst with gouts of steam when pulled apart. The unseen band struck up a classic melody, and the men began to eat.

They were a strange company to be gathered for such a meal. Smatt himself, the only Walthorian other than their host, came from a lowborn family that only tasted goat and lobefin on high holy days. Beneath his finery and pretense, it was clear Sdubb came from a similar station. Garong looked like a street urchin that had somehow outlived and outgrown his lot in life. Oo'ogrin just looked like a slave. Only Kyrik seemed to belong in such a room as this, and he belonged as a guard at the door, not a guest at the table. The conversation proceeded in Saspian, the only tongue they all had in common.

Smatt found that his appetite was unaffected by issues of appropriateness, and soon his beard was running with grease. He considerately tried to avoid getting anything on the girl in his lap until he dribbled some sauce on her by accident and she licked it off her bare arm like a starveling. So he started offering her morsels, one small bite for each of his huge ones, and a sip of beer for each gulp he took.

"I don't know what I think about going to war with a man who's kind to animals," Garong chuckled, never one to let the slightest kindness go without mockery.

"Your Highness," Oo'ogrin said, prudently changing the subject between bites of grassfowl leg, "I'm afraid some of us are at a disadvantage, missing what others have."

"How do you mean?" asked the "King," in an exaggerated tone of shock at the thought of such a breach in manners.

"Well, sire, it seems you have a past connection to our dear commander, yet he has never told us the tale, as I'm sure you would have by now, had you known of his omission."

"Indeed," Captain Kyrik said, looking irritated at the fact that a lovely, mostly naked young woman was seated on his knee. "It must have been an unusual circumstance, and thus a worthy tale to tell, that brought your kingdom and our empire together."

"To be honest," Sdubb replied, likely not being honest, "I can barely remember. The Silver Sillies, was it?"

"Yes, that was it," Garong said, himself annoyed at being cornered into bringing his business to light. "An unusually well-armed band of them. It would've spelled the end of Inirriu if they'd taken over here, and then years on top of that for the senate or worse, the Society, to root them out."

"A most unfortunate circumstance. My royal guards could have handled it, but I was glad for the help. Garong is more—discreet than a troop of spearmen when it comes to putting down a cult, but quite as effective."

"To the Commander," Oo'ogrin said, his face a bit quizzical as he raised his goblet. Everyone repeated his words and drank.

"You take away what holds an army together, you take away the army," Garong expounded. "In that case, it was charisma. A cult falls apart without its leaders egging it on from day to day. In our case, it's gold. Take away the gold and we have no army. What holds your guard together, Your Highness?"

"Why, magic of course! The same thing that holds all of Inirriu together." He roared with laughter, but not necessarily the kind that followed a joke.

"My men,"Garong said, "were quite curious about what all that entails."

"It's almost the Age of Jaw Courser, by Walth," Sdubb said indignantly, though with a good-natured smile, his words mixing Saspian calendar with Crescentine god. "You'd think ancient rumors would be put to rest by now. But no, here we are. It doesn't start with me, you know. I'm just here to rein it in, so to speak, keep it from getting too far out of hand."

When it gets to be known as far away as Vajra, or even Torkiz, that Alth Dawdanna has a ceremony that helps find lost gold, or Green Yizian can cure tumors with his hands, people come all the way here with their complaints and their money. And by the time they get back, everyone at home will be saying Dawdanna's a fraud, Yizian a fake, but Thrak Mahorn brews a truth serum for the Service, and will let it go to others for the right price. And then you go to him and let the right price go, and come home to find out Thrak is discredited and Dawdanna is famous again, with his fish-finding wand, all past frauds forgotten. And so on.

"Whoever you go to for your spell, they'll tell you they need stuff to get it done. Mandrake root, of course, but only if it was gathered by the Wenzyr family, who claim to have a charm that lets them harvest north of where others can go. The dried organ of some wilderland beast, which I'm sure Hehemo Yuzz is holding for you in one of his little jars. Maybe a spark of the lichfire itself, forever sealed in a tiny box that none dare open. A good business that is, right? You buy a box that's either empty or sure to kill you if you open it. Then, of course, your friendly necromancer will gladly take it from there, for another fee."

"The only business better," Oo'ogrin pronounced, "is religion. And how has the world turned out."

Smatt imagined this dull-eyed man would prefer a world where people still went to hill witches instead of surgeons for their medicine, fought wars with bamboo bows and reed arrows, and paid for things with rice and fruit instead of money. He'd always felt contempt for his fellow men of conquered races who looked back as if the forward march of time could be reversed. For his part, Smatt had headed straight to the heart of the empire as soon as he was able, tasted its cruel pleasures and learned the most violent of its arts. And it had served him well enough, so far. He wondered again why he was risking it all on this expedition, but there was a risk of taking an arrow through the neck on the most routine and least remunerative of jobs. A good mercenary was a good gambler, nothing less, nothing more.

"And if, for some reason, none of it works," Sdubb concluded, "back home, they'll tell you that you found the wrong Inirriu, since there is another town of our name, with a pretender to my name, and wizards who go by every famous name of ours, from Yizian to Dawdanna. That's why I had the painting done, so there'd be no such mistakes. And yet—people are fools."

With another crash of the gong, the next phase of the entertainment appeared, a trained ape with no attendant in sight. At no one's apparent prompting, this prodigious creature, about the height of a ten-year-old child and covered with coarse grey fur, began by refilling everyone's goblet with beer, kissing the cheeks of each of the girls in the guest's laps, and kneeling before Sdubb just like a human minion. Then a dozen wooden balls rolled into the room; the ape raced around catching them all, and proceeded to juggle them. Garong laughed with childish delight, and even the stern Captain Kyrik was moved to grin.

"I present to you Momo the Blue. I consider him to rank highest among my courtiers."

"I'm sure he gives excellent counsel," Oo'ogrin remarked.

"So," Garong said, his speech beginning to slur over his fourth full goblet, "what would Momo advise us of our journey tomorrow?" Sdubb grew serious, and Momo took up a place beside him, looking equally stern, as if he really were some gentleman at court.

"All true spells have one thing in common. Rather, there is one truth in all spells. They work on the mind. A mind in which a spell can work, is a mind on which a spell can work."

"Is it really true none have returned from the witch country since the Fist?" Kyrik asked, as usual trying to steer the conversation in a practical direction.

"Not really, no. None that you'd have heard of in your cities,"

Sdubb said. "Before the Fist, when the road was somewhat more in use, they'd take a toll from the senate—no one's sure exactly what, or how it was paid—and stay up in their Roost. The theory goes that it's still possible to pay them for passage."

"Theory," Captain Kyrik repeated dismissively.

"The Valley is under control of whoever lives up in the Roost. Control, I think, not who, is the key point. The places just south of there, the part no one has been able to pass, is to the witches what the outland is to you. Their people are there, but not their law. Before the Fist it wasn't so, but now it is. In my time here, I've met a few who wandered that way and made it back. Their tales have been different, colorful even, but the theme is always the same: they felt confused, but then found their heads and knew to turn back."

"Or perhaps they were confused into turning back, if the danger was all in their heads," Garong said, still managing to provoke as he settled into a drunken stupor.

"Perhaps. I suppose you'll find out tomorrow, one way or another."

As the night went on, Smatt's memories, the sequence of events in particular, grew hazy. There was more music and dancing and a wrestling tournament involving the naked dwarves, and in the midst of it all, he had a chance to learn the girl's name and exchange a few words with her. Ennenia had been born a slave in Walthor, but taken to the outland by her mother as an infant, so she had no recollection of homeland or empire or any place besides "Inirriu." Here, her mother had done the same job as her until her comeliness faded, at which point she was reassigned to the palace kitchens. The turmeric butter on the fish was one of her most prized sauces.

None of this meant very much to Smatt, but deep in the night, after she'd led him stumbling to the sumptuous chamber where he was to spend the night, he bade her close her legs and cover herself when she lay down on the bed.

"I don't please you?" she said as she sadly obeyed.

"It's not that." He felt quite sober all of a sudden. "I'm a soldier of fortune and I've led a far from exemplary life. I've bedded whores and even slaves. I find it's not to my liking when a woman gives herself other than freely."

"But I like you," she said, "and I am free."

Free how? Smatt thought. She could hardly run off on her own. There was no real law here, no one but the "King" to protect her, and she wouldn't get ten steps from the palace without someone snapping her up. If she allowed Smatt to pile his fat, hairy weight on top of her, it would surely be for want of better options.

Instead, he lay down next to her and cradled her head in the crook of his arm. She nestled in like a child, as if out of pure instinct. Her skin felt cool against his.

"What do you know of the witch country, Ennenia?"

Though still puzzled at his refusal to take her, the girl, apparently under orders to give him everything he asked of her, answered freely.

"I have served Per Wenzyr in this house as I now serve you," she said, "and he told me the charm they use."

Smatt vaguely remembered the "King" mentioning a charm that kept one safe further north than one could go without it.

"And why would he tell you such a thing?"

She looked him in the eyes for the first time. Her eyes were brown and long-lashed. They could have been his own eyes as a boy her age.

"Men put things in me. They like to. They need to. They have put two babies in me already. But the thing they mostly like to put in me is their secrets."

Smatt paused to consider this, thinking of the times he'd overheard men babble things they wouldn't tell their best friend into the ears of prostitutes.

"It's why I like you," Ennenia said. "No secrets. If you had one, you would have put it in me by now. The men with the worst things to hide, it is like another sack they need to empty. They can't wait to spill it into me. You, you are a clean man. Clean inside. I don't meet one like you very often."

Smatt thought about explaining to her that it was easy not to have secrets if you weren't ashamed of anything, and that it was easy not to be ashamed of anything if you didn't have any scruples. But in the world they lived in, he had to concede his having nothing to hide still counted for something. Most men in his situation, for example, would have a plan in mind to fuck his comrades out of their shares of the loot, and this was exactly the kind of thing they'd brag about to their whores. Smatt simply wanted to fulfill his terms, take his contracted share, and go home. It seemed a low world that made a man good just for being straightforward, especially when his profession was knocking down walls and sinking ships.

"So, what is it?" he asked. "Or is that a secret you keep?"

"On the left side of the Witchroad, just before you reach the other town called Inirriu, there is a blue spruce growing in the midst of some Nydhian pines. You can tell it by its sweet smell, sweeter than any other spruce you have smelled. Take a sprig of that tree and tie it to your right wrist, and the witches south of the Valley won't bother you."

"It seems a bit silly. A magic tree?"

"Not at all. It's just a sign. The Wenzyr have a compact with them."

"But if there's no law there, not even witches' law, what's to make them honor the compact?"

"I don't know. I only tell you what I was told. But I do know the Wenzyr always return, and they bring the best root. My mother cooks medicine as well as food, and she sings praise of their mandrake."

"Hmm."

It was all a bunch of nonsense to Smatt, but of course he was going to get a sprig of that tree, and sprigs of it for his best men as well. Ennenia moved her head to rest her cheek on his chest. He couldn't tell if she was trying to arouse him or just using his ample flesh for a pillow. Either way, the small, soft weight of her head helped him fall into a deep sleep.

The next morning, he had but a short window of time to put the plan into action as the column approached the grove.

"Commander, by your leave, I'd like to break off here with a few of my men. We'll rejoin the column briefly."

"Having the shits?" Garong asked with an overly interested, prurient leer.

"We've some minor repairs to do on the frames of the engines. That looks like good pine, better than our spare timber. We'll cut down a young one—won't take but a quarter-hour."

The commander looked a bit suspicious, but gave his leave. When Smatt returned with his men and a freshly cut pine log for appearance's sake, he demanded to know what was meant by the sprig on his wrist, and why all who had left the column now wore one.

"Can't you smell how sweet it smells? It's going to be a hard ride today. An old Walthorian trick, freshening yourself with a sprig of spruce."

"You people," the commander sneered, "are all just girls." But he left off his inquiry there.

They rode on toward the witch country, their coursers three abreast on the wide road. Past the second "Inirriu"—a more typical outland town than its southerly namesake, built of wood and set behind a crude palisade—the commander called a halt and ordered that some of the expedition's stock of firebeetle be distributed to both coursers and men. The idea was to stay awake and keep moving until they were through the witch country, where the authorities unanimously recommended against sleeping or even allowing the night to fall on you. There'd be no way around the nightfall—the Roost was at least three coursings off, and the maps of the region tended to underestimate distances. So the plan was to stay awake, keep moving, and hope that most of the stories were just stories.

Smatt used a little firebeetle now and then; every soldier did. He was no fiend, had no love for the stuff, but sometimes in battle it was a choice between that and death. Engineers were particularly vulnerable if they dozed in the field, since everyone wanted to steal their pieces. Though his stomach was still sour from "King Sdubb's" generous pouring of beer, he promised himself a skin of wine once they made it through, to tamp down the heart-pounding and jitters from the drug. He was never thrilled to ride a hopped-up courser, either, but at least the one he'd been assigned was a gelding and relatively docile. They never gave the fast, fierce ones to a fat man.

With his senses heightened by the beetle, Smatt noticed changes in the plants and in the earth itself as they progressed. The soil smelled damp with something other than rainwater, and whatever that was appeared to have discolored the foliage, which on every tree and plant seemed either ruddier or bluer than it ought to be. The ancient cobbles of the road began to disappear under a half-dry, greenish mud that didn't bother the coursers but would've been foul for a man to walk on. Out of this mud grew long, creeping vines of a species Smatt had never seen before, and at the corners of his eyes the vines seemed to writhe like copulating serpents.

They passed through a cloud of bugs too tiny to see, but loud to the ears and unmistakable by the buzzing they made. Smatt covered his mouth and his ears but still they came in through his eyes and his nose. The itching was prodigious but stopped as quickly as the creatures had appeared. All around him, he saw men tugging at their lobes, covering one nostril to blow the other out, rubbing their eyes. It seemed a minor nuisance, but it was strange how vigorously and thoroughly the insects had attacked every orifice of each man's face.

As soon as they were gone, a mist, greenish like the mud, arose and covered the whole ground, obscuring even his courser's feet. The ocean was not far off, but it did not seem to be the source of this fog, since it came from all sides at once. Smatt told himself these must all be strange but natural things, the likely true source of the region's reputation.

Once the mist was on them, the column moved in fits and starts as one lizard after another caught its feet in the vines. The coursers were able to pull themselves free with obvious effort, indicating that a man would not be able to do the same, being so much weaker than a courser in every respect. Smatt resolved not to set his own feet down in this mist no matter what happened. He'd stay mounted, at least until his mount tried to mount him.

Despite these delays, they were able to ride a whole coursing before coming to a halt that was long enough for Smatt to make for the column head to find out why. The answer became clear as he rode up the flank. There was a hut in the middle of the road in front of them, a crude one built of bark planks with a roof covered in dry branches. A strange and ominous obstacle to be sure, but one that seemed dispatchable with half a dozen fire arrows. The foresters on their antelopes had gone off to the flanks while the coursery column stood before the hut, with captain and commander at the front, surrounded by their hand-picked men.

"Looks like you have need of an engineer," Smatt said jovially as he approached, only to be met with an angry shushing gesture from the captain. It was then he saw that a small, comely, young-looking woman in a plain drab dress stood between them and the hut. Her nostrils flared as Smatt approached and her eyes darted to his wrist. Just as quickly, she returned her eerie gaze to where it had been set before: on Commander Garong.

The mist began to fade all at once, and Smatt could see that he was on the road, while the column had gone off it. Ahead of him it passed obliquely through the crowd of foresters then stretched free and clear to the horizon. To his right, where he'd believed the road to be, there was only the hut and behind it, a field so thick with vines that the lizards couldn't go a single step without getting caught.

Garong and Kyrik and their guards apparently didn't see any of this; it was as if the mist hadn't cleared for them. Their eyes were just as set on the woman as hers were on Garong. The obvious choice, to regain the road and follow it around her and her house and her garden of wicked vines, was not occurring to them. It seemed the mist had faded for Smatt alone.

He had his priorities. Once a long moment had passed with no one saying or doing anything, he turned his lizard and rode back to where his men and engines were. By the time he returned with them, nothing had changed. The officers and the young woman—*witch,* he supposed—were still just staring at each other.

He brought his men to a halt a few strides behind them.

He was about to call out to the commander when Vixprin, his best loader, a big hefty man of Cucuthian origins, softly warned him to stay his tongue.

"We have the sign, they don't," he whispered. Smatt supposed he had experience with these things, coming from the hills of Outer Grendishland where witches still served as doctors. "If you tell them, you betray her. Who knows what that will bring?"

"Nothing, would be my guess," Smatt said, annoyed but still not raising his voice. "I don't see why they don't just take a moment to chew right through her and her hut, especially if they don't know it will just wind them up in the weeds."

"She made us see mist, then let us see through it."

"I'm sure she's just exploiting a trick of the light. But I have to give her credit for standing up to an army all alone like that."

"If she is alone. If she's even here at all."

Without directly acquiescing, Smatt heeded Vixprin's advice and quietly brought his little train forward, bypassing both witch and witch's hut. The foresters parted to let them through, their antelopes rearing and snorting at the nearness of lizardry.

"It's a trick," he said quietly in his best Nydhian as they passed. "This be the roadway."

One of the foresters nodded, but apparently thought enough of witchcraft himself to wait a while before doing anything with this information. Instead, the ragged ranks of antelope riders closed behind them and stood their ground. Smatt hoped he wouldn't be long without their escort.

The land changed again, the greenness of the mud turning to a black that would've been comforting if it hadn't been more like charcoal than rich soil. Somewhat addled by the beetle, Smatt wondered if they'd already gotten past the witch country and into the Wreck, where the Fire of Walth—the Saspiards' *Fist of Za*—had burnt the land. The plants here were sparse and took on a purplish tone at the edges of their leaves.

The road began to rise, which was a good sign. After all, the next named place they were supposed to reach was Witches Valley, and since they'd been on a flat plain all day, he reasoned there must be a hill before it. The return of sensible thoughts brought his mind back to his money.

"There's supposed to be some kind of toll ahead. It isn't mine to pay. We'll wait at the top of the ridge for the commander."

"They say it's not wise to stop or wait here," Vixprin replied. "Our orders were to keep going no matter what. The commander isn't following his own command, so perhaps he won't be joining us at all."

"Perhaps." Smatt looked back and laughed. "Or perhaps not."

Behind them, a column of black smoke was rising where the hut had been, and the advance scouts of the foresters could be seen coming up the road in the distance. It seemed someone had figured out that the insurmountable obstacle before them was nothing more than a frail, small person and a pile of sticks. The mist had apparently been dispelled along with its apparent summoner.

He told himself it was all just tricks, the fogs and fumes and mind-altering effects that could be obtained by mixing ordinary things, sent through secret channels in the ground, worked with hidden levers. Yet the firebeetle was throbbing in his bloodstream, grating his nerves with every pulse. Whatever protests his mind might conjure, the drug made him feel like an incomprehensible evil infested the very air he was breathing.

The road grew steeper, the soil even blacker and more bereft of plant life. *A fire, a simple wildfire came through and burnt the grass on the slope. That's all.* He chased off notions that it was the black of dried blood, of unconsciousness, of death itself.

With reason, against instinct, he dismounted at the top of the hill and bade his men follow suit. The engines were left hitched while the lizardmen spread feed before the brutes that pulled them. The lizards were nervous themselves from the beetle they'd been given, and perhaps a sense of the strangeness surrounding them, and they barely touched their fodder.

"This is no good place," Vixprin said.

"Look over here!" Smatt replied. He was standing at the top of the hill, looking down to the north. The fabled valley of witches seemed quite ordinary compared to the nameless lands behind them. Huts like the one they'd burnt stood behind roadside farmsteads, like ordinary peasants' huts in any river valley. He couldn't see the source of the stream that ran alongside the road at the bottom, but he could see the break in the hills where it exited the valley, and beyond, a glint of ocean.

"I think we've been through the worst of it," he said.

"You think?"

It was a woman's voice from behind him, speaking in Walthorian with a quaint accent. He turned and saw the same woman, he thought, who had faced the column in front of her hut and was surely dead by now, food for the first rank of coursers. But now she was wearing a black cloak over her dress, or a cloak so purple it was almost black. She seemed paler than before, and more crazed in her expression. In one hand she held a basket covered with a pure-white cloth.

"Surely you are hungry after your journey."

Smatt almost laughed, since the dose they had taken would dispel all hunger for a day or more. But when she lifted a corner of the cloth, a smell reached his nostril that instantly banished this effect of the beetle. It was like it had wafted all the way from home, from his mother's hearth, sweetened by the loving touch of her hand as well as the finest goat butter.

"I doubt you would refuse one of my honey barleycakes," she said, "for they are delicate, and fresh as the dawn."

Vixprin already had his hand out, and his tongue, letting his drool run with abandon. With no fear of the lizard he mounted, the witch—young woman—walked over to him and placed a cake in his hand. Smatt's own hand itched as if stung by bees for want of one.

But as he chewed his first bite, Vixprin started to look tired. The skin around his eyes went dark and began to droop. He seemed to age. The lines around his mouth, barely visible before, grew long and deep. His skin greyed and began to break in places, revealing brownish, putrid flesh beneath.

The other engineers were shouting and crying in various tongues, but Smatt was dumbstruck. There was no such thing as a poison that could turn a man old. This was worse than that. Soon Vixprin was well on his way to becoming a skeleton, the last of his facial tendons still moving to chew the fell cake until its mealy mass dropped to the ground through the gap in a fleshless jawbone.

In the end, even his clothes and weapons rotted through, as if corroded by the nearness of his body's corruption. And then it all fell away in a downward sluice of greyish dust, leaving a riderless courser where Smatt's best loader had been. The witch still smiled. Smatt still wanted a cake. He could feel his beard growing damp with his own slobber.

"It seems he got a bad one," she said, "but surely this one will be better?"

Looking at the cake, he found her words made a terrible kind of sense. It was golden, perfect, the steam curling from it like the lush hair of a maiden. What could possibly be wrong? It was only a cake.

He shook his head furiously and raised his right wrist, displaying the blue spruce. "Go away with your cakes. Our passage is paid. You won't be harmed if you let us pass."

"Your friends killed my sister, or one of her," she answered, still smiling. "Yes, your passage is paid. I leave these for you."

She set her basket down by the side of the road and, with a flourish of her purple cloak, disappeared into the mud. The cloak stayed behind for a moment, crumpling and sinking into the earth until it was gone, or turned into earth itself; Smatt couldn't say which.

He looked to his men. All their eyes were on the basket. Smatt himself could barely break away from it. His mouth reeked with want.

"Vixprin was right!" he shouted, as much to admonish himself as to rouse them from their stupor. "We should've kept moving. Let's go, now, and never speak of this to anyone!"

By the time they met the toll taker, they were deep enough in the valley that they could see the ocean through the gap in the hills to the north. There the shape of the Roost, much as stories described it, breached the clear horizon. All was quiet, the fields and houses seemingly empty, until they came upon her pulling up some roots by the roadside.

She was more the figure of a witch than the others they'd encountered, an ancient-looking woman in a robe with a long hood. As they approached, she rose from her labor and stepped into the middle of the road in front of them.

The commander, the captain, and their guards were riding ahead of the foresters in anticipation of this encounter. Smatt had chosen to join them, hoping that perhaps his sign might count for something even here. The others seemed not to remember the hut or the young woman that had stopped them before. The chill that came over Smatt on seeing her seemed to come over him alone.

"You bring many men and many lizards into our house," she said in accented Saspian. "We are not fond of men, nor of lizards. There is a price for bringing them into our house."

"We have gold," the commander said with a note of contempt. "Tell us the price and you will have it, but let us pass."

"There is no need for gold here. But my fields need weeding."

"Conchist, signal for the slaves to be brought forward."

"Your slaves are not enough. Everyone must work. You can take shifts tending to your lizards and antelopes."

It was dusk by the time they finished pulling up the weeds, Smatt toiling alongside his men and stripped to his loincloth like the rest. Only the commander himself refused to work, to which the old hag said:

"He is but one of many, yet thinks he is more. Yes, we can spare his labor and we can spare his men." She implied what would not be spared with an ominous smile. The commander had scoffed at her.

Perhaps he'd been right. This woman had no apparent power other than the men's fear of her. When the weeding was done, and everyone began to dry off and dress again, she said:

"Your next task is to dig a ditch to bring water to my hempfield. Will you join your men in this?"

"Never," Garong said. "My men will lose all respect for me if they see me toiling like a slave." Yet he commanded them to do same, even his officers, even Smatt.

The firebeetle was beginning to wear off and the moon had risen by the time they finished the ditch. Smatt had done his share of digging in the past, but always with a bronze spade, never the fire-hardened stick of a common laborer. It was bone-rattling work that sapped him to the core, and it took a long while to stop sweating and catch his breath when it was done.

"Your ditch is dug, and night falls on us, my lady," the commander said. "Surely we have paid you toll enough."

"Your men have paid their toll, but you have done nothing for me. But I will let you go if you give me a kiss on the lips." She grinned, revealing a maw infested with sores and shot through with decay of every kind.

At this the commander smiled, as if he'd fooled the woman based on her assumption that he was not a man of the deepest depravity. He seemed the type who would enjoy kissing something so hideous, not despite but because it was hideous. He proved this in the act, lingering like a lover as if he savored the very vileness of it.

They rode on.

V

Captain Kyrik preferred the Fistwreck to what had come before it. After stopping at King Sdubb's court in Inirriu, they'd gone up the Witchroad without stopping, spurred on by dire warnings from the superstitious outlanders and a generous application of firebeetle to their lizards' gums. The riders, too, got their share, not enough to get them beetledreaming but enough to keep them from dozing. For his part, Kyrik never touched the stuff, wouldn't even take it on a wound, remembering the number of good men he'd watched the beetle drag to the gutter. He had other tricks to keep himself awake in the saddle, old sailors' tricks from a past long left behind.

He wanted it to be nonsense, the things they said about the road. To him there was one world, a big, dumb thing made of dirt and leaves and stone, flesh that needed blood to keep from rotting, and blood that only flowed until it stopped. He'd abandoned the gods of his birth when he joined the legions, and everything he'd seen since then made him sure he was alone, like every other man, with neither friends in the sky nor enemies down below. Like every brute on earth, he had food and drink to get, enemies to crush, and a warm, dry place to claim when he needed sleep.

In the end, they were all going to the same nowhere. Burying was just a time of day to Kyrik, between battle and camp. When the slaughter called for pits wide and deep, he'd been up to his armpits many times, fighting layer after layer of hardpan until his pride was so far gone as to let him whip off his filthy loincloth and mop his face with it. Someday, his toil would be done, and the pit would be his.

But there was something in the Witchroad legends, something

he couldn't deny any more than he could deny a hidden column of foes rising from the tall grass, or a storm on the horizon. He couldn't remember much of what had happened the last day and night before they went to work for the old lady in the valley, but he knew it had been enough to convince everyone not to argue with her. A dozen men had vanished on the journey, no great loss to a column of this size, but most troubling since he didn't know the cause.

So it came as a relief when they arrived at the burnt rim of the Wreck, where the road itself had been swallowed by rivers of molten rock, in places still glowing red. There were the familiar skeletons of villages on the outskirts of the old capital, the pillars black as charcoal, the inhabitants baked in ash wherever they'd been standing, preserved as grotesque statues. But this zone of ordinary burning was narrow, and gave way to the Fistwreck proper before they could find a suitable place to make camp between the lava and the corpses.

The Wreck proper was a plain of bone-white rock. Gone were the recognizable shapes of structures and people and animals and the familiar ravages of ashfall and molten rock. In their place was a level expanse covered by a smooth layer of a rock the captain had never seen before. It was much harder than chalk, but just as white, and not limestone either—he could break off chunks of it with his sword. He was leery of digging too deep, though, for peppered across the entire surface were tiny round holes that emitted a strange and eerie kind of fire.

This was something other than ordinary fire, bright and dark at the same time, as if both burnt and burning. Earlier in the day, one of the Nydhian foresters, dismounted on a halt, had brushed by one of the jets and pulled his boot off just in time to save his foot and perhaps the rest of him. The boot was engulfed in moments, faster than anything that wasn't soaked in oil should have caught fire, but then it kept its shape and sustained the blaze long after it should have been reduced to ash. Indeed, they'd left it whole and burning when Kyrik decided they had no further time to spare for observing the eldritch. For all he knew, the boot was burning still.

He didn't like this kind of thing, and certainly harbored no curiosity about it. He supposed he'd signed up for some weird stuff when he contracted to raid the ruins. The jets of flame grew denser as they went deeper into the Wreck, and they had to pick their way around them with caution. Still, it was better than that last stretch of Witchroad. If odd-looking fire and a lost boot were the worst of the Fistwreck had to offer, he'd be more than pleased.

The coastline was flat here, but not flattened by the Fist like the buildings; it had always been so. The erstwhile capital had stood on a narrow neck of sea-level land, only two thirds of a coursing from ocean to Mirsa, the land-ringed sea that Kyrik had once called his Goddess and his home. Another thing he could say for the Wreck is that it would never put him out of sight of saltwater.

He was a Glindishman born, about the saltiest thing a city boy could be, and his clan was surely out on the water, perhaps not far away, even as he coursed across this strange, white, fiery wasteland. The songs he'd been raised on were sailing songs, and they mapped in verse every harbor great and small on Mirsa's girdle of shores. As a boy he'd done every job on every kind of vessel from raft to roundboat. At times he wished he'd kept to the sea instead of jumping ship to join the legions.

But that he had done, at a tender age, and it was a decision no boy or man had ever been allowed to reverse. Now he could barely remember anything but war on land, though the sea songs stayed with him. As a mere child in the light infantry, he'd been sent to the jungles of Min Khune, where they said more legionaries would be buried than shipped home alive. Kyrik returned a corporal, and soon was recognized for his knack at sitting a courser. The Saspiards were always unduly impressed when someone who wasn't one of them could handle a lizard.

He went on to serve the bulk of his twenty years as a centurion in the coursery of the line, fighting Cucuthi bandits in the Grendish Hills, Shadaghi barbarians on the burning desert sands, and even his own people when the fishing clans of Kleerak revolted. For all the death and dismemberment he saw, he seldom took a drink and of course never touched any beetle, and to this he attributed his general avoidance of the lash and the more grievous punishments the Army was wont to inflict on its officers and men. He watched others of his rank cut and flayed, sometimes justly and sometimes unjustly. It didn't matter. Like every legionary, it was Kyrik's duty to witness the wrath of the Army.

When he reached his twenty, he took the gold instead of the land and formed his first company, mostly because at the time he hadn't been able to imagine any future besides fighting on until the fighting took him. Centurion Kyrik became Captain Kyrik, but they were much the same person. He still thought of the Army as his home and viewed his slingspears as a regiment of soldiers. He divided his men into troops of fifty and put them under corporals, and the corporals under centurions, with a trooper-conchist attending each officer. The signals they used were drawn straight from the field manual. Under Kyrik men lived and fought as coursery of the line, and if they didn't like it, they were free, unlike legionaries, to leave and sling spear for some looser captain.

Truth was, Kyrik was no one's soldier anymore, on his own side now. Even his men were tied to him only by chains of gold, susceptible at all times to brighter and weightier chains. He seldom knew exactly who was paying for his missions, or why.

But his enemies were about the same as they'd been in the line—Grendish headhunters, Copper Sea pirates, his own people again when Klorcsport declared independence—and he suspected that he was often working for high-ranking Saspiards who needed to keep some of their military activities off the senatorial books.

In typical fashion, Kyrik had been kept in the dark about the purpose of his current mission, which as far as he'd been told consisted only of a single objective to reach and take. The Fist had flattened just the top two-thirds of the Great Pyramid of Za, and this landmark, visible for coursings in every direction, made it a simple matter to orient the column toward the objective. But only the shady, though apparently well-connected, commander actually knew what they were supposed to be fetching from there. The captain assumed it was something under the ground, a piece of the treasure of fallen Sasp, which was the topic of five decades' worth of legends and lies. He assumed the men who had joined him for this expedition were drawn not by his reputation for fairness and discipline, nor even for the pay as contracted, but by tales that promised so much more.

The lizards were flagging, and with the commander's leave, Kyrik ordered a stop for the day. They made a ragged-looking camp, impossible to keep straight around the jets, where he hoped they could sleep off the horrors of the Witchroad and the beetle most of them had ingested. Kyrik was leery of putting stakes down into the source of the black flames—"fistfire," the men were calling it—so the coursers had to be drugged to their eyelids with sandbeetle paste to keep them from running wild. No matter, Kyrik thought, there was nothing to fight out here. He gave the men an extra ration of wine and went to bed feeling somewhat smug that he didn't feel the need for any himself.

The next morning, he awoke in a high dudgeon. He felt rested and ready to conclude the mission quickly and return to the world of the living. As usual, the mission had something else in store.

He found that on top of his objective, someone had put up a little wooden fort, makeshift and completely unexpected. He had his conchist blow the call for parley, and whoever was inside the fort responded in kind. *Could it be some of ours inside?* He had to remind himself that he wasn't a regular soldier anymore, and he couldn't be certain he was working for the senate, so encountering imperial forces out here didn't necessarily mean they weren't in for a fight.

The fort itself was hard to place as one nation's or another's, as the toehold of a colony or a pirate base. It was the same fort anyone would put up if they were wrecked or otherwise done with their clinker-built ships and aground in a woodless country. Kyrik could see in its timbers the curvilinear forms of strakes and futtocks, ill fits for a land wall striving to be straight.

He wondered if the occupants might be just another band of treasure hunters with an old army conchist in their ranks. It surely made more sense to come by sea from Glind than travel the Witchroad, as he'd stupidly agreed to do. But it also meant the occupants were sorely outnumbered. Unless they were stacked in there like firewood, the little fort could have held no more than fifty mounted men, or a hundred-odd foot. Minus the handful they'd lost on the Witchroad, his side numbered nearly four hundred, each one mounted on a decent courser or stag, though he only grudgingly included the hundred Nydhian rogues in his count.

He kicked his lizard to a slow trot, planning to close half the distance between his front line and the gate before dismounting. As he rode, he watched the gate, expecting it at any moment to open and eject the commander of the fort, likewise on courserback and unaccompanied. This was the custom for parley, and Kyrik expected one who knew the proper conch calls to adhere to all the other rules of war.

The ground here was no longer flat, but crossed by a series of low ridges. The captain's camp-soured stomach was far from soothed by the ups and downs. Looking down to catch his breath, he could see that the ridges were arranged in a pattern of concentric circles, like ripples frozen in a pond, with the fort at their center.

It was dawning on him that his objective must be the very place the Fist had struck. The ripples in the bony rock seemed proof of that. For the first time, he wondered why this supposed divine punishment and his company had been sent to the exact same place. Not just some place under the city it had felled, but the very place where the Fist struck earth. Surely one had something to do with the other. Although not particularly religious, he shuddered at the thought.

For its part his courser didn't even notice the terrain. It could go vertically if need be, though the rider certainly hoped for no such need. The one thing its claws avoided were the jets of fistfire. It was a relief that his lizard had sense enough to keep away from it. There were enough jets that steering to avoid them would have been next to impossible. Controlling a courser, even for the best rider, was not so much a fine craft as a gross exercise of will.

The gates didn't open as he approached. He wondered whether this fort even had gates. Perhaps whoever it was had nailed themselves in there. Kyrik felt a chill as he considered what might cause men who knew the proper conch calls to withdraw into such a desperate redoubt. When he reckoned he'd closed half the distance between fort and front line, he pressed his knees into the courser's ribs. The lizard took its usual two defiant paces before coming to a jaws-up, claws-down halt against the incline of a ridge. The position put more of its spiny crest in his line of sight than Kyrik would have preferred.

"Avast!" a voice boomed out from behind the wall.

It was a queer old word, and he couldn't remember exactly what it meant, but he thought it was something like *stop,* which he had already done. The speaker must have been using some device to project his voice. Kyrik wasn't sure even his old centurion's battlefield bellow could be heard and understood at such a range.

"I be the Great God Kom, Lord of Dominance, and I am come to scourge the apostate!"

The words continued to come strange and ancient-sounding to the captain's ears. But there was one thing he was sure of. He cupped his hands around his mouth and shouted back, "Za is the Great God of Dominance, and Emperor Asb Aq the Fourth of His Name is Vicar of Za on this earth." He put no stock in any of it, but these were religious facts that any child would know.

"The lizard boy Sa, sayst thou? And thy chief be nought but his vicar?"

A sinister laugh echoed over the flame-pocked plain. Kyrik wondered exactly how one laughed into a hollow tusk, which is what he imagined this "God" was using to greaten his voice.

"The path to mine temple be paved with shards of the erstwhile idols of Sa."

"Your temple? Where is that?" He was already beginning to feel hoarse from the shouting.

"Mokkom. Yonder, to the west!"

Now it was Kyrik's turn to laugh. West of them was nothing but more ruins and the ocean. He suddenly felt he knew everything he needed to know. They'd quickly put an end to this perverted charade. He kicked a heel into his courser's flank to start it turning.

"Yea! returnst thou to thy ill-favored rabble! To Kom they are but playthings of clay, all serried up by a babbie!"

Kyrik rode away wondering what it took to keep up that kind of talk. It seemed like "Kom" would've had to read nothing but scripture for years, while speaking to no one but others doing the same, to take on such a manner in the first place. Awe at the effort mingled in Kyrik's mind with strategic thoughts about what it might take to snap him out of it. Perhaps the followers of this "Great God" would wake from his influence if they heard him swearing like any common, modern person.

Back at his lines Kyrik found Yoya, centurion over Claw and Fang, the two forward troops, had left his own post to act as captain. Commanding the senior squadron, Yoya was by office first lieutenant, charged with leading the whole company in the captain's absence. But Kyrik hadn't really been gone long or far enough to warrant it.

Yoya was a purebred wild Cucuthi from Far Outer Grendishland. He never said much about where he came from or why, but Kyrik suspected he'd jumped from a slave caravan before he was ever really made a slave. He had the typical frame of his people, which made him appear almost as wide as he was tall. White ripreed cloth and bronze armor looked incongruous on him, and in truth, Kyrik wasn't sure how fit he was to serve under real military discipline. But he was the fiercest and most blooded fighter in the company, and the men would stand for no one else as the captain's second. Besides, hardly anyone could sit a courser like Yoya. His personal lizard was a fine Reticulate that he called, for some reason, "Sweetmeats."

Kyrik wanted to rebuke him for taking command so quickly, but he was still too excited to have learned how piddling an obstacle was really in their way.

"Centurion Yoya, good, keep to this post. I'm going rearward to confer with Commander Garong."

"Yes boss. But them say him sick."

"Sick? With what?"

"Flux, boss."

Kyrik choked down a curse. He didn't like showing any emotion to his men, but the commander catching the flux at this far point could be a killing blow to their mission. Chances were, he'd have to be evacuated through a Salt Folk cuttlefish station called Yeguadda, the nearest human place to the ruins, six days to the southeast at wagon speed. All told, if he lived, it would take more than a month for Garong to get to Glind, receive his treatment, and return.

Even if they took the fort and found within it a passage into the bowels of the earth, without the commander's guidance there would be no telling what to look for down there, nor when to stop looking. The opportunity to sack the vaults might make the whole adventure worthwhile for him and his men, but Kyrik didn't dare return to whoever had paid for all this without their prize. People with the means to risk one army on such a strange quest would likely have the means to raise another, after all. And it had to be something specific they were after, not just plunder in general. The whole train immobilized with ordinary loot would be at best an even break for the financiers. And if he asserted the truth, that he didn't know what the prize was meant to be, they'd assume he was lying and had sold it to someone else.

With these dark thoughts the captain rode past the files. His men were a mixed bag of savages and cutthroats, but they all sat a courser nicely, and their motley origins were covered over with clean white tunics and cuirasses of polished bronze. Half were armed as lancers and half as classical light coursery, with javelins for a few softening volleys before closing the deal with the jaws of their mounts. Most were sitting cheap but sturdy lizards of the dark brown Shadaghian landrace. Against the chalky ground these cut a splendid contrast. His only complaint was that his ranks were a little jagged, but jags were necessary in places to avoid the fistfire.

Behind the coursery, the Nydhians made an unruly cluster, swollen in the middle, a ludicrous way to be formed on any field. Kyrik supposed they simply didn't know—they were only good for what they were good for. He wanted them to start picketing the fort immediately, but he'd have to wait, since they'd only take orders from their own commander, Yharalon, and good luck finding him in the mob. These outlaws looked alike on purpose, he thought, to make themselves tough to tell apart. Yharalon was still avoiding the captain, thinking they might have a score to settle over a little incident with a herald's mace, though Kyrik had long ago shifted blame for that to Garong's madness.

Past the Nydhians, the wagons were formed into a circular redoubt next to the engines of war, two medium bolt-throwers and a light catapult. The latter seemed just the thing to breach this "Great God's" shabby little wall. Smatt, the expedition's chief engineer, and Oo'ogrin, wagonmaster and chief lizardman, were already standing by the machines as if they'd been anticipating a conference with the captain.

"Hail," Kyrik lazily greeted his fellow officers as he pulled up nearby, not so close as to threaten them with his courser, since both were on foot.

"Hail, Captain," said Smatt. He was a paunchy Walthorian with the classic Walthorian hirsuteness reaching parts of his person that would have been left unexplored by the body hair of other races.

"All engines in good fettle?"

"Aye, Captain."

"Good. Let's haul the catapult into position and make a door in their little wall."

"Captain," Oo'ogrin said, "if you don't mind my asking."

Oo'ogrin was a strange kind of mongrel person from a Rivereen father and Cucuthi mother, respectively the smallest and biggest races of people in the empire. The coupling was comical to consider, as when a Black Mountain camprat bitch whelped a litter of squirms off a common bilge stud half her size. The result, Oo'ogrin, was a man of normal height and girth, but features so mixed up one might think he was of a different species, not quite human, perhaps not even of this earth. One eye, for instance, was noticeably higher and much darker than the other, and his nose and mouth seemed crookedly misaligned.

Kyrik, in fact, did mind him asking, but answered, "No, proceed."

"Do you know who's in there." Other than the falling tone of his questions, Oo'ogrin's speech was proper Saspian.

"Oh," the captain smiled again at the memory. "Whoever they are, their leader is one of the Silver Sillies, the worst case I've seen. He says he's a god, greater than Za Himself, and he's full of *thou dost this, thou dost that,* as if he walked off the wall of some ancient temple with a mouthful of glyphs. I'm willing to bet anyone dim enough to follow him isn't going to give us much of a fight."

"What are they doing way up here, then?" This time Smatt was the asker, taking the captain's permission to his counterpart as a general invitation to ask questions, shedding light on why Kyrik hadn't wanted to give it in the first place.

"I didn't ask them," he said, "because I don't care. We'll crush them without spilling a drop of our own. For all I know, this is the last place they thought the Society would catch them."

The Silver Prophets were a band of either madmen or charlatans who had convinced a swath of the free lower classes that the ancient Saspians were returning from their lost isle across the ocean. With them would come death and suffering for the unfit and comfortable, land and slaves for the faithful and strong. This was preposterous, since the Northwest Current had reversed soon after the Saspians arrived, seven centuries ago, and the ocean had only swallowed ships since then. The tale got even taller with their magical armor of silver, supposedly stouter than bronze, hence the name of the prophecy. Ridiculous, since bronze shears were used to cut silver coins to make change in every marketplace in the world.

Smatt grinned, that crafty grin of a Walthorian smelling gold in a situation.

"Two talons on each of their heads, then," he said, referring to the bounty the Society of Za had placed on every Silver Prophet, "even more than I was expecting to haul up from the crypts. What do you suppose there are, fifty in there?"

"Smatt," Kyrik's voice sharpened a tad, "instead of making up stories about what's inside, let's just knock down that gate and find out."

Oo'ogrin was first to jump to it, making at once for the circle of wagons to pick a lizard and men for the detail. The expedition's cartlizards had come as a uniform batch of the type vulgarly called "dickhead" for their bacillar crests. The brute they brought out was a mature, blue-skinned, black-billed, and very dickheaded male with sprays of orange stripes on its shoulders and rump.

Oo'ogrin's lizardmen were mostly Delta Rivereen, one of the empire's great slave stocks, little men with sun-proof skins and a knack for handling the big ones. The two he'd selected for this detail wore nothing but loincloths and short rawhide jerkins, and they carried blunted pikes. These they used to steer the nearly brainless thing by poking at the nerves in its sides and haunches. Dull though it might have been, the cartlizard was, thanks be to Za, just as chary of the fistfire as the captain's far more sentient courser. Its greater size, though, made for a circuitous route to seek adequate passage between the vents.

Smatt, noticeably slower to respond than the wagonmaster, sauntered off to order his engineers. Kyrik observed him swapping two men from the bolt throwers onto the catapult. He didn't know whether to be pleased the Walthorian was picking his best for the detail or wary that he might have someone who needed moving. Kyrik had promised Garong the best. Those the captain had contracted with, at amounts unskimmed by him, had promised him the same. But it seemed like a bad time to start nurturing suspicions.

"Left, right, or center, Captain," Oo'ogrin asked once the cartlizard was harnessed to the catapult.

"Center," Kyrik replied, "hit 'em right down the middle."

This didn't really make sense as an order, but it conveyed his desire to get the business done straight and quickly. Smatt, for all his fat and foibles, had knocked down a lot of gates in his time. At a snap of his fingers, the engineers pulled the chocks from in front of the catapult's wheels, and the lizardmen prodded from both sides at once. The brute strained and trumpeted, axles screeched, and the rig began to roll, its frame creaking and whining at every rise and dip in the rippled ground.

Satisfied, Kyrik dismounted and made for the gap in the wagon circle, which had been temporarily widened to permit the cartlizard's passage, with one vehicle wheeled out nearly perpendicular to its neighbor. The commander had located his headquarters tent within the circle, a wise defensive move that would've exposed him day and night to the stench, were he actually staying. The brutes were crowded together on one side, snorting and panting, ranging in color from blue-grey to purplish brown, in size from large to massive, but otherwise nearly alike. He could see that Oo'ogrin had picked one of the biggest to draw the catapult to the front.

At the entrance to the command tent, one of the Nydhians was standing watch, an ungainly fellow in a floppy hat and hempen clothes that might have been clean once. As he drew closer, Kyrik could see that the man's eyes were beady and his nostrils enormous. In his hand he held a longbow without exactly knowing how to hold a longbow. A strange choice of bodyguards, but the commander was a strange man. Kyrik recalled he'd also given this fellow the job of tallying votes for the chief of foresters, a job for which he seemed, if such a thing were possible, even less suitable. But perhaps he was the only one of these benighted rogues who could read.

"Good day, Captain," he said in a pleasant tone. "Naihard Shig, at your service, squire."

"How fares the commander?" Kyrik asked, not returning the least hint of pleasantness and dismissing the name at once as a false one.

"Ill. We have him on the bucket but I'm not sure his legs'll hold up much longer. We've already emptied it twice."

Kyrik suppressed the urge to grimace. "Can he speak?"

"Not clearly."

"Draw the curtain."

"Are you sure, Captain?"

The rogue looked fearful, as well he might be. Flux was highly infectious and it did kill men, especially in its bloodier manifestations. In Kyrik's experience, it struck every camp—

it had struck his own gut more than once—and he'd learned it was best just to go about his business and take his chances. The recommended precautions didn't seem to work very well, anyway. Garong was a surgeon, after all, and what good had that done him?

"When I'm not sure, I don't speak," Kyrik said sternly, "so draw the curtain."

"Aye."

The rogue opened the tent to reveal a pathetic sight, the commander with his tunic hiked all the way up, squatting hug-kneed over a tin slops bucket. His pockmarked face was gleaming with sweat, and his hair looked even greasier than usual.

"Commander!" the captain said forcefully, as if trying to blast a breach in the walls of his delirium.

No answer came other than a loud and noisome report from the end of him that didn't usually do the talking.

"Commander. You're going to have to go away for a while."

A moan and more shitting.

"It's a tough break, Commander, but you're the only surgeon on this expedition. We can't treat you here. There's a harbor a few days from here where we can get you on a boat to Glind."

"Dust."

The word was a croak from a skeletal place, as if Garong had been roused from his tomb by Kyrik's words, as if all the fluid in his body had long ago drained through his ass and his pores.

"The dust? Gold dust?" But no, two of his trains laden with gold dust wouldn't have paid for the expedition. "Ruby dust? Ultramarine? Is that what we're here for? Commander, it's important you tell me what we came here for!"

"Dust!"

Was he wanting the beetle? A surgeon would have known better than to take beetle at this stage of the flux, and wouldn't have called a beetle flour "dust" like some common fiend. Or was it a metaphor? Was he calling for water, saying his throat was dry as dust? A strange way to speak, but he was a strange man in a strange state. Just in case, the captain unfastened his own canteen from his baldrick and tossed it into the tent. The gourd rolled all the way to the commander's feet, but he just looked down at it and up again at Kyrik, eyes shot with blood and gloom.

"It will be more than a month before you can get back here, Commander, and by then the rogues will be gone and my men will be eating their sandals and sword-belts. You need to tell us what we're here for or else we aren't coming home with it." He pronounced each word carefully, loudly, forcing each syllable to ring like a ship's bell.

"Dust," the commander croaked again, his voice fading.

No more time to ask what *dust.*

"Commander, where is the dust?"

"Crystal," he coughed, just before toppling face first to the canvas, followed closely by a sluice of the upturned bucket's contents.

The rogue shouted for slaves, then said to Kyrik, "Dust in a crystal, sounds like a fool's prize to me."

"What would you know about it?"

"Oh, well, you see, I've had the commander's confidence in certain matters."

Far off, Kyrik heard the familiar dull thunk of beam striking frame through a bumper of coiled rope. Since he heard nothing more, the stone had either sailed over the target or dropped short of it, as he'd expect from the first load of a catapult salvo. The machine's arm groaned at being drawn back for the second.

The rogue was trying to lead him down a path. It seemed quite plausible that he knew certain things, given his position outside the commander's tent. But he was a rogue, and for him to seek influence was beyond suspicious. It was a ploy to gain advantages that would likely prove harmful or fatal to others, most notably Kyrik himself. But what was he supposed to do? Who else was there to follow?

For his part, Commander Garong seemed completely unconscious as two slaves, neither of them wearing anything but a bronze collar and a vinegar-soaked rag tied across the lower face, attempted to clean him. Kyrik reminded himself to check that night and make sure the slaves weren't being raped. He'd forgotten for the past few.

He turned to find Oo'ogrin behind him, a few paces off as if wary of vapors from the tent. It seemed to Kyrik that a man who spent his life inhaling lizard dung and the flies around it had nothing in addition to worry about here, but he knew men were funny that way, blind to the everyday hazard that, being everyday, was most often the thing that finally felled them. Yet they saw in every stranger a thief, in any unknown plant a poison, in any odd weather an evil omen. Since most lives were monotonous, it was easier for most to live that way, treating only the novel as noxious. For a soldier it was a good way to carry oneself if one wished to die young. But a lizardman, even one on a military train, wasn't really a soldier.

"Catapult's in position, Captain. Left my detail up with Smatt in case he needs it moved."

"Very good, Oo'ogrin. But now we're going to have to let go your best-sprung cart, a lizard and a spare in the fullest health, and at least two of your most reliable men. The commander requires transport to the harbor at Yeguadda."

"Very well, Captain, but if I may, no one lives at Yeguadda. Won't it be weeks or months before a ship puts in."

"True, the place has no inhabitants. But cuttlefish is caught by jig and beacon, so the Yeguadda fleets gather at each new moon. She's waning now, so if they're held up on the road, they'll just barely catch them. If not, there's drying-sheds for them to bide a few days and try to keep the poor commander in this world."

Oo'ogrin grimaced slightly at the thought of what he was being asked to put his men through. Far from being annoyed, Kyrik thought this the mark of a good leader. He himself wouldn't have liked to put his two best corporals on a slops detail.

"Very well, Captain," Oo'ogrin said, composing his misbegotten features. "Are they to have an escort."

"Oh, yes. You can tell Yoya I promised you ten men. He'll make the selection from his troops."

"What about guides," the lizardman asked, now pressing his luck.

At this, the Nydhian laughed. "Us? Not a one of us is going to leave now's we're well nigh tasting of the gold."

"I wouldn't trouble myself about it," Kyrik suggested, "since the rogues don't know this country any better than we do. You can have my map—I won't need it to follow the Witchroad home."

"Generous of you, Captain," Oo'ogrin said, clearly not meaning it. He walked away acting like he himself had been consigned to the ignoble duty of bearing the ill after being so close to buried treasure.

The slaves, with great efficiency, had swaddled the commander's loins and loaded him onto a litter at the entrance to the tent. The evacuation seeming under control, Kyrik left the corral and found his courser tended by two lizardmen.

"Did it feed?" he asked.

"Yes boss. Hungry boy. Three rat today."

Kyrik wasn't sure how he felt about that. They'd been fortunate enough to replace the lost rats at the rim of the Wreck, in the parts burnt by ordinary fire, where rats were apparently the first life to return. But he might have wanted his courser hungry. There was going to be a battle, though not likely much of one. He'd never quite decided whether he preferred a sated courser to a starved one in battle. It all depended on the tactical situation, really, whether a calmer or fiercer mount was the greater advantage. If fighting classically, using only the jaws in close combat, one risked being disarmed when the lizard's belly got full. Kyrik resolved to get his hand on a lance before joining any fray that day.

In the distance, a crack of stone against wood reported that the catapult had found its range. Without further delay, Kyrik mounted his courser, praying to Ha to make the front line before Yoya decided to do something stupid. At a brisk trot, his lizard still pranced nimbly between the little round holes in the ground and their dark, fiery exhalations.

The commander's escort rode past him in the opposite direction. He noted they were all young lads on expedition coursers, not their own. Of course Yoya wasn't going to send his best men on this detail—Kyrik wouldn't want him to, since they were ultimately *his* men—but the centurion could've spared at least one veteran to keep the rest of them cool if they ran into a fight on the way to Yeguadda.

Nonetheless, he reminded himself, he'd given the command over freely, and specifically told Oo'ogrin to ask Yoya to select the detail. If anything happened as a result, it would be, as usual, the captain's fault. Perhaps Yoya didn't understand that Garong was their insurance, or rather his insurance: a person to take the blame for mission failure above Kyrik.

Another catapult load struck home with a splintery-sounding pop. The beams of the gate were cut to float, not take blows, and had probably been put together into a wall by a ship's carpenter rather than a proper siege engineer. At any rate, they seemed to be giving quickly. As Kyrik rode by the ranks of Claw Troop, the fort came into view. He wondered how the "Great God" Kom felt now that his playhouse was getting knocked down.

The air was cool and the sky a uniform gray, promising neither rain nor sunshine. Kyrik supposed this was everyday weather for such northern climes, but it happened to be the best for battle, providing long, clear lines of site without glare. A part of him was looking forward to this; not the bloodshed itself, but the potential for a perfect execution, the craft of war raised to fine art, officering as choreography.

The catapult was set up ten paces ahead of the front rank. The lizardmen had the brute uncoupled and off to one side, feeding on a mound of stale ricecake. Oo'ogrin and Smatt were conferring with each other as the engineers hauled back the machine's arm for another load. All were grinning like men who'd found their stride and had only to finish the job now.

"Oh, Captain!" Smatt said in greeting, "we were just discussing what to do if we run out of shot, and it's still your pleasure to lob a few more rounds."

"There's extra shot in the train," Kyrik said, "but I doubt we'll need it. Gate looks close to buckling to me, and that's all we need it for."

"As you wish," Smatt said.

Kyrik wondered whether the artillerist knew something about the fortifications that he was holding back, or if he was just making some kind of underhanded comment. It was worse than torture—he had been tortured before—to consider such things, to live life guessing at what other people concealed in their heads. The sentiments and schemes and secret agendas, that was, not the actual pink stuff, which one only had to learn to step around to avoid slipping in it.

As a thing to navigate, he much preferred the Army's straits of iniquity to the murky comradeship among partners in a mercenary venture. This was why they really needed Garong, since there was no provision in the contract to give full command to the captain in case of the commander's incapacitation. Kyrik had suggested it; Garong had balked. So now they were fated to decide things by council.

Once the gate was gone, Smatt could walk away for all Kyrik cared, but no one was getting home without Oo'ogrin and his train. So he kept his peace as he watched the next stone arc over the flaming white plain. It hit home with a crack, deepening the dent, promising a conclusion to the bombardment in the near future.

But then, as if the stone had been a friend's fist knocking, the gate began to lower with a clink of chains. Slowly and smoothly, proving better engineering than Kyrik had previously suspected, the drawbridge descended. He noticed that the stretch of ground where it was about to make contact was free of the fistfire—probably why they'd placed it where it was. He'd thought about using the fire in battle somehow, but if the walls burned on and on like the boot had done, it wouldn't really help him get inside unless he wanted to burn as well.

The open gate felt like a gift, but not a large one: three more loads, the captain reckoned, would've had the same outcome. If anything, it made him distrustful of his senses, particularly the sense he'd had of an easy victory. The well-built drawbridge, and the seemingly empty bailey he could now see behind it, did not seem like marks of a desperate redoubt.

Kom!

The syllable filled the air, sounding like a hundred men in unison. A bass drum took up the rhythm of an ancient Saspian hymn.

Kom! Boom! Boom! Boom! *Kom!* Boom! Boom! Boom! *Kom!*

He couldn't fault the discipline of the voices, nor the steadiness of the drummer. Whatever else they were—mad fools, to be sure—they were organized, as soldiers were organized. They did things as one. The captain looked over his shoulder for the reassurance of his own neatly ordered troops.

When he looked back, the first enemy had appeared at the gate. This must be the great Kom, he thought, since his getup was so elaborate. The man and the courser he rode were encased from the lizard's claws to the top of the rider's head in plates of white metal. It looked like pewter, judging by the color, but since few men could wear the price of a fleet of ships, Kyrik assumed it was darkened tin. Mummer's armor, used in mock fights to amuse little children.

But this wasn't like any mummer he'd seen before. In days long past, when chariots ruled the battlefield, chieftains had ridden to battle in plate from head to toe, but the suits were so heavy they could manage at best a shortbow, while their seconds and thirds did all the real fighting. The main purpose of the armor was to have the leader on the field, so he'd be able to say he fought but avoid risking his life. Long ago, this was how tribes became nations.

Perhaps Kom meant to hearken back to those days by encasing himself in tin, but there was no precedent for doing the same with his courser. Kyrik had never seen a lizard barded past the belly line, and never in plate. This one had articulated panels encasing all of its legs, its belly, its head, and even the tail right down to the tip. As far as he could see only the fangs and the eyes were exposed. In his hand, Kom held a short-handled battle-axe, also obviously of tin, since a blade that size made of bronze would have made the thing unwieldable. All in all, if his purpose was to align his appearance with prophecy, it seemed he had done much more than he needed to. But what did Captain Kyrik know about the business of charlatanism?

The much greater surprise came when the second rider appeared as elaborately costumed as the first. With each successive man and lizard, he grew more shocked at the effort someone had put into this fraud. It was like a mirror to his own embarrassingly well-provisioned expedition. He had no idea what this cult might mean to accomplish by standing off against real coursery in their suits of tin.

Kom! Boom! Boom! Boom! *Kom!* Boom! Boom! Boom! *Kom!*

A battle of sorts was assured now. Coursers, even wild coursers, even his own coursers for that matter, could always give Kyrik something to worry about. But the riders, it seemed, would be dead before the fight even started.

"Should we bring up the bolt throwers, Captain." Oo'ogrin had quietly slipped up beside him to watch the spectacle. He was mounted himself now, on a fine Red Racer like the captain's own.

"I don't suppose there's any need. What's their range?"

"About here," Smatt called from a few paces back.

"Good. Place your best men on the throwers, and order them to shoot through any stray coursers before they make the reserve line."

Without saying as much, the captain had made it obvious that he was ordering a charge. The wagonmaster bit his misshapen lower lip. Kyrik thought he might have been touched by the silly prophecy himself. He supposed a person couldn't be blamed for feeling superstitious, standing as they were on a plain of bone-white rock and tiny black fires, in the place where justice was said to have rained from the sky on the wicked old world of their grandfathers.

"And the catapult."

"I don't see any need to drag her back just yet," Kyrik answered. "Why not bring up another cart of balls? We can lob a few into their ranks before we take them."

"Very well."

Oo'ogrin expertly turned his courser around to detail some men to the corral for ammunition. Smatt already had his boys drawing back the arm of the catapult.

Kom! Boom! Boom! Boom! *Kom!* Boom! Boom! Boom! *Kom!*

The enemy, if you could call them that, were forming up in a kind of miniature echelon, a chitboard of little nine-man squares in front of the wall. There were five squares total. That made forty-five men and forty-five lizards, all dressed in tin. *Nice of them to make themselves so easy to count.*

"Loose!"

Smatt himself had set the range and given the order. This time the first shot scored a hit on the enemy's right flank, knocking one man out of his seat. Kyrik was sure his own lizard or its neighbor would chew him apace, but they didn't bother him at all. Surely it wasn't the plate that kept them off. A courser could chew through tin like the skin of a grape. Kyrik hoped the phony armor was keeping their jaws clamped shut.

The fallen man didn't rise at once, and the courser, not a patient kind of animal, was soon running free of the line. Strangely, it seemed more encumbered than it should've been wearing that amount of tin, but its armored claws ran freely over the fistfire without catching it.

Set javelins! called the conches. Kyrik didn't want a whole volley wasted on a single stray, but figured he ought to give it to them, for morale. In his experience, there was nothing like a little overkill to fill a unit with the bloodlust, and it would take a surfeit of same to get up any enthusiasm for slaughtering a herd of tin-plated coursers.

Loose javelins! The conch-blast sounded up and down the lines, followed by successive rushes of spear meeting air. Though most flew long or short or wide, many javelins hit the running lizard. They bounced off its armor like wooden spears flung against a stone wall. A lucky throw caught the courser in the mouth, and it chewed the weapon greedily without pausing to mourn a lost fang.

"We need to get behind the lines," Kyrik said as the blood drained from his cheeks.

"But what about my catapult?"

"Stay with it if you like, Smatt." He was already wheeling his courser around. "I've got a charge to lead. But Oo'ogrin."

"Yes." The lizardman, too, was turning his courser.

"Let's make sure we get that good lizard back to the corral."

"Yes, captain."

The master hastened back to order his lizardmen, who promptly and in righteous fear for their lives began prodding the brute into motion. Smatt, looking furious, trotted along beside them, his big paunch bouncing with each hastened step. His engineers followed, occasionally glancing back at their catapult like forsaken lovers.

For his part, Kyrik didn't like having his back to a charging courser, but that was the way to safety. Close to his lines, he heard the twang of a bolt-thrower string, followed closely by the thick, familiar, satisfying sound of flesh and armor pierced by a brutal force. Looking back as he slowed his lizard, he could see the metal-encased courser on its side with a bolt in its neck, though none too deep. *What is this plate that can slow a thrower-bolt like bronze against a brigand's dagger?*

He was wary now of what seemed to be serious armor, no mummery at all, and, though he hadn't thought it possible, better than his men's. If the riders' weapons were made of the same stuff, they could slice through greaves and cuirasses of bronze like quilted cloth. Kyrik couldn't help but think there was sorcery in the metal, which he'd seen resist the fistfire, after all. For the second time that day he commended himself to Ha, despite his fixed belief that war had no god. At least he had the numbers, which was as close to a god as had ever existed on *his* battlefields.

"They kind of tough after all," Yoya said as he pulled up alongside his front rank.

"Indeed, centurion. I don't like that stuff they're wearing. I think we'd better charge them now while their back's against the wall. Pretty sure we're faster than they are, so we've got that going for us."

"Yes boss. Now?"

Kyrik swallowed. There was never a good time to start a battle.

"Now. Just your troops. The rest in reserve."

His command, followed by Yoya's, set off a chain of conch calls, and the ranks began to move, creeping at first. The captain didn't know what the walls still hid, and expected a volley of arrows or sling-stones at any moment. Across the plain the enemy stood, impassive and unmoving in their little squares. Their helmets, which he hadn't paid much mind before, covered their whole faces like masks with no features but two slits for the eyes. It made them look more than ready for what was coming.

Kom! Boom! Boom! Boom! *Kom!* Boom! Boom! Boom! *Kom!*

He wondered if he should have brought the bolt throwers up before charging. It was a bad habit to second-guess oneself on the battlefield, but one that no officer failed to indulge. His troops were picking up the pace now, the coursers maintaining a brisk trot, impervious to the terrain, as the riders clutched scruff to keep their seats. Kyrik scowled as he realized his ranks were breaking up into threads following the most direct paths between fistfire jets. Out of formation, their greater numbers would hardly matter against a better armed and armored enemy.

A pair of conches sounded, and the air filled again with the noisy whisper of javelins. The men selected as javelineers had true aim, and their missiles made it home more often than not. But the foe's body armor proved no more penetrable than the loose lizard's had been, and true or not, the javelins only found their way to the ground. Kyrik thought he heard laughter from the enemy ranks.

"Well boss. I go now. You join?"

Yoya was right. It was about time for the officers to join the charge. Without answering he dug his heels into the courser's flanks to get it moving. The centurion was somewhat ahead of him, the Reticulate being more pliable to command than the twitchy Red Racer.

The enemy hadn't changed position. Kyrik imagined all sorts of games they might be playing. Perhaps the trick was to lure his men into the bailey, pull shut the gate, and slaughter them from the walls. But most battles never came to tricks. More likely, they were just confident they could meet and best the charge from their current position, and perhaps they were right.

As to Kom himself, if he was among the enemy riders, he hadn't distinguished himself in any way, not with banner nor headdress nor gilding on his armor. The troops were more uniform than any Kyrik had ever seen. More likely, the man who'd spent more of his life learning to talk funny than training with weapons was cowering inside the fort while these mounted fools who thought him a god did his dirty work.

Kom! Boom! Boom! Boom! *Kom!* Boom! Boom! Boom! *Kom!*

As his first rank came within lancepoint of the foremost foes, the chanting and drumming stopped. For a moment there was an unnatural quiet, with only the faint, eerie rushing of a thousand fistfire jets to accompany the scene. Then metal met metal and the screaming began, along with the hissing of coursers fired by rage at their own kind.

Across the dustless, shadeless plain, Kyrik saw it all. The impact was less disastrous than he'd expected. Though the points didn't pierce the enemy's breastplates, the force was in most cases sufficient to unseat the rider. Two of the five squares were cut in half in moments—in half, that was, if he were only counting men.

On his side, the shock left the first wave with lodged or broken lances in the midst of riderless, armor-plated coursers. The screams, first from Kom's men as they were uncoursered, now came from his own, much more balefully, as the jaws fell on them. Kyrik saw a leg nipped off at the knee, just above the greave, and another man pulled halfway in two by lizards clamped on each leg and moving at cross purposes. *The horrors of war, as usual.*

Just as the second wave was achieving moderate success against the coursers by ramming lances into eyes and teeth, the rest of the enemy began to advance. Their squares moved intact, coursers stepping right in the fistfire with their metal-clad claws, and Kyrik was suddenly awed by the advantage that represented. His troops were getting strung out as they advanced, forming into a series of big, long, loose flanks for the enemy to nip to pieces one by one.

Kyrik slowed as he approached the melee, not sure what he could do in terms of actually fighting. He'd never got himself a lance, and his only weapon other than the Racer's bite was the shortsword at his waist. This was the standard army sidearm, not much more than a dagger, which a courseryman was meant to use either as last-ditch defense against his own mount should it turn, or else on himself to avoid a much more grisly end. Kyrik carried it because it was the proper weapon for him to carry, and because he very much approved of both these purposes. For the moment, though, he wished he had something much longer.

Some of the dismounted enemies had risen and were getting to work with their longswords and battle-axes. He watched one pull his shoulder free of a courser's fangs without blood, and another pull his head from the jaws. Bronze would stop fangs as well, but to be encased in something as strong and still be able to move was the stuff of fairytales. He watched the risen men kill three of his own and their coursers, then remount both armored lizards and the naked ones of Kyrik's fallen.

Meanwhile, the enemies that had been at the rear were now sweeping past the melee and attacking the flanks of his troops as they arrived. This turned quickly into a bloody slaughter, with swords, axes, and fangs proving all equally deadly from the flank, and the lances of his own men useless other than frontally. By the time he'd observed a dozen taken down, shucked of their breastplates, and gnashed to bits, the captain had brought his own lizard to a complete stop.

He looked back, wondering if it was time to call the reserves. From what he'd been witnessing, he was in danger of losing both Claw and Fang Troops to a man, though they outnumbered the enemy two to one. The grey metal armor might as well have been sorcery. In all his wars, Kyrik had never seen mere difference in equipment make such a change in odds before.

Vein and Bone stood tensely in their ranks against the grey

horizon. The forest of upright lances gave the captain hope. Beyond them he could see the bolt throwers arrayed to their right rear flank, the circled wagons, and the rogues still sitting their antelopes in a bloated, disorderly mass, doing nothing.

Of the men now at the front, the reserve troops might save a few at the cost of twice as many of themselves. They might also just lose and be butchered to a man. There was no reason to risk such gallantries, not when he had two bolt throwers to even the odds if he left the troops where they were. As for the others, he would spare a tear after he found time to weep for the hundreds, perhaps thousands of lives before theirs that he'd squandered in battle.

Turning back to the carnage, he saw one of his coursers had fallen into the fistfire. By the time he looked, the lizard was completely engulfed, the rider shrieking like a little girl as the red-black tongues of flame took him from his pinned leg up. His suffering was brief. Soon both courser and rider were fused into the black core of the fire, flames dancing red and dark all around their prone and motionless shapes. The sight brought back every premonition of hell Kyrik had ever had on a killing field.

By now, despite their gains, the soldiers of Kom were surrounded, yet it was by no means clear they were bested. Man after man, good men who had followed Kyrik in a half-dozen campaigns, threw themselves into the fight. Soon the enemy was defending from behind a pile of corpses, men's and lizards' stacked together: a forward redoubt of sorts, even as their gate stood tauntingly open.

A cheer, and the sound of hoofbeats. The rogues were charging now, four abreast behind a single leader, looking much more organized than they had standing still. The leader was not Yharalon, the man he'd contracted with to gather the foresters, but instead one who was unrecognizable from this distance but wore a familiar-looking floppy hat and dirty hempen clothes.

The cheers turned to curses as the stags rode past the fight and toward the open drawbridge. The sound of their hoofs on the wood was more maddening than the enemy's kettledrums had been. As the tail of the column pulled into view, Kyrik saw what had become of Yharalon. He was bound tightly with rope and laid across the crupper of a back-rank man.

Feeling half a fool, he heeled his courser to go after them. The reserve troops and the bolt throwers would do what they needed to do on standing orders. Having no weapons to contribute to the fight himself, he had no reason to stand by them. Survival would be the only commander they needed.

It was the risk to his own skin that made him feel foolish as he kicked the Red Racer to full speed. He'd soon be alone inside the fort with hundreds of rogues plus whoever or whatever else was still there. But his chances outside didn't seem much better. More men and coursers lay engulfed by the dark fire. It seemed that once there were a few lying around, they multiplied as others stumbled into them. The grey armor made the enemy impervious to this hazard, which seemed like it might be enough on its own to turn the battle.

Above all, what made him choose the fort over the field was the rogue with the big nostrils. Facing Kyrik, he would only tell tales. It wasn't in his nature to be honest, and he'd never confess to anything under any circumstances, even with two hundred blades at his accuser's throat to insure him against any consequence. Instead, he'd give an excellent reason why he'd tied up Yharalon and led the foresters into the fort. It would all be for the good of the mission, *you see.*

A load of dung, obviously, but by pretending to buy it, Kyrik would gain the opportunity to look for—and here he felt the fool again—a crystal full of dust.

VI

The servants were swirling around Herrin, making him as plain as could be. He had to wear ripreed, coarse-woven to prove his austerity, bleached or black or starkly striped to show the honor of his house: the livery their family shared with government and god, and no one else. But Herrin liked the feeling of silk against his skin as much as the next man, so the process of readying him was even more elaborate than Gihha's. He needed to be tied into his silks ever so carefully to ensure that no one saw a slip of them, and his body, once so fit, was no longer suited to dressing discreetly. For her part, Gihha favored silken gowns with slits that hinted at the finer silks beneath.

She had one leg raised on a kneeling slave's palms to allow another to fasten the buckles of her sandal around her calf. Her face had been done in the morning, as always. In Herrin's mirror, over his shoulder, her cheeks looked as shiny and smooth as a baby's, as they should have, since the cosmetic putty she used was made from the fat of babies, and she paid a fortune for it.

Anyone would find it hard to believe she was the same age as the senator, but it wasn't his place to stay young. Her calf was as hard as when she claimed first in the running javelin toss at Water Lily Peak, the year before he started courting her, when he was still the handsomest boy in the world, as well as the richest. Since then, he'd grown fat on his wealth, on his slaves, on sitting in rooms where decisions were made at great length. Fair enough: she would have opened her veins in the bath before settling for a husband with less.

"You shouldn't wear a tunic," she said, without directly mentioning the size of his rump, "the skirts flare out and it looks clownish. Robes are more dignified, anyway."

"It's midsummer," he answered peevishly, "you want to drown my very manhood in sweat?"

The slave holding up his options, a white robe with a single black stripe and a white tunic with a checkered hem, looked terrified at being caught in a dispute between master and mistress. Whichever outfit Herrin chose, the one who brought it forward was likely to be punished for it. Gihha smiled. Life could be delicious, if one learned to enjoy the small moments.

"If you tried wearing silk like everyone else, you'd have all sorts of options for the hot-weather days."

"Bah!" Herrin spat. "You're always trying to make a fancy-boy of me. If you could grow a prick, you'd shove it up my ass without a moment's hesitation." He turned vulgar very quickly these days when she annoyed him.

"If that's how wearing silk makes you feel," Gihha smirked, looking his plump, silk-encased form up and down, "so be it, sire."

Herrin growled as he cocked his head to allow an eyebrow to be trimmed. She wondered what would happen to old men if they didn't receive such treatment, if they'd eventually go blind from the hair growing into their eyes. All manner of unkempt people could be seen around the capital, but they didn't live long enough to test her theory.

"I still don't understand your purpose in this," she remarked. "Why not just confine him to the dormitory, and let him be the Chancellor's problem?"

"The dormitory!" Taz pulled away from his groomer and sneered at her. "A den of Crescentines, purple halfbreeds, and provincial louts. You think he'll grow into a better senator there than he would here, in the finest house in the empire?

"He means to be a surgeon, not a senator."

"Youth is a time of folly. At least he isn't claiming to be a poet."

Gihha couldn't argue with that. She was now fully dressed, the last of thirty-two eelskin straps firmly buckled around her well-kept leg. Herrin was still half-naked, the choice between tunic and robe unmade, and the slave, who had not been selected for physical strength, visibly straining with the effort of displaying the two options for so long.

"Well, I'm ready to go. Nydhian food, is it? I must admit I feel an appetite for the taste of sealizard."

"It's always Nydhian food," Herrin grumbled. "No one likes anything Saspian anymore."

His nosehairs reduced with two painful-sounding clicks, he dismissed the grooming-slave and finally gestured for the robe to be pulled over his head. Two others ran up to help him into it while the dressing-slave scurried off to bring forward a selection of headdresses. Herrin chose a shiny black vulture-feather piece that made him look like a fat old bird, but Gihha refrained from comment.

"He didn't break any laws," he said as they descended the stairs, Gihha looking down to admire how the torchlight caught the green silk of her new dress. She had no idea how to respond. *Tell him about the beetle smoking?* The timing didn't seem right.

"He's a man, a Taz," Herrin continued. "As the law sees it, he killed one of his own slaves in his own house. If that was against the law, there would be no law."

"Killed and ate," Gihha added, "and not in that order."

"As is done, at times. That's why this must be treated as a purely family matter. To burden the college with it would be unseemly."

"So, what are you going to do? Put him over your knee and spank him?"

"I'm going to scare him. Scare him into thinking a little bit before doing whatever he feels like doing. I consider it part of his training. We all went through something like this as boys."

"If you say so, Senator. But if you're getting into the business of scaring your son, you might wish to consider scaring him away from that Capaz girl." It came out sounding supercilious even to Gihha herself.

And perhaps that was the problem. Herrin had long ago courted her for her pure blood, the Red Saspian blood that made her nose long and thin, her cheeks high and narrow, her muscles firm, her blood cold. That was all she'd had when she was a girl, as she came from an ancient family of Old Sasp who'd lost everything but their nostalgic appeal to the Fist. Indeed, her father and most of her relatives lay buried under the ruins, and it was only by accident that her mother, with Gihha in her belly, had been away at the salt baths in Traspor that day.

She generally assumed, or worked under the assumption, that Herrin found her fetching as well as suitable. Her fire, the challenge she brought to their conversations, the hardness of her body as she pushed back against him in bed, these were the things a Saspian man was supposed to want. But Gihha sometimes wondered if they really did. When she was at Water Lily Peak, back when only pure Red Saspian girls were allowed, all the boys had gone for Ayin Yasba with her soft eyes and easy laughter. Gihha's beauty, on the other hand, was acknowledged but not much pursued. Herrin had drooled over Ayin along with the rest, and probably had her, since he'd never foregone a single thing he wanted. Now their son was running around with Ayin's slut daughter by the wastrel Wan Capaz, an older man of decidedly purple blood who'd always been in the market for badly used goods.

"He's young," Herrin reiterated as they walked out into the garden. "Expect folly. Don't encourage it, but expect it."

"You don't care." She spun around and stood in his path. "You want his wineries!"

"Woman, you speak of things of which you know nothing."

"You've wanted them for years, you old drunk. Why else would you always be going up to that wretched hole of a—"

"Torkiz," he said, naming the wretched hole of a frontier town, "Capaz wineries and all, is worth less than the bricks it's built from to me. Save our house, of course. It's a fine house, you know. You should spend more time there. The autumn weather isn't bad. Besides, a man can't make a dowry out of that which already serves as collateral. Especially not to the father who holds most of his markers."

"It's too late for Irrian to be dallying, though. The suitable girls his age I can count on one hand. Unless you want to marry him off to the Zata infant, if I were you I'd be just as anxious as I am to see him a few steps down the road. We may be the richest, but we aren't the only rich family in the world, you know."

"I wish there were a brother and sister for them," Herrin mused, turning to approach their palanquin. "That way we could just mark up some clay and everyone would get to keep what they have."

"Are you ill? When have you ever missed an occasion to give a little and take a lot? But profit commands that Aga marry down, and Irrian, well, he marries as close to us as he can get."

"These are our children, Gihha, not chits on a gambling table. Next you'll have them marrying each other. We could all move to an island and cloister ourselves, as if one mad emperor wasn't enough."

"I'll take that as an endorsement of our son running around with the Capaz slut. What are we punishing him for again? Or is he being rewarded for his good table manners?"

It was a rare cloudy summer day in Za'ar. The eunuchs had brought out one of the larger palanquins, too big for just the two of them, as if Herrin didn't want to touch her accidentally on the ride. The peaked roof had been covered with an oilskin fly as a precaution against the looming rain. He used the process of boarding the conveyance as an excuse to avoid responding to her question. It was an elaborate process, designed to ensure that master and mistress had neither to stoop nor to climb. At the end, as they'd been trained, the slaves licked their palms in gratitude for having been allowed to touch the soles of their owners' shoes.

As they rode through the streets of the West End, it was hard to remember not to raise her voice. The interior of the palanquin felt very private, like a canopied bed, and the neighborhood was too genteel to remind her of its surrounding presence with stink or brash noises. Yet prying ears were all around them. She resolved to hush her tone as she proceeded with her inquiries.

"I don't suppose you have any idea why he's chosen the Surgery course," she said as softly as if they were already seated at the tavern, with senators and senators' wives at every nearby table.

"It is rigorous, to be sure. In a way, I'm pleased he's chosen to challenge himself."

"I don't see it that way. Our family's challenge is the running of the empire. He wants to be some fancy West End surgeon and a man-about-town, carrying on with little tarts like the Capaz girl. Not much of a challenge when you compare the two."

At this, Herrin grew unexpectedly sullen. "I have a few good years left. He can spend them having his fun if he wants. I was nearly twice his age when I first sat in session."

"As long as his kind of fun doesn't wind him up in a gibbet," she murmured, thinking the words would linger in the air for a while, making it crackle with implications.

Instead, Herrin responded at once, and forcefully: "The day a Taz is put in a gibbet on Saspian soil will be the fall of Za Himself."

They arrived. Thunder cracked the moment they came to a halt, and the rain followed abruptly; guards and slaves hustled to set up a portable awning to raise over them on their way to the door. Like many of the fashionable places on the West End, the tavern had rustic pretensions, with a little courtyard evoking the mythical charm of the Nydhian countryside. Big eunuch hands steadied them as they negotiated the sloped walkway of rough-hewn stones, already half in flood from the sudden downpour. At the bottom, a door of knotty pine was flung open, unleashing warmth, pink-tinted lamplight, the smell of searing meat, and the polite clink and murmur of upper-class dining.

"Your son is seated at your usual table, Senator Taz," said a man with a thick Nydhian accent. They all looked alike to her, but Gihha deduced that this was the owner of the establishment, whom she'd met on a number of occasions. There were at least sixty tables in the place, and every one seated a senator or his kin. To be the ones he greeted at the door made Gihha feel warm inside. She resolved not to let good food and good etiquette soften her stance.

Irrian, sitting at their table by himself, looked shrunken and young. It was as if all the girth and bluster he'd gained in the past two years was just a show he'd been putting on. Underneath, he was still her little boy, albeit not a sweet and innocent one. Indeed, she couldn't think back far enough to remember him as either harmless or affectionate.

As soon as they were seated, the serving-wench brought out a board of Dhulari dumplings: chopped tapir kidney, green onion, and water chestnut steamed in wrappers of antelope lung. To accompany this perennial favorite, they were each presented with a flute of rare grapewine, clear and sparkling, cool enough to bead up moisture on the crystal. The way the lamplight twinkled in each droplet was elegant, like fine jewelry, and she did allow it to distract her briefly from pressing concerns.

"So how does it taste?" Herrin asked while the boy's mouth was full. "Better than last night's repast?"

Irrian swallowed prematurely, bringing water to his eyes. "It was wrong of me, wasn't it."

"Wrong? Wrong? Of course it wasn't wrong. To take the highest sacrament is right and fitting for the Master. This you've been taught, and this you know."

Gihha, enjoying her own dainty bite, smiled discreetly. One of her favorite things about Herrin was how he used religion at his convenience. It was so much more Zalike than actual piety.

"In manhood, however," he continued, "you learn to balance what is right with what is prudent. When Za gave His commandments, He meant for us to follow them with a clear and level head. We must eat of that which is sacred. It is the Way. But son, there are fifty slaves in our house. Each, from the eldest to the youngest, from the strongest to the weakest, from the cheapest to the dearest, would have served just as well for the purpose."

Herrin let his comment sit for a while, and after a respectful interval, Gihha put in, "What your father and I would like to understand is the *thinking* that led you and your friends to eat Krakwin."

Irrian's eyes filled with contrition, but his mouth was full again, so he had to finish chewing before he spoke.

"It was late. The four of us were getting back from—supper, a late supper. We went into—"

"Four of you?" Herrin asked.

"We were with the Zata boy, Kini, whom you know, and Corth,

a foreign student at the college. Walthorian. He's sort of a mascot to us."

Gihha suspected Corth served the boys as more than a mascot, but she kept her peace. Irrian was allowed that, the same way he was allowed to drink wine, come home late, and eat the household slaves. He was a "man" now; the Grandmaster had proclaimed it at his commencement. Only things forbidden to men were forbidden to him, but that apparently didn't keep him from those, either.

"The fourth?" she asked.

"Mother, it was—you know. It was Hhule Capaz."

She stared back icily. Nothing needed to be said.

"Shun love of boys and women," Herrin put in, quoting Zaist scripture again, "but only take possession, and pleasure in thy dominance."

"Yes, Father. So it is written."

Gihha couldn't hold her tongue. "There are better ways to impress a girl than making a late-night meal of your father's best scribe."

"Please, Mother, it wasn't like that. I invited everyone into the atrium because they wanted to bathe."

"I wonder why." With her look, she made it clear that she did not actually want to know what her son had gotten up to with the Capaz girl, the Walthorian boy, and rat-faced Kini Zata that made them all need a bath.

"I suppose we were making a lot of noise in the water. We'd had wine. Krakwin came in. We were all, well, we were naked. We almost died laughing at him but we also didn't like the way he was staring at us. It would have been eerie, like he was trying to cast a spell on us or something, if we didn't know exactly what it was really all about."

Gihha believed this. The scribe had a twisted way of looking at anyone comely, hinting at twisted predilections. She'd noticed the same of her husband and son, but they weren't slaves. She always thought Krakwin smart enough to confine his interest to the younger slaves, of whom there were plenty in the house, but perhaps he hadn't been able to control himself in this instance. She wondered if it was bathing alone he'd happened in on.

"So then he launched into this speech, about how he is a scholar and we young people have no respect for scholarship. As if I weren't enrolled at the Imperial War and Mining College!"

"I have to admit," Herrin said, "that was an outrageous thing to say. And bookkeeping isn't exactly scholarship, even if you use a secret code or two."

"That's what I thought, only I wasn't really thinking, I suppose. Because of the wine, that is." Gihha squinted at him, bringing forth a tinge of red on his cheeks. He continued with a stammer: "H-Hhule got really angry. There was something about listening to a slave talk like that right after he'd ogled her. Imagine if someone behaved like that around Aga," he concluded, turning to his mother.

Gihha did imagine it, and she imagined Aga handling the situation better than her brother had.

"Indeed, it is quite nasty, when you put the two things together like that," Herrin conceded. "Our slaves see us undressed all the time. We can't abide letting them get any peculiar notions. He should have been flogged, at least. But I also think he should have been flogged—at most. Why did you feel the need to inflict the ultimate punishment?"

Irrian shook his head. "It must have been the wine. Maybe we were hungry."

Gihha already knew the whole tale from Gurgatha, their captain of guards, who'd observed the proceedings without being noticed.

The boys had used the chains under the dining table to set old Krakwin up for the *faga numm'zahhoy,* the Banquet of Ultimate Humiliating Dominance. Usually the victim was nailed down for this, but Irrian had been wary of damaging his father's table, so they just chained him at four points. Indeed, they hadn't done anything like a true *faga numm'zahhoy,* as scripture called for all the slaves of the household to be gathered to bear witness. It was supposed to be a formal, solemn affair, not a drunken debauch. Simply devouring someone without bothering to kill and cook him first, with no regard for the other protocols, did not count as ritual, at least the way Gihha had been taught.

Only Irrian and the Zata boy partook. The Capaz slut, by the captain's account, had taken a small taste—a sharp, bloody little kiss on the cheek to remind the victim of what he would never have again—while the Walthorian, predictably squeamish about such things, just stood by and watched. In all, they would consume only about a twentieth of his total weight, but it killed the slave all the same. The places they had chosen to bite were particularly cruel and injurious ones.

"The loss to me is great," Herrin said sadly, but without anger in his voice. "Krakwin had figures the way sages have letters. There was no limit to the number of books he could add while keeping them straight in his mind, and across his undecipherable little tablets. Our accounts are tossed because of what you've done. Tossed! I'll be dead before we get them back in order."

"Father, I'm sorry. I accept whatever punishment you and Mother feel is appropriate."

"No. *Sorry* is for slaves, and punishment is for slaves and wives and children. You are a man now. You did what you did. The consequences will come to you. I'm leaving it up to Za this time."

Gihha saw in Irrian's face the same puzzlement she was feeling.

There were occasionally times when he looked and thought like his mother's son. *What do the gods have to do with this?* To her, reining the boy in was a practical matter, and neither Za nor any other god was known to be helpful in practical matters. It seemed, as she feared, that Herrin planned to do nothing at all, and the next incident was sure to be worse.

"Za," he went on, "presides over all. He is the Giver and the Taker. The Senate is one thing, the Emperor another. But Za stands over them all, and where our house stands in relation to them and to Za—well, I leave that to your own observations.

"One thing is clear. The more of the world we own, the more Zalike we are. Whether or not we are the Most Dominant is for Za Himself to decide, and not the laws of men that make men senators, slaves, or emperors. To own the world is a heavy burden. It means some things cannot be left to politics, or policy. We must protect what we own."

Where is he going with this? Gihha squirmed inside, unused to the feeling of not anticipating him perfectly.

"Krakwin kept books," he continued. "The Senate keeps books. The Ministries keep books on behalf of the Emperor. The Society of Za keeps books. The Army and the Navy: books. Together, they press enough clay in a year to build a small city. But Krakwin was unique among them for marking into his books the form of none, and the function of all. If you think this family does not make war, he's beguiled you along with the rest of the country."

Gihha chose to stay out of this side of the business. She supposed she'd be sucked into it now that Krakwin was gone. Why, after all, had Herrin summoned her to this little family repast? Her presence wasn't just for Irrian's benefit.

"War is expensive," the senator continued, "war looks to most men like a loss. War is made with taxes, not investments. What is gained by war must always appear to be gained by peace. What do you think I kept Krakwin for? His occasional insolence, or his foul breath?" He laughed drily. "It's my fault as much as yours, for entrusting so much to a slave."

"Indeed," Gihha agreed, knowing she wasn't meant to. Herrin glared at her briefly. Irrian still looked confused and even more childlike.

The wench came back to clear the dumplings and set a clean board, followed by two slaves with chunks of broiled sealizard on copper skewers made to look like swords. The fat was still bubbling on the charred white flesh, the black skin imbued with aromatic smoke and puckered to a perfect crispness. It was a pity Herrin was ruining everyone's appetite, except perhaps his own. He gestured for them both to eat, an unwelcome sign because it indicated he was far from done speaking.

"It so happens that you had your little escapade at the worst possible time. And it also so happens that both of the matters of greatest concern to me, those in which our finances were most delicately balanced at the time of Krakwin's demise, may be of personal concern to you."

Irrian's face said *To me, father?* without help from his tongue.

"Yes, you. There's something dear to you at stake in each case. First, the matter of Torkiz."

"Where Hhule's from."

The guileless look that accompanied these words told all. Irrian had no idea what it meant to be a provincial, a second-rate person, and, conversely, he had no clue yet what it meant to be a Taz. Physically and emotionally he showed all the coveted traits of a dominant man, but mentally he was either still a child, or a fool for life. Gihha had a brief precognition of her old age, with Herrin dead and Irrian in charge of family matters. It wasn't pretty, and it wasn't the first time she'd pictured it.

"I'm doing what I can," Herrin said, his expression a beautifully crafted mockery of regard for the safety and well-being of others. "Krakwin had a complicated scheme to move gold for the defenses. If the town is lost now, your friend will have nothing to her name."

Lost. Gihha had overheard Herrin discussing another invasion by the desert tribes, but he'd never sounded so sure about it before. *Torkiz in flames. Oh, well.* At least it would throw a Taz-Capaz union entirely out of the question, since everything the Capaz owned was in that dirty crack of a border town.

"Second," Herrin went on, "is a matter so secret I haven't even mentioned it to your mother. Suffice it to say there is an order from His Dominance, and it involves the War and Mining College. But perhaps you have nothing to worry about there."

She'd seen Herrin do this in many conversations, disarm his adversary right before the kill. It was always the same routine, in which the food on the table or whatever else was at hand—tablets and scrolls, perhaps, or a slave attending him—became a prop in his studied performance of casualness. In this case, he used a chunk of flesh, pulled neatly from its skewer, chewed unhurriedly, and washed down with a sip from his wine-flute. He was certainly going in for the kill, but she was at a loss as to what this might entail.

"No, really, I suppose you don't. It's my own stake in the college that's on the table. For those who stand on their own merits, it shouldn't matter whether Senate or Society is in charge."

"The Society of Za?"

"Yes, son. *That* Society. The college is the Emperor's, and His alone by law. It's only by grace of tradition, and purse-strings, and our friendship with the dear Chancellor, of course, that the Senate controls it. Should we fail to please His Dominance, the first thing He'll do is order Azag out and have the Society take charge of instruction. Things are as tense as ever between us. They accuse us of moral laxity, we accuse them of graft. You can imagine how zealous they'll be in uprooting any imperfections in the student body."

Gihha could almost hear the chits falling on a gameboard. Herrin was playing his terrifying revelations hard and fast. The facts that his father knew of his dabbling; that others could soon find out; that the literal wrath of Za, in the form of His holy vicars' lashes and chains, might indeed come to visit the House of Taz if he wasn't careful; each of these facts in turn, unfolding out of such bland-sounding words, made a deeper abyss of the boy's gaze.

"But of course, there's nothing for you to worry about since you aren't involved in smoking firebeetles or anything like that."

Herrin grimaced the way he did when he was trying to prolong a spasm of ecstasy. Gihha followed his look to Irrian, and back. The boy had gone so pale she thought he might be sick at the table. As for Herrin, his expression was too knowing, more familiar with the topic than he was supposed to be. Perhaps he had lost his composure to the joy of terrorizing his son, and was giving away more than he wanted to, but he showed no other sign of being out of control. *I know what a filthy fiend you were and probably still are, but you're telling him now?* It was a parting of the curtain between parent and child that Gihha could hardly believe, let alone accept.

"If I were you," he went on, "I would enjoy myself. Mark my words, but understand nothing has come of this yet. I suggest you enjoy that for as long as it lasts. Go on, eat your lizard. Drink your wine. Tomorrow, we may pay for what you've done, but that's tomorrow."

Yet it seemed young Irrian Taz had lost his appetite.

The thing she hadn't thought possible had come to be, in the form of a raw patch at the bottom of her stomach. The "fiend's pit," they called it, a body part that slept in innocent bellies, but squirmed and rumbled and pleaded for more once it knew what beetle was. Each roll of thunder chafed it; the splash of every raindrop seemed to open it wider. Aga Taz was becoming a firebeetle fiend.

As it turned out, the fiend's pit had no respect for wealth or privilege. In Irrian, it ran deep, and rode him hard. His schoolmate, Kini Zata, who suddenly seemed to be his best friend, was even worse. Kini hadn't even enrolled in the college, commencing instead into idleness and a neverending quest to stay high. But the one who had it worst of all was Hhule Capaz. Throughout the week, despite the extreme strictness of the Maids who ran their school, Aga would catch her sneaking dabs from a tiny gourd, especially before meals, since food was hard to keep down when the pit was raging.

Aga didn't have it so bad, yet. Each week she'd been able ride it out until Spineday, confident that, once she was home, her brother would come through for her. He shared what he had out of love, and for the cruel comfort of dragging her down with him, and in fear she'd tell their parents if he didn't, a tangle of emotions and motivations that would have made her feel even sicker if she could afford to think about it.

But this Spineday, Irrian hadn't been home at all, and now he was at the tavern with Mother and Father, a family gathering to which Aga had not been asked. She knew what was happening. Her mother had decided even before Irrian was born that he would marry an equal and Aga would marry beneath herself. It was assumed some provincial senator would be so keen on the Taz name that they could cut her dowry by half or more. But now Irrian was running around with the sort of person she was meant to marry, and she was sitting alone again on a Spineday afternoon. At the finest tavern on the West End, their father would feed Irrian, weaken him, reason with him, and finally threaten him, in an effort to set things in proper order.

She'd be glad to see Irrian separated from Hhule Capaz, but shuddered at the notion of being married off to one of her brothers. The neat, nasty little way things tended to work out made it seem like more than a possibility. The Capaz boys had never been seen in the capital, but word was they ranged from the thoroughly insipid to the utterly depraved. For all she knew, Wan Capaz himself was at the table with her brother and parents, and they were drawing up the agreement that would keep Irrian away from Hhule, with Aga traded off in a subclause. It was sickening, but not so sickening as the blaze in her belly. She would have married ten ogres and a score of rustic simpletons to quell that.

So it was almost inevitable, with everyone out and the summer rain drumming so oppressively it seemed to rattle the very stones of the House of Taz, that she'd find herself in Irrian's room, on hands and knees, crawling from one of his—formerly their—secret hiding-spots to the next. Under the loose floor tile by the chest of drawers where they kept his silks and linens, she found the niche they'd once used as a dungeon for insects captured in the garden, still there but completely empty. Under his bed he kept torn-out parts of a medical scroll detailing the technical aspects of copulation and related acts. Those were still there, more faded and rumpled than she remembered from the times he'd made her look at them. But nothing else was with them.

In the crack in the stone below his windowsill, she found money, more money than he was ever supposed to handle at his age and station, but none of what he had it for. As she ran out of places to look, her pit raged louder and louder until she couldn't even hear the storm. She told herself it was a stupid errand anyway; he would keep his beetle with him, or leave it somewhere else, before risking discovery by her or anyone else in the house. This only made her more keen to turn the place over, defiantly now, as if her reason itself was an insolent servant saying unwelcome things. She reached under his bedding and rummaged through his underclothes. She found nothing.

So she sat on the bed and pictured Irrian in his room, alone, doing the things he did. The answer came to her so quickly that she felt like a fool for all her prior efforts. In the past year he'd grown nearly as tall as his chest of drawers. When she imagined him next to it, she saw how easy, how natural it would be for him to place something on top of it. Excited, her pit nagging a bit less at the mere thought of finding something to fill it, she dragged a stool from by his dressing-table to the side of the chest. She'd had her own spurt of growth, and she reached the surface easily, though she was still not tall enough to see where she was groping. The wood was crusted with dust as if it hadn't been cleaned in years. Not finding anything at first, she braced for another disappointment when her fingers lit on something round, with the texture of clay: Irrian's pipe. But there was nothing to put in it.

She brought it down anyway, though the sight of it was sure to make her craving worse. The end was crusted with burnt resin, glossy and sticky. The boys loved to joke about becoming gutter fiends, sleeping in the plazas and prostituting themselves to sailors and carters for a taste, and amid this banter she'd heard them mention scraping pipes out of desperation. Aga didn't share their relish for having things in common with the worst of the city's rabble, but at the moment it felt like her salvation. The resin somehow seemed even more reminiscent of living insects than the chopped-up flour Irrian got, and her stomach warred with itself between desire and revulsion. Desire won. She pried a bit of resin loose with her thumbnail and rolled it into a ball.

Then there was the matter of fire. The oil lamp and the flint-and-bronze set, innocent objects on their own, had been left in the open on Irrian's bedside table, but she found herself even less handy than he was at making a spark. After she nearly sliced her finger on the bronze, she opted for a different approach. Tucking the pipe into the folds of her shift, she went back to her own room, dimmed the distilled-oil fixtures, and clapped twice for a slave.

"I have a terrible headache from the pressure in the air. Light me a lamp."

As soon as she'd given the order, she felt she'd made a mistake. One needn't explain one's whims to slaves, and to have done so might inspire more chatter than the odd request for a lamp in the afternoon. When the slave returned, Aga studied him—it was a young male—more intently than she'd normally look at a slave, but his face revealed nothing.

"Latch the door on your way out."

She'd never done this alone before. While she only half-trusted Irrian not to tamper with her during spells of incapacitation, whatever he might do was nowhere near as bad as the consequence of anyone else finding her like that. But the pull of the fiend's pit was stronger than her misgivings. She touched the flame to the end of the pipe, recalling the way Irrian had done it for her many times now.

The smoke from the resin tasted bitter compared to what she was used to, the way burning any food would change its flavor. There was less spice to it, more oiliness, and she understood at once why only gutter fiends resorted to this method. The first few puffs merely numbed her, taking away some of the discomfort without adding pleasure. Up to this point, she'd been pretending to herself that was all she was looking for, but with the agony out of the way she only wanted more. She lost count of how many times she fired the sordid little ball before the smoke finally carried her off.

Her beetledream was always some version of the world being made, then unmade: cities rising and falling, herds of lizards sprawling across the plains then brought in for the slaughter. She would see what seemed to be vast swaths of the world over a staggering procession of eons, but would feel herself neither larger nor smaller, elder nor younger for it. Rather, it felt like her senses were finally open to things that had always been there, surrounding her, forming her. The best sense she could make of it was that the drug knocked her mind into pieces that needed to be picked up and put back in their proper places. Sometimes when she was quite far gone, she would feel the thick hand and stern gaze of her father guiding her back to the world.

This time, for the first time, Old Saspia stood at the center of the world that formed out of the red darkness. She watched the first men climb down from their homes in the trees to stalk lizards at night, timidly at first, growing bolder as the meat made them stronger. She watched as they cut down their homes to throw up longhouse walls and palisades of joined logs, forms she knew as stone flourishes on fine buildings. Here were the wooden originals, practical and brutal in their obvious intent. Conquering the forests and the greatest of lizardkind, the first men turned to each other for prey and sport, finding among their own species much greater danger and much more to be gained. Za Himself was a man in those days, becoming the Most Dominant as He surpassed all other chiefs in war and ownership.

She watched as the first armored soldiers were dressed in

bronze, red and gleaming at first, blossoming green after seasons on campaign. She watched the first brave man throw his leg across the back of a courser, and the first of the courserback legions forming. At spearpoint and swordpoint the tribes had long fought, but now men fell mostly to fangs. Cowards and the defeated were led away in chains of bronze, to slavery, buggery, and finally the stew-pot.

There was nothing for show in those times, nothing to delight a girl's fancy nor to soothe a woman's need for elegance; nothing for any of the senses. Clothing, if worn at all, was made of hides and grasses, for her people had learned to dress in metal before they learned to weave, a Crescentine art. The food for the whole tribe was boiled and put out in troughs, and the people would crouch and feed together, each class in turn, from chief and princes and blooded warriors down to the slaves and women. The best people, first in line, got the better morsels, but all ate of the same slop. The only music was war-music, the only songs ballads of bloodletting, the two tempos: march and battle.

And so it went on for ages, with the Crescent and its native tales— the flight of the liches, the rise of Walth from the ruins of Uthu— as little more than shadows on the far horizon. At times, the world of her ancestors grew so monotonous that she strained to see what was happening beyond the ocean. But then she'd realize what she was doing, the same error all her people had made, losing sight of what had made them great in favor of foreign and exotic things, softer, more intricate, seductive and enervating. *No,* her father told her, *not that way. Look to your own past.*

And there the Beheader, Great Zoba, was becoming another Most Dominant, the first fully Zalike man since Za Himself, uniting the chiefdoms in a feast of blood and terror. No one before Him had ever frightened so many, killed so many, nor brought such humiliation to the great and mighty. To be descended from one who carried an ax in His bodyguard, and from another member of His horde who got his lands by shield and spear, Aga swelled with pride. Where before she had seen the Capaz or nameless warriors, her own ancestors came clearly into view this time, fighting, killing, beheading their way to ultimate victory.

But when Zoba crossed the ocean, He was as gone from her vision as the Crescentines were as He brought them to heel. Instead, she watched His empire crumble in His absence, the isle becoming as it was before, a vast woodland dotted with the timber strongholds of proud sovereigns, every route between them a warpath. Za Himself, as the everlasting spirit of Dominance, was neither dead nor diminished, but shattered, scattered across the various principates as a contradiction waiting to be resolved.

They discovered a new metal, dull and grey in the ground, that would gleam like silver and slice like bronze after laborious beating and polishing. At once, every fighting man had to have his panoply of the stuff. The smiths got ahead of the unblooded warriors at the feeding-troughs and demanded use of their wives. Soon there were no fathers and sons among them, no clans, no lines of inheritance; only the strong and the weak, the sharp and the dull.

She could see how they were right and she had been wrong. They had started the same and grown different, but in the homeland they had grown more Saspian while their cousins in the Crescent grew less so. She watched the storms churn up the wide ocean channel between Old Saspia and new, forbidding all traffic, but this final separation seemed like nothing more than a symbol of her own decline, beginning long before, when her ancestors cut themselves from the true soil of their roots.

The Taz had guarded their blood but not their ways from the

purpling of the nation. The soft silks about her loins were their own accusation. She could feel the fabric cloying and belittling her, amidst her frothy cloud of bedding, as she watched a new Most Dominant rise and make Old Saspia whole again, with His troops of silver coursery crossing the forests and besting their enemies. The name *Kem* or *Kum* rose in vast chants above the din of the world below.

Soon she was just ticking off the moments until His return, His inevitable return across the water to punish all her wasted kind, not excluding herself. With a gasp she realized there was no one else to blame. She tried to cough but could not dislodge what was in her. She had asked it in, set pure Crescentine mischief alight and drawn it up into herself, not just willingly but longingly. More than transgressing, she had surrendered herself, given up, become one with all that was small and weak in the world. *And so easily. And at so young an age.* A silver blade was at her own neck. They'd found her, smelled her out. The feeling as everything went black was justice, for the first time in her life.

Aga came back scolding herself for letting the foolishness of street preachers, outlaw ones at that, invade the sanctity (as it were) of her beetledream. Of course there was no such thing as a silver sword. As far as she knew, her people had died out on Old Saspia long ago. They said the Fist of Za had caused great ocean waves; perhaps the seas had covered the island over. There were no such people as she'd seen in her dream. She had used in the manner of the gutter and fallen prey to gutter delusions.

Her parents and Irrian were still out, the whole house strangely quiet for a Spineday evening. The rain had stopped, but that wasn't all of it. The slaves seemed to be hanging back, shirking anything that needed to be done near her, as if they knew something was coming from their masters and didn't want to be first to encounter it. The pipe was still in her fist, an ugly, soiled thing. The lamp was sputtering. Glints of silver armor encircled her in the gloom, and for the first time she truly wished she had never tried firebeetle.

VII

Qabba Tek, in his heart still Grandmaster of Moksa, sat in the vault waiting for his captors to defeat some local savages above. An iron chain, cuffed around his ankle and fitted to the wall by the smiths of the "Great God," afforded him just enough liberty to reach all the strange objects Kom had commanded him to study, name, and count.

For now, Tek sat, since everyone was fighting and none could come to scourge him for his idleness. The tiny black beetle kept him awake; he had not slept since discovering it. But for a spell after each application he found he could do little more than sit and try to draw together the thoughts that kept racing away from him. He had lost so much, and the spell of the beetle overwhelmed him with the urge to fix it all in his mind before it slipped away into the darkness of oblivion.

Four years had passed now since the fall of Moksa. Qabba Tek was no stranger to slavery. As Grandmaster he had enslaved scores of his own people for cowardice and other unpaid debts. But he had always expected to be killed, not made a slave, should the stronghold fall. This new life was something he had never prepared for.

Great and brutal changes had never daunted him. His use of his Dominance under the Way of Sa had been broad. When he learned that some of the tribe's bravest warriors were in love with their wives, he had confined all the women and girls to a longhouse where they were used in common like the food in the troughs. When he saw that the men who were always held at the back of the line had taken to relieving each other, he had made them women by law and put them in the longhouse to share the women's burden.

Dominance, Sa, the One Real Thing, did not change because Qabba Tek no longer held it in his fist. But Kom brought something new to Dominance when he took it for himself and changed its name from Sa's to his own. The laws of Sa and of the Great Chief Mok had always been applied without measure and without record. Only Masters of the Way had known the sacred glyphs that were used to count the suns and moons and the years that had passed since the Founding, so that sacrifices could be made at the appropriate times. Now, under the Way of Kom, the glyphs were used to count everything that could be counted, with the former Masters of the Way of Sa enslaved as scribes to keep the tallies. Where before the calendar had been carved in stone and kept in a secret place in the forest, now the sacred glyphs were scratched in the dirt at the whim of Moksa's new ruler.

Under Sa's law all food belonged to the whole tribe, Chief and Masters eating first with the bravest warriors. Then the smiths and common soldiers would sup, followed by lizardmen, hunters, and fishers, leaving the dregs for women and children and slaves. So it had been decreed by Sa at the Dawn of Time, so Mok had affirmed in the Morning of Time, and so it had always been done.

But Kom decided that repute alone was no longer sufficient evidence that a warrior had earned his meat. Instead, he wanted daily evidence from each man to justify his sustenance. Right hands it was at first, until someone noticed the hands growing smaller and softer on average, and one-handed women and children began to appear among the new captives. So Kom changed the unit of proof to the one part that left no doubt as to the sex and maturity of the person it was taken from. To spare the edges of other blades in his service, Kom's master of smiths fashioned a new iron tool for the harvesting, and the anvils of

Mokkom, as the stronghold was called now, rang day and night with an order of one for each soldier.

Though he never removed his iron mask in the presence of any man, Kom seemed to Qabba Tek full of pleasure at watching a Grandmaster reduced to his chief trophy-counter. The tallying became more tedious as the food began to be measured as well, with different portions going to men who turned in more or fewer units. But Tek applied himself to this work as dutifully as he had kept the calendar of his former god, because he had faith in Dominance above all, and Kom had indeed bested Sa, and Dominance now rightly bore his name. *At least in the Land of Mok, at least for now.*

The trophies piled up in their thousands as Kom used his new base to attack the neighboring lands and strongholds. It was not long before they ended up in the food. They were no one's favorite, and, as a slave, Qabba Tek resorted to them frequently in moments of great hunger. The taste was a far cry from the delicate bites of preserved human flesh he had once ingested as the prime sacrament of Sa. But it nourished him like any other meat.

Then one day all of Saspia was gone, become the Komlangn. There was no one left to fight, nothing left for the warriors to harvest. Without currency for admission, two factions formed around the door to the longhouse at Mokkom, and fistfights for control of it soon rose to iron and murder.

The morning after the second or third spilling of blood in this manner, the warriors and draftlizards were all sent to camps in the forests around the stronghold. From dawn to dusk, Tek could hear the thunking axes and the crack, fall, and drag of giant trees being taken. The eternal prohibition on love between men was also lifted, and at night squeals of pain and roars of pleasure from the lumber camps joined the rutting howls of the camprats and the screams from the longhouse. With everyone thus occupied, peace was restored in Mokkom.

No one told him or any other slave where they were going when they marched them in chains down to Pink Bay, named for the many times its waters had been dyed by bloodshed on its waves and shores. But when he saw the fleet of bright new ships of the new and ingenious pattern brought recently to Saspia by some unfortunate visitors from across the water, Tek knew at once what was in store. Needing more lands to conquer, Kom had set his eyes on the legendary Crescent, the vast, rich ring of lands to the east conquered by a Saspian chief named Sopa, long ago. The visitors were thought to have come from there; though, having stumbled upon the Feast of Hearts in Komhek, they had not lasted long enough for anyone sober to ask them anything much.

When Kom set out in just two out of his forty ships, with but fifty of the best of each from among his thousands of men and coursers, Qabba Tek thrilled within at this first sign of weakness from the new "Great God." His path to Dominance, it seemed, up to this point as straight as an unpulled bowstring, had gone sideways into some foolish urge to glory.

It seemed Kom still had some measure of prowess to prove to the men beneath him, at least in his mind. If he were truly driven to conquest by the restlessness of his horde alone, he would have brought them all at once. This had to be Kom's own mission, not the mission of his entire nation. His pride proved he was only a man. Qabba Tek prayed it would destroy him.

Even as the ship rose, plunged, and rolled from side to side, dousing his wasted form over and over again with icy bilge, he prayed to Sa with all his remaining strength that the storm would take them, and with them drown the heresy of Kom. In the darkness of the hold, he knew not how many days and nights passed on the voyage. By his beard it must have been a moon.

It began to seem like the voyage might outlast the men attempting it. His tiny crusts of food stopped coming and the warriors no longer sang on deck. The rowing stopped, and he was not sure whether they had caught a favorable wind or lost their strength. He prayed it was the latter.

But then the water calmed and his gaolers came and unchained him alone among the bilge slaves. It was his lore, after all, that had kept them from killing him so far, since they could not both take his head and keep what was in it. For this reason, Kom wanted Qabba Tek, though he was nothing but a worm to him, among the first to set eyes on the new land. It was a strange sensation, as a cuffed and starveling captive, to have the "Great God" wishing to know his thoughts.

When he saw the coast, flat as a pond and whiter than cinder, Tek remembered his father Oksa Tek, who had been Grandmaster before him, telling of a strange light in the sky to the east and how the whole earth shook when it fell into the water. The old songs were full of such heavenly omens, but this was the only one related to him by a person who had seen it with his own eyes. Perhaps this was where the light had landed, flattening and burning the ground it touched. So Qabba Tek told Kom. The faceless mask nodded.

Ashore, they found a surface of hard, seamless, bone-white stone pocked with little round holes. Each of these emitted a jet of a strange fire, black and white and red all at once, a color that seemed impossible. There were volcanoes in Saspia, and at first Tek thought them some strange, flat, foreign version of the same sort of thing. Kom seemed bored by this idea, and sent him back to be chained with the rest of the slaves as they formed to unload the ship.

He had perhaps been right to do so, since Tek turned out to be wrong about the fires being tiny volcanoes. As soon as the flame first touched a thing that was not made of iron—the wooden wheel of a cart laden with sacks of feed—it quickly revealed itself as something less mundane.

Cart, lizard, load and lizardman were engulfed in the fire in moments, faster than fire had ever taken flesh or wood. Yet it did not seem to consume its fuel—if fuel it could even be called. The fire burned on and on without reducing any part to ash, instead preserving the familiar contours of a lizard-cart like the eerie silhouette of a thing in the heart of a furnace, somehow failing to melt down. A lizardman who chose to test the flaming lizard with his prod met the same fate, and he stood by them like a burning idol, his long wooden shaft forming a permanent flaming bridge between the shapes of footman and vehicle.

Kom cursed the loss of load and lizard, then ordered his column forward. The iron-clad feet of his men and coursers had been treading on the fire without consequence for hours, so he simply cautioned his cartmen and the barefoot slaves to avoid driving or walking over the flames as they advanced. They picked their way along in zigs and zags trying to keep up with the straight-marching coursery, an exhausting task for a man still starving and no longer young, with a weight of chains to lift with every step. The war drums thundered as they marched, and Tek's legs wobbled and buckled beneath him like a wild syncopation to the beat.

He silently praised Sa when Kom called a halt, but it was only to send them back at once to the shore. The "Great God" had found where he wanted a fort, and it was up to the slaves to dismantle the ships where they sat in the water, haul the wood back to land through the icy, churning surf and then through the maze of fires to where the warriors rested. A pile of raw fish heads was set down and the slaves went at it like a pack of wild animals, swallowing bones and fins, taking nips at each other after the meager meat was gone, until their gaolers yanked them back. Later, in the cold saltwater, Tek was glad he himself had not been bitten.

The hardest part was getting to shore, half-walking, half-swimming while keeping a grip on the biggest load of lumber one could carry on dry land. They fed one young boy to the coursers for letting a piece float away, and, with his screams ringing in their ears, the rest of the crew somehow managed to get the rest of the wood across. When he finally sat down to his bowl that night, in a camp already surrounded by the timber skeleton of a redoubt, Tek barely had the strength to bring the lukewarm gruel or its single, tiny piece of cartlizard gristle to his lips.

The next morning, he awoke to the cold sting of mailed hands wrenching him up by the armpits. The soldier led him stumbling to Kom, who showed him why he had chosen to build a fort in this place. All around, though the dawn was just breaking, the hammers and saws had already begun their frantic race against the coming of the night.

The reason was a hole in the ground, the first breach in the strange white surface that had none of the dark fire. Instead, it revealed the top of a rough-hewn stone stairway leading deep into the earth. They pushed and dragged him down these treacherous steps and chained him in a great vault at the bottom. At first, he did not know why.

Over the course of the day slaves went back and forth, down into the crypt and back out to the vault again, bringing familiar and unfamiliar things for him to count. Tek knew what they had in mind for him before they brought in stylus and fresh clay and gave the command. The madness of Kom for counting, for tallying, had perhaps found its match in the piles the slaves were making. He praised Sa that he would not have to carry another piece of wood, then cursed himself for praying selfishly. Better to carry wood, he thought, than secrets to the vain.

For the great thing to be gained here was not arms, nor goods to trade, but the secrets of the Crescent, this strange land that had long been nothing but a legend to the people of Saspia. To conquer it, Kom would have to know it. And there was much Qabba Tek did not understand. For each thing whose purpose he could guess—the brightly colored feathers, obviously used to fletch arrows; the cutting and piercing instruments of polished bronze; the sewn garments and stacked-up rolls of a material somewhat like basketry or hide, but finer than the one and lighter than the other, which he knew the Crescentines to use for sails on their ships—there were at least ten other things that baffled him completely.

There was much of gold, which he knew as a kind of copper too soft to be useful, including tiny disks, carved with symbols and images, in numbers too great to be counted. There were stacks of clay tablets engraved with similar markings. At first, he had no idea why these things were preserved, but soon he began to see patterns, familiar forms amongst the images—lizards, insects, human figures, parts of the body. A few of the symbols were like the calendrical glyphs he knew. It was mostly dots and scratches that meant nothing at all to him, but here and there he saw a glimmering of knowledge, and these were the parts he pursued.

It was thus he found the black beetle. He saw it first depicted in clay, then found the cage full of living specimens. The clay suggested that he set one ablaze and breathe in the fumes, and he did so at first not knowing whether the instructions were meant for a poisoner.

Here was a new path to power, to Dominance. And Kom would never know of it, even as the servant of Sa used it to bring about his destruction. The servant would scheme, and never sleep, and to his captors always hold firm that the black beetle was but a source of dye, useful enough but nothing like what it truly was: the most precious of his treasures. As a matter of course, he had come to think of all the things in the vault as his.

In the first moments after burning a fresh beetle—he was always alone, and never sure how long the spell lasted—Tek would dream first of Moksa before it was Mokkom, the order over which he had long presided; the drums, the taste of blood, the screams of the vanquished. In his dreams, the fall was brief as he watched Kom and his minions fall in a thousand ways to the Spirit That Does Not Die. To Sa, to the true Lord of Dominance.

Sometimes he saw them conquered by force, but he was dreaming of poison and treachery when the two strangers came in. Their faces were alien to him, brown-skinned and oddly misshapen, but one was dressed as a Saspian warrior from days of old, in quaint bronze armor. Tek remembered similar pieces in the Chieftain's Hall before it was burned by Kom, with the bronze and bones of the ancient chiefs and the great Moksan heroes of yore hung up for all to see, forever. But this man's armor was newly made.

The other must have been a slave by his look. He wore a strange woven helmet that reminded Tek of the pathetic way slaves and women would sometimes hold giant boya-plant leaves over their heads while gathering food in the sun and rain. *Of course a slave; a man who shades his head from anything but iron is not a man at all.*

As they approached him where he sat, he recalled the tales of Sopa. Could it be that these were men of Sa, long lost and reunited with him? Had they kept the Way here over all these eons? Could men so swarthy even be men, and if they were not men, could they keep the Way at all? The questions were bubbling over in his mind even before they addressed him in a rude version of his own tongue. Oddly, it was the slave who spoke first.

"Yo. Gonna free yer ass," he said.

The warrior, who had an iron axe despite the rest of his gear being bronze, made short work of Tek's chain. What was left attached to him was longer than he would have liked, but he was in no position to complain. Despite being free, he still sat. The mood to get up had not struck him yet.

"Who are you? What happened to Kom?"

The slave chuckled. "Oh, him. Yup. We kinda, y'know, like, stole his fort."

"They goin' crazy outside here now," the warrior put in. "Not real-real happy, nope, not one itty-bitty bit, but we left 'em plenty to deal with out there."

"He ain't kiddin'," the slave affirmed. He was already stuffing the treasures of the crypt into a huge sack. The warrior had one too. Both rapidly began to sweat as they bent, shifted, picked and chose among the treasures.

"Any of that-there, good-good stuff down here?" the warrior asked.

"Not really," Tek lied. "Just what you see. Gold, feathers, clay, if that's what you want."

Almost as soon as he had said this, the slave let out a whoop as he lifted the cage of black beetles from its unobtrusive corner of the mess, a place carefully chosen to make no one think they were anything important. *Of course they know what it is. They are from here. What if they leave me none? Almost better to be in Kom's hands still.* The idea of forfeiting his supply made his mouth taste like rust and his stomach cramp painfully.

The warrior sneered when he saw the cage. "That shit gonna kill yer ass."

"Whoa!"

The slave had found the clear tube. Other than the strange material it was made of, Qabba Tek had seen nothing interesting about it. Some glyphs he did not know were inscribed in the gold that stopped the ends. The contents, as far as he could tell, were the ashen remains of a person or an animal. *Some strange funerary rite, or a burnt offering, and nothing more.*

But the warrior wept with joy when he saw the thing, and the slave seemed nearly as delighted. After carefully picking over the rest of the collection with an eye to gold and colored stones in particular, they left the place with full sacks, grinning broadly. Tek got the sense that the grins were a little less broad than they might have been—that there was better news for these men than they wished to share with their comrades.

"Boys!" the slave shouted as soon as they emerged. The light dazzled Tek at first and he could not see whom the slave addressed, but the strong smell of an unfamiliar animal filled the air.

"Check it out, suckers!" he yelled, holding up his sack.

Hundreds cheered. It was clear that the slave was hardly a slave, but some kind of leader of men in this alien world. Perhaps he had raised a rebellion of slaves. As his vision cleared, Tek saw a crowd of lightly armed and armored men, each mounted on an animal like a giant camprat with an extremely heavy snout, a pair of horns on its head, and two blunt, black toenails instead of claws. He had never before known of any hairy beast that was neither rat nor man.

"But them fuckers outside," the slave continued, pointing a thumb over his shoulder at the drawn-up gate, "we gotta do something about 'em first. Reckon they're a teensy-weensy bit ground up out there right about now. Ground meat!" Laughter. "I say drop the bridge hard and hit 'em with all we got!"

Another cheer, and the men at the edges of the cluster began riding out and circling the fort's perimeter to stand ready behind the gate. Tek was impressed with how quickly they formed, despite having no appearance of discipline. But a charge by men in hides and scraps of bronze at best, with little wooden bows and spears, against Kom's finest? Unless their strange mounts had some kind of sorcery in them, it seemed unlikely to succeed.

The gate went crashing down, and the rat-riders stormed out all at once. The din of the animals' blunt claws against the hard earth was like nothing Tek had ever heard before. At a gallop they rushed out, with their leader and his antique-armored friend standing by and urging them on.

They still stood there after the last of the riders had passed them and gone headlong into the iron and fangs and the forest of black fire. For the first time, Tek noticed how the shifting colors of the eldritch flame were like the distinctive color of the beetle. It was black, to be sure, as all dark things were black to him, since his tongue named only three colors. But it had a tinge of red as well. It was also white, the third color, like the shiny shell of the beetle where it caught the lamplight. He was sure there was sorcery in a thing that could be every color at once.

Tek looked at his new companions meaningfully, asking without words when they planned to join the fight they'd started.

"I ain't goin' anywheres near that-there mess," said the "slave."

"We gonna be heroes by gettin' outta here," the warrior added, "Stayin' here, we ain't gonna be shit."

They waited a long while before slinking out around the side of the fort, while the battle raged in front of it. Qabba Tek commended himself to Sa as he cursed their cowardice, and told himself he was a captive, and so remained innocent.

Besides, they have my beetles.

VIII

At first, as usual, the plan seemed perfect in every way. They even thought to kill Yharalon, the fool that the other fool had put in charge of the foresters. It seemed prudent to end him on the distant chance he'd otherwise make it back somehow and tell tales. Once the rest of the stags had been sent out on their ill-fated mission, they lifted him down from the saddle where he'd been slung like a felled game animal.

After some consideration, Shigius cut his own antelope loose. Riding her might have gotten him home faster than walking, but alone, even mounted, he could carry less treasure. More importantly, an antelope seemed less useful than two armed companions in the likely event he'd be waylaid.

So he cut the tether, knowing he'd end up with sore feet, but also knowing he wouldn't miss the sore ass. The antelope, still saddled, ran off to rejoin her herd in its charge toward certain death, the animals for once showing no more wisdom than the men who rode them. That left only Yharalon to deal with, lying on the white ground with the ropes wound around him and hatred smoldering in his eyes.

Kyrik, who was already beginning to think like a proper rogue, suggested that a murder with weapons might rouse suspicion, even on a battlefield, if the authorities ever visited this place. So instead of doing him in with an axe, they untied him, pushed him onto a fistfire vent and let him burn. He did not scream, just kept glaring at them as the red blackness engulfed his body, for as long as he had a face left to glare with. Shigius was, for the first time, impressed by the man.

"That's the last piece of work for us to do here," Kyrik said, forgetting he was no longer captain and henceforth would possess only opinions, not facts.

"You call that work!"

Shigius laughed loudly at the notion. Work was driving a cart. Work was killing a sealizard. Killing a man was either business or sport. Knocking him into some kind of sorcerous trap that did everything for you was nothing at all. He would have liked to have had the fire by him all along, at hand for all the things he'd ever needed to dispose of completely. He had no love for spadework or the smell of burning flesh.

"For me, there's been no other kind," Kyrik said.

They then argued briefly over who would carry the dust. Kyrik, of course, wanted the cylinder in his own sack, since he was the one who had the biggest stake: it was on his head to bring it in. Shigius disagreed. In truth, he understood the old centurion had the best chance of surviving the journey on his own, and he wanted to hold something that would bind them together. But instead of mentioning that, he said:

"You're the fighter. I'm the smuggler. You break things, I hide them and keep them safe. We should each of us keep to what we're best at, or else the Wreck and the Witchroad are likely to get the better of us."

Kyrik relented quickly, as if he himself had had no thought yet of abandoning the others. *He'll learn,* Shigius thought, *or else he's already so good I can't tell.* The one who called himself Qabba Tek had nothing to add. Although Kyrik and Shigius spoke to each other in Saspian, he seemed not to understand very much of it, just as they struggled at times to understand his quaint diction. Perhaps it was for the best that he didn't get it all. Or perhaps he understood more than he let on, but sagely held his peace. Either way, he wasn't an oaf, and Shigius didn't mind having him with them as long as he was able to keep up.

"So?" Kyrik asked. He was awkward, unused to not giving commands. He wanted to get them out of the fort but didn't know how unless it was by bellowing down a chain of command accompanied by conch-blowers.

"Yes, let's," Shigius replied, and the three of them stepped onto the drawbridge.

The battle still raged in the not-so-far distance. Shigius was betting—and Kyrik, of course, was betting a lot more—on not a single one of the foresters living to tell of their treachery. He turned away without taking stock of how many dark flame-shapes of man, beast, and lizard were piling up around the battlefield. He hadn't caused this carnage for its own sake, and he had no desire to look at it or think about it.

Once they went around the corner of the fort, he could see the ocean, barely distinguishable from the grey of the sky. Of the ships Qabba's people had arrived on, there was sadly nothing left to sail, but at least the shoreline would guide them south better than the sunless skies and trackless plains of the Wreck. Prudence and a vague recollection of something genuinely witchy bade Shigius fear the journey ahead, but his heart wasn't hearing it. The pleasures and the profit at the end of the road seemed like more than a dream, and he felt young again, alert and fearless.

Mostly, he was buoyed by the thought that he had plenty of firebeetle now, even with the dregs of his personal supply forgotten in his saddlebags. The mere idea of a stock even better than Yaay's was almost enough on its own to carry him off. The little beauties seemed to have crawled right out of his fondest dreams and into his treasure-sack. The load, though great, was a delight bearing down on his shoulder, playing a sprightly tug-of-war with the hand that gripped it. His mind filled with puerile visions of endless wine, parading whores, ferocious merriment.

They stole away along the wall of Kom's makeshift fort, taking care not to be seen by anyone. Shigius, as most experienced sneak of the bunch, took the lead. A few paces along, a jet of the fire stood in their path. He led them around it, straying farther from cover than he would've liked, but reasoning that the consequences of being spotted could not be worse than stepping in the fire. As soon as they passed, the noise of the jet grew louder, rising from a whoosh to a roar. They all turned around at once, unsure whether the sound meant something to fight, something to flee, or nothing at all.

The jet had grown taller, from ankle to waist height, and the bright parts of its flame were much brighter now, almost blinding, though somehow still deep red in hue. The dark parts remained absolutely dark, darker than anything Shighius had seen outside of his blackest beetledream. As they stood frozen, momentarily dazzled by the display, the rock around the jet began to bulge and fail, as if pushed up by a force from below. One of the faults began to lengthen in their direction. It forked in two as they backed away from it, and another pair of cracks branched off just a handsbreadth or two below the flames.

"A person," Shigius said before he had finished thinking it. The faultlines were quickly growing to resemble arms, legs, a trunk, like a child's scribble of a man with the mouth of the jet as its tiny head.

Kyrik dropped his sack of treasure. His axe went up in a studied guard, but Shigius could see the grey blade trembling. Qabba Tek staggered back three paces and retched. Shigius froze, having no idea what to do.

The rock continued to crumble around the original faults. New cracks formed into shoulders, hips, jaws and an eyeless skull with a gaping, fire-spewing mouth. The broken rock kept bulging upward until it formed a figure like a white stone statue that had fallen and shattered but kept its shape.

Up to this point, Shigius had been wary of taking his eyes off the thing, but now turning his back to it was the only conceivable option. Kyrik apparently felt the same. He grabbed up his treasure and lowered his weapon, and they ran. Qabba Tek, unnoticed by Shigius, had already recovered from his vomiting and gotten a few strides ahead of them. Each time they passed another column of flames, they could hear it happening behind them: the roaring fire, the breaking rock.

But Shigius didn't hear footsteps close behind them, and after a while caution gave way to curiosity. Barely slowing his headlong hurtle, he waited for a clear stretch ahead, and craned his neck around.

Their pursuer appeared to be a man engulfed in fire. All day long, Shigius had seen men swallowed up like this, but until now they had lain as if dead, which he'd assumed they were. This one was up and moving with the gait of a healthy man, and just behind walked another like it, a bit slower, as if more encumbered, but not shambling or stumbling.

The second one was different, its head seeming to belong to some other creature, not a man at all; perhaps a goat or an ox. It took a few moments for Shigius to recognize the underlying form as a man's head in a horned helmet. Yharalon, too, then, had risen as a wraith to pursue them.

The poor fool had fancied himself some kind of noble stag, despite being as much of an outlaw as Shigius, and just as lowly born. For all his horns and fancies, he'd probably never imagined getting up from his grave as a fiery spirit to take vengeance on his murderers. That wasn't the sort of legend a would-be hero saw himself in.

But it was beginning to seem like a legend. Up to this moment he'd never considered Garong's "Dust of Rhll" as anything but the ashes of some poor orphan caught skulking around the college, a gimmick cooked up by the last person sent on the same fool's errand some hundreds of years before. But now elements of the tale began to return to him, a few lines of song and verse that he'd picked up without meaning to, the images carved or painted on Walthorian religious buildings. He had never really pictured a wraith before, faceless and featureless as they were. Now he wondered if he was dreaming, the way any child might have nightmares after hearing a fearsome story.

At any rate, it was time for a boost. He'd never taken live beetle before while running, but he somehow managed it. A costly bauble or two might have bounced out of the sack as he got the cage out, but other than that, he managed well enough. Opened with a thumbnail, the beetle released its essence for a revolting but welcome assault on his sinus. It was a hideous way to use live firebeetle, squandering much of its potency and leaving a sting that would last for days, but it got the job done.

Qabba Tek, already a devotee—Shigius didn't like the word *fiend,* at least when he was talking about his partners—managed as well, though he only had to crack and snort the beetle he was handed. It was enough to keep them running. Kyrik, the most fit of the three but the only one making the escape in armor, refused his portion. Some people, Shigius supposed, would always stand on their principles.

With a burst of speed from the beetle and the wraiths not running but walking after them, they soon gained enough of a lead to rest for a spell. As they squatted, raining sweat from their faces onto the bare white stone, Kyrik began to complain of an ache up and down the left side of his body. When he unbuckled his breastplate to clutch at his chest, Shigius knew something must be deathly wrong with him.

"Tell them in Glind," he said thickly.

Shigius moved in close to him. Though he didn't plan to give anything up to help the man, even if he could, his apparently dire state made him feel solemn and gentle and regretful of his less-than-exemplary life.

"Tell them," Kyrik gasped, twisting his tunic away from his left breast, as if the thin cloth were a great weight that was keeping him from breathing. "Take me back."

"Where do you want them to take you?" Shigius asked, his voice just a notch above a whisper.

"Mirsa."

He had named the goddess of the inner sea, asking to be buried in Her house. In his mind, Shigius quickly retreated from any such responsibility. Deathbed wishes were one of the few things he'd normally try to honor, but he wasn't about to die himself trying to drag this boulder of a man across the Wreck and the outland all the way to the Mirsatic coast.

"Nonsense," he cooed, with two different meanings in mind when he added, "no one's taking you back to the salt. You're going to be fine. You just need to catch your breath."

Within moments, though, Kyrik was dead. His body, it seemed, had been overtaxed by making such a run without help from the beetle. They said taking the beetle would kill you, and Shigius knew it would, but Kyrik's fatal error had been the opposite. So they cracked another shell apiece and Shigius grabbed the dead man's bag of loot, which they agreed to take turns carrying as they ran. If Tek prayed to Za or whatever god his people knelt in front of, for his own or Kyrik's or all of their souls, Shigius didn't hear it. For his part, the beetle itself was his prayer, though he was only taking enough to keep him going, not to carry him away.

And so they ran day and night, through dusk and moonrise and on into the next morning, never stopping, slowing only to take more beetle. Half the time they spent getting out of the Wreck, so flat and white it might have driven a saner man mad, with jets of lichfire growing sparser as they got farther from the center. Still, each time they passed one, another wraith would break the rock and rise behind them.

As the day faded, the white rock gave way to black lands where the lava had flowed after the Fist. They said it was pushed up out of the bowels of the earth by the same great force that flattened Sasp. The result was much like an ordinary eruption, the land all black and ashy grey, the surface jagged or mounded up in thick, ropy coils. The corpses here, ensconced in ash, did not get up, but still offered ample reason to keep moving apace. Their twisted forms were awful to the eyes.

Mercifully, night waited to fall until they were out of the scorched land, with dirt and weeds under their feet again instead of burnt rock. They stopped briefly to allow Shigius to light the coil of slow-match that he always kept under his hat for such exigencies. The match was so inundated with sweat that his flint-and-bronze was no use on its own, so he made a little fire of dry grass to get it started. And so it was that he finally got his chance to smoke the legendary beetle from the crypts of Old Sasp. He was in the middle of handing the match off to Qabba Tek when the lights of the world went out.

They would have no choice but to pause and dream a while, Shigius going off to visit his dead. There was a clarity to this beetledream, a substance he hadn't felt before, a brightness hitherto unseen. It was more crowded, too. Along with a swell of the faceless, a few recognizable people joined the rising ranks of the lost and the betrayed: a pair of young foresters he'd thrown chits with in camp; Kyrik, who had only wanted to complete his mission by any means; Irrian Taz dissipating in an elegant bedchamber.

For some reason, in this dream Irrian had a twin sister who had also fallen slave to the beetle. She smiled at Shigius with sad, famished eyes. He wasn't sure what it all meant, but at least one thing was verified: this was the best firebeetle he'd ever had, more than rivaling the stuff only Yaay could get back in Za'ar.

He returned to himself with a newfound vigor, ready to run without stopping for another full day or more. Tek seemed to feel likewise, his pale features all aglow, and Shigius wondered what things, what dead, what strange apparitions had come to visit him in his dream. They grabbed up their treasure-sacks, pissed out the last of the fire, and started again to the south. Shigius was glad again for the ocean, since he'd awakened with no other clue as to which way was which.

The wraiths were well behind them now, and their path had grown straighter, no longer tangled around lava flows and lichfire vents. Traces of Witchroad began to appear in the dirt: sunken paving stones, the cornerstones of what might have once been inns or roadside shrines. Without immediate hazards to distract him, Shigius began to wonder if he was still dreaming, the wraiths almost on top of him as he lay blissfully by the embers of his little grass-fire, running to the south end of nowhere but his own head. A beetledream could have layers, he knew, especially when one mixed different beetles, which he hadn't—as far as he recalled.

He thought back to before the first wraith had come up through the rock, to the last time he'd smoked before that. He couldn't say when it had been, which made him even more suspicious.

Whenever it was, it had to have been some really good stuff, better than the flour he'd had with him, to derange his mind like this. Had he smoked some of the stock from the crypt before leaving the fort? It would have been foolish to do so, but his past was far from bereft of foolish acts, especially ones done in the name of filling himself up with more and better smoke.

Supposing he wasn't dreaming, though, he thought he'd better remember as much of the tale as he could. The wraiths were supposed to follow the liches. There was something about that in the story, he was sure. They'd all fallen up into the sky together, liches drawing the wraiths behind them. Everyone remembered that much. When the foresters rode through Inirriu, he'd seen pictures of the scene carved into the walls—unless he hadn't; unless that memory, too, had been part of the same beetledream he was currently in.

He had trouble grasping how his mind could conjure so much of an old story he barely remembered, but he kept returning to the conclusion that what seemed to be happening must not be. The day before—whatever day that had been—he wouldn't have believed his own telling of it. He considered that the legend of Rhll might itself be part of the dream, a whole figment of his own diseased mind, untold in the waking world. This argument was an endless circle, though, because even at his most dubious, even when he was sure he was dreaming, the only thing he could think to do was keep acting as if it all were real.

That meant running, and running, and running, all the while retracing the steps that had brought him here, or hadn't. They were going in silence across a land long dead, so the only sound to distract him was the jingling of his companion's broken chain. Memories unfolded as Shigius imagined each version of himself that might be dreaming this.

Had it been in camp, the generous merrymaker throwing chits and passing a reed around with the outlander boys? Or the drunk leaning back on his bench in The Prow, the night before he left Za'ar? Or had it been earlier, perhaps much earlier? The teenage boy sent out of this world by firebeetle for the first time? His whole past, the decades of smuggling and skulduggery, began to waver in his mind like a once-doubted mirage, as if it had all been part of a fond youthful reverie, soon to end when his father called him down to the family dock to swab or haul something.

What finally brought him out of these gloomy and confounding calculations was their first sight of a tree. He had almost forgotten about trees, and being reminded of them made everything seem at once more dreamlike and more real. Before long they were in a forest: a witchwood to be sure, all sinister with glowering mossbeards and unfamiliar creeping vines, but still a sign that the most perilous parts, the parts devoid of all life, now lay behind them. Likely the trees afforded no protection at all from the wraiths, but Shigius felt much better under cover than out in the open.

Nightfall was again drawing near. He knew they needed sleep. The effort of running felt as easy as floating down a stream, but even with the best firebeetle, a body had limits. He'd seen many a fiend fall this way, just when they thought they could go on forever. The warnings against bedding down in witchy places weighed little against the certainty of collapse. The wraiths, by his reckoning, were half a day behind them by now, and the fire in their blood, even drenched with wine, wouldn't let them rest for very long.

"Qabba, friend, we need to rest." It had been long since anyone broke the silence, and his own voice echoed in his head as if it came from someplace else.

"I feel not weary."

"Nor do I, my friend. But trust me, we're in danger if we don't. You can only go so long on firebeetle alone."

This seemed to convince the old monk, or whatever Tek was, and they went eastward off the road, coming to a stop in a clearing under the arching limb of a giant oak. There they set down their treasure and started gathering fuel, breaking fallen branches against thighs and splitting long sheets of bark into kindling. Tek went about it like he'd never done any kind of work before, but followed along and learned quickly. The only food they had was the captain's field rations, which he'd had the presence of mind to put in his sack while all the others were thinking about was their loot. Soon, as the sky darkened from dull to black, they had the dead man's ricecake and dried meat boiling down into porridge over a bright and crackling fire.

Staring into the pot, Shigius tried to collect himself. The ichor was still lively in his blood as he stared into the flames, making everything around him seem to dance in a slow, ineffable circle while somehow remaining in place. His heart and limbs, relieved after lengthy effort, felt as fluttery as the wings of moths. There was only one known cure for this. The captain had been parsimonious in this respect, bringing just one skin, as a sober man does when anticipating the need to raise a toast or numb a wound. But Shigius had gone so long without a drink now that the wine would hit him as if he were a sober man.

"This'll fix us right," he said as he unstoppered the sloshing vessel.

Qabba Tek sniffed and sneered. "Thy drink hath turned, methinks."

Preparing to be devastated, Shigius brought the muzzle of the skin to his nose, but detected only the all-too-familiar bouquet of a military-standard imperial ricewine. It was brewed to dull the senses, not delight them. There was nothing great about it, but nothing wrong with it.

"It's good," he countered, wiping his mouth after a tart swig. "You need to drink some too, or else you won't sleep."

He passed the skin across the fire. Tek took it weakly, reluctantly, as if it were something dead or cursed.

"Go on, drink."

"In Moksa, the slaves that gather in our food press a potion of berries, that maketh them dance as if mad. On pain of death it be forbidden them, yet every year they dance."

The firelight smoothed over the wrinkles in his clean-shaven face, making Tek look like a spirit, not quite in this world and surely not from it. Shigius could see much reason to believe this truly was a man from across the ocean, from the lost homeland of the Saspiards. Even if it was all just a show, it was good enough for Shigius, and he was harder to deceive than most of the empire.

"Your slaves were making wine, of a rude sort. Here, it is not forbidden, not even for slaves, unless they steal it. It can bring men low, like the beetle can bring men low. But if you know how to use it, you'll find it beneficial to your, um, overall well-being."

Tek looked pensive for a moment, plausibly struggling to grasp the modern and Crescentine form of his language. Then, without saying more, he brought the skin to his lips and took a drink. He gulped it down grimacing, with great determination, as if a god had shat in his mouth and commanded him to swallow.

"You get used to the taste. Grow to like it, even, when you see what it does. Much like with the beetles."

"It tasteth of rotten things."

Shigius tamped down the urge to tell him that was because it was made of rotten things; *fermented,* if they were being polite. Chances were that he knew this already, but if Tek was putting

Shigius on, he could put anyone on. If they played it right, they could make a handy profit off the Silver Sillies back in Za'ar.

"It's safe. It won't hurt you unless you drink too much of it, and you're in no danger of that. I wish we had enough that you were, but we don't."

Tek had another pull at the skin and got it down with a bit less difficulty.

"The stench abateth." He took a third drink and gazed at his abdomen. "Doth it warm the belly? Methought a coal had caught, and this strange hide were smoldering."

Shigius grinned, and received something akin to a smile in return. They'd found Tek naked and chained; the "strange hide" was an old master's robe they'd discovered while they were looting. It was quite a stroke of brilliance to pretend unfamiliarity with woven cloth as well as wine. It fulfilled the vision of a harsh Old Saspia, an untilled country amid the primeval forests, where food was coarse, women were and wore nothing, and all of life was devoted to war and the rule of men over men. Shigius was already coming up with ways to turn this Silver legend into gold.

"Don't take more than your share, now!" he chided as Tek took another long drink.

For his part, Tek looked like he was about to speak, but instead remained silent as he passed the skin back. The only sounds to be heard were the crackling of the fire and the chirping of some unfamiliar creature of the night. It sounded like a cricket but with more of a warbling tone, as if a cricket had learned to bend its legs the way an expert player would bend the neck of her fiddle.

"Porridge is close to ready," Shigius said, after drinking again but before wiping his mouth on his sleeve. "With a bit of this and a bit of that in us, we'll have a fine sleep, though a short one."

For a while they stared silently into the flames, the glutinous foam overspilling the pot, hissing where it met the fire; the red embers creeping along the bottom of the wood. A tiny insect, not much bigger than a flea, landed on the end of Shigius' nose. *There's the old problem with a fire in the woods at night.* Brushing it away, he only managed to drive it halfway up his bridge. Another swipe and the bug scurried into his eye. It itched at first, but stopped after he blinked a few times and squeezed out a tiny teardrop. Another swig of wine and the irritation was all but forgotten.

When Tek received the skin again, he seemed to hold counsel with himself before he drank. His brows knitted, and he held the wine in his mouth for a long time, making Shigius unsure whether he'd started to enjoy the taste or was merely distracted. Then he drew a sharp breath and braced himself as if expecting a blow before asking:

"Be it custom for thy dead to breach the earth and walk as shades in flame and darkness?"

"No. Only in stories. Old stories, like the story of your people coming over the ocean. The singers tell them, but few think of them as they go about their daily business."

"Do the shades draw nearer as we sit?"

"Surely. But they walk, and we've been running. We have a few hours. Let's regain our strength."

Tek nodded. "The beetle calmeth. I sense it in my very blood. Thy potion be potent."

With a wry smile, Shigius took the skin back and sucked down a big, belch-inducing draft. The wine was more than halfway gone, and the night itself seemed to be settling. Whatever had been chirping had gone away or stopped. The dazzlement of his beetledream was fading, too, the toxic gyration of the whole world slowing until it was hardly more noticeable than its turning in a sober light.

His stomach gurgled and hunger soon followed. He dipped the captain's spoon into the bubbling pot. Even after a lot of blowing, the porridge was still so hot he could barely taste it, which was fine by him, since the rice had no flavor and cartlizard meat was foul. After a couple more bites he passed the spoon to Tek.

"Delicate," he pronounced after his first spoonful. "Thy meat be fit for a chieftain, thy meal of a seed unknown to me, but finer by far than the tall grass of Moksa that our slaves and wives gather in. Dost thou dine thus nightly in these lands?"

"Indeed, this is everyday fare. There's finer things to taste than cartlizard porridge!" He paused to study Tek's expression, noting a glint in his eye that could mean a number of different things. "You do understand we're going to be rich men, right? I mean, I wasn't short on gold before, or anything else for that matter, but now, we're going to be rich. Like the Luls or the Zatas kind of rich. We'll be able to buy anyone or anything we want."

"*Rich. Buy.* Thy words be strange to my ear."

Shigius drank again. They were nearing the bottom of both pot and skin. If Tek was putting him on, it was getting to be annoying. He didn't feel like explaining the concept of money.

"You know trading, right?" he sighed. At least the topic would help him feel tired.

"Indeed. When one chief hath much wood and little iron, and another much iron and meager wood, he maketh trade with him, and this be done under truce, for though that which belongeth to one endeth in the hand of another, it be not as war nor plunder, for neither suffereth, and none be the victor." He sniffed and added, "It pleaseth not the gods."

Iron, Shigius assumed, was the name of the white metal Kom's people used. But there would be plenty of time to ask about that.

"Here, you can trade anything for gold, and gold for anything.

When you have more gold than anyone else, that's when you're rich."

"The white copper? A word not spoken oft, for gold be dross. I know not why we carry so much of it. It cutteth not, nor can it halt a cut."

Shigius laughed. "Wait 'til we get to Za'ar, my friend. Wait 'til we get to Za'ar."

He kept repeating this in his mind as he drifted off to sleep with one eye on the dwindling fire.

A flash of light across his face awoke him. He'd had no intention of sleeping until daybreak, and before opening his eyes, he thought the captain's wine must have been drugged to put him out for so long. But then he saw it was still the middle of the night, long before moonset by the glow filtering through the treetops. Their cooking fire had gone out, so the light he'd sensed hadn't been that, either.

Then the night darkened, as if a cloud had fallen across the moon. Shigius tried to discern Qabba Tek in the gloom, but it would have been impossible to tell his figure from his sack or thrown-off robe, so low was the light. As Shigius' eyes were adjusting, there was another bright flash. Wide awake now, he could see the all-too-familiar redness about it. Under its illumination, the face of Tek was again made to seem otherworldly—this time, of some realm below—as he slept peacefully with his head resting on a rock and the master's robe tucked up around his shoulders.

"Wake up, they're here," said Shigius quietly, not knowing whether the wraiths could hear or not, nor if it mattered. He was just a quiet man, when it came down to it.

Qabba Tek rose at once, and grabbed up two sacks, his own and the Captain's, without being asked. Shigius considered whether to arm himself or keep a free hand. He chose the latter, since the wraiths, as far as he had seen, could not be fought with weapons. They left quietly, not knowing but not wanting to find out if their pursuers could hear. When they reached the Witchroad, cut clear and straight through the forest, Shigius looked to the north and saw the source of the light that had awakened him.

A mighty spruce, taller than all the other trees in the wood, had caught the lichfire, and stood in the night by the side of the road as a giant, unmoving, conical wraith. Below, its human-shaped brethren were advancing in a crowd so thick it made the road look like a river on fire. A few other trees besides the spruce had caught, all on the left side of the road—the side where their camp was. Tek seemed to notice this at the same time as Shigius.

"They follow not the road," he said. "They follow us."

Shigius didn't want to think about what the deceptively small difference between those two things might mean. He was starting to feel the dearth of beetle in his blood.

"We need to crack a couple of shells," he said. "No time for smoking now."

As soon as he reached into the sack, he knew something was wrong. The cage had a powdery coating that shouldn't have been there, and when he took it out, he saw that his hand was bleeding from a painless cut. When he realized what had happened, he almost dropped everything to fall to his knees and be sick. Lich or no lich, it was no good to have the dust of the dead on his hand, much less entering an open wound. But he wasn't letting his cage go for anything. He'd think of a way to clean himself once he had a little ichor in him. He was always putting off thinking until then.

So he expertly unlatched the tiny door with his thumb, opening it just enough to let two specimens out, then closed it with the same motion he used to trap the beetles against his forefinger. Again, something was strange; they'd emerged too quickly, as if pushed to the entrance before he opened it. He didn't recall them being crowded enough for that, not even close. After passing one to Tek and cracking his own, Shigius held up the cage to examine it before putting it back.

Sure enough, the beetles had multiplied, two- or threefold, since the previous day. He'd never seen such a rapid brooding in all his time as a breeder. Perhaps there was something to the Dust, after all; he could see where it had gone through the bars, and the beetles were eating it, just as they would eat of anything small enough to get in their mouths. Or perhaps it was in the nature of the strain to increase so quickly. At the moment, it hardly mattered, but if the little beauties kept this up in Za'ar, he could double or triple his prior dreams of wealth. He'd be richer than the Taz! *And have the whole fucking empire higher than the very walls of Palace Island.*

With the ichor draining nastily down the backs of their throats, the road felt easy again and they soon put a low rise between themselves and sight of the wraiths. This first undulation in the land was a sign they were nearing the mouth of Witches Valley, an unwelcome prospect under any other circumstances. But it occurred to Shigius that the old hags, who apparently had power enough to make an army weed their fields and dig their ditches, might best be left to deal with wraiths and lichfire while others, not so blessed, could slip away to safety.

The forest grew sparse as the road climbed higher. Near the crest of a hill, Shigius made the mistake of looking back. The wraiths were lighting up the road all through the forest and beyond, their awful glare fading, but not vanishing, where the night grew thick below the horizon. The straightness of the column was terribly purposeful, made even more alarming by the string of wraith-trees marking where it had veered off toward their camp. It seemed as if the whole population of Old Sasp had risen from the grave to come after them.

Tek was looking back, too, with fear in his eyes, the first time Shigius could remember him showing any such emotion.

"Tell me," he said, "tell me the tale. I must know."

Shigius knew which tale he meant.

"I'm afraid I don't know it well. There was a man called Rhll who came back from the dead as a lich, and the wraiths followed him."

"Where be this Rhll now, if he liveth after death?"

"The sun god burned him up and put his dust in the crystal tube with the gold at the ends. The captain was supposed to bring it back to his people. So much for that."

Shigius could see that Tek didn't understand all his words, but enough to start the gears in his head turning.

"So it be the dust they follow. Returneth this Dust of Rhll to earth, and to earth the shades shall return."

"We can try, but the damned thing broke. It's spread everywhere and the beetles are eating it. I even have it on my hand."

Shigius wasn't sure whether or not he believed the dust was causing their predicament. He certainly didn't want to believe it, if it meant leaving all his loot and especially his beetles. By Tek's look he could see the latter was just as unimaginable to him. Whatever they did, the cage was coming with them. In comparison, the gold and baubles he had stuffed in his sack were nearly worthless. Besides, they had the Captain's share to split, so with one sack less they'd be no poorer than when they started.

"So, we move the cage to the Captain's sack and leave mine."

It still turned his stomach to think of leaving all that for some lucky bastard, but he had to keep things in perspective. Even if none of this was real, he didn't want the dream to go bad. Men died from that, too; not from the beetle itself but from fear of things they saw in bad dreams.

Tek, still not knowing what money was, seemed indifferent to the proposal. Without ceremony, Shigius dropped the price of ten farms in the roadside dirt. He took the real riches out, a cage so full of life now that it vibrated in his hand, and tucked it carefully into the sack that Tek handed him.

They went on, load lightened by a third, hoping their sacrifice would end the pursuit but moving as if it wouldn't. Soon they had put enough terrain between themselves and the wraiths that they wouldn't be able to tell one way or the other. Up and down the road went, and the ichor was strong enough in Shigius' blood that he soon lost count of how many hills they'd put behind them. He didn't have a number in mind, anyway, since he hadn't bothered to memorize the route on the way up. Without at least the foresters at his side, he'd believed back then, he'd be as good as fucked anyway, so why bother to map? The idea made him chuckle now, for some dark reason.

Day was breaking as they reached the final ridge before their descent into Witches Valley, and there they paused to study the road ahead. The Roost was obscure but unmistakable, the dim form of a crooked spire rising above the waves in the greyness to the west. Just visible where the road curved around a finger of the hills that stretched almost to the surf, the first rays of dawn were twinkling like coins on the mouth of the little stream that fed the witches' farms and gardens. Shigius remembered the backbreaking work they'd made him do, and hardly looked forward to seeing them again.

"Witches Valley. Roost's yonder, but the causeway will be out until low tide. They're prickly old hags. They might know what to do about those." He pointed back with the thumb of his free hand.

"As for ourselves, I'd say it's best we just keep moving and hope they don't bother with us."

"Hags, thou sayest. This be a land of women?"

Shigius had never seen Tek look so aghast.

"Witches, yes."

"I know not this word."

"They're wise women. I won't say sorcery, but they know tricks. And things like that," he pointed his thumb over his shoulder again, "are more their business than ours."

Tek scowled. "A woman cannot be wise. She maketh not war, and from war cometh wisdom."

Shigius shrugged. "These ones have little need to make war. *Methinks.*"

At that, he started again down the hill, and Tek quickly followed. Despite the cool and the early hour, the meadows had already come alive with the sounds of tiny creatures, the chirps of some kind of locust, the buzz of bees or flies, the occasional sound of something larger blundering through the tall grass. It occurred to Shigius that what was making his own beetles bloom so vibrantly might be in the air here, infecting both wild and captive creatures. He could feel it in himself, too, an invigoration that entered him with each breath, beyond what the beetle provided.

He wondered, briefly, how he'd missed all this the last time. But then a tiny bee appeared just a handsbreadth from his face, falling back as he went forward, and he found it difficult to focus his eyes on anything else. Did bees fly backwards? He was sure his beetles didn't, and he didn't think he'd ever seen a bee do it before. But he'd never thought much about an insect that couldn't get him high or earn a profit.

He batted the bee aside—it was too small to worry him about getting stung—but as soon as he lowered his hand it was right back where it had been, in the perfect spot to keep his eyes crossed and blurring. Glancing to the side, he saw Tek engaged in a similar struggle.

"Fucking bees!" he spat, "do I look like a fucking flower to you?"

As soon as he said this, he realized he might indeed be starting to look and smell like that other bee favorite, a pile of rotting meat. *What a state to be in, he thought, richer than a god and scummier than the lowest tramp.*

His eye began to water, just the right eye, and he vaguely recalled something flying into it, though he couldn't remember what or when it had happened. This made his vision even blurrier on one side, while on the other, the bee looked bigger and sharper, as if viewed through a glass. For the first time in his life, he was looking at an insect that seemed to be looking back at him, just like any animal that had ever looked at him, shrewd and inscrutable.

Its wings were working so frenetically they looked like smoke puffing out from its tiny thorax. Shigius could hear the distinct sounds his ear would normally combine into a monotonous droning, the clicks and clacks of every minuscule member striking each other. As the road began to flatten at the base of the hill, the noise of the other small creatures around them grew louder and more insistent, filling the air as well as the underbrush.

The road curled around the base of the last escarpment, edging into the sand along the shore. The sun was higher now, high enough to catch the ocean water, and Shigius wanted to pause to breathe in the air. He'd never felt nostalgia for home before, a place of endless toil and the penetrating stink of rotting sea life, which wasn't weak here, either. But his sojourn in the Fistwreck had been enough to make a man homesick for anywhere.

He kept his pace, though. The bee seemed to pull him along, like a lizard and a cart, the one little more aware than the other of the forces that were coupling and impelling them. Around the bend, the warm air of the valley replaced the ocean's cool breeze. With the change in temperature came a new smell and a rumbling under his feet.

The smell was like a pasture or a livestock market. He didn't remember pastures on the way up, but they wouldn't have been out of place in the valley as he did remember it. Really, though, it was more like a circus, the fragrance from multiple varieties of beast pissing and farting together under a huge tent. And it wasn't just wafting on the wind; the air seemed to be saturated with it in every direction. He strained to look past the bee, up the stream and into the valley to see what was raising such a stench, and making the earth rumble so.

To his surprise, the bee acommodated him by flying out of the way. Even more shocking, it looped around his head once and flew into his ear, going deep inside before he had a chance to react. He slapped at his temple and cheekbone, yanked the lobe around, dug in with a finger or two, forgetting what they were dirty with. The buzzing continued and the itching deepened as the insect remained alive and restless in his ear canal. Out of the corner of his eye he could see Tek making similar gestures, with just as little apparent success in dislodging the invader.

Without pausing to ask why two bees would behave in the same strange way, Shigius studied the route ahead. Not far off was the ford, with a rope strung across it for use as a handhold between the two ruined abutments of what had once been a wooden bridge. The tide was falling back, and past the breakers he could see hints of the causeway, the sunken rocks in lines too straight to be reefs. They were practical people, these witches, he thought—and mostly, it was a comfort to think they were people. If they were everything else they were said to be, they'd have no need for causeways or ropes to get across the water.

Beyond the stream, the road veered inland into the now-familiar landscape of Witches Valley, rising gently toward the next range of hills. But his view was obstructed halfway up the slope by a great herd of animals, just as he had suspected from the rumbling and the odor. He could see they were of many kinds, the tallest among them showing their distinctive shapes—long-necked draftlizard, gleaner, tusker, memuel—in silhouette against the morning sun.

He'd never before seen so many animals nor such an assortment of them in a single place, not even at a circus. It seemed impossible. To begin with, the gleaner should have been attacking everything around it, and everything around it stampeding at the sight of a gleaner. Instead, all were advancing at an even pace with the sparest gaps between them, more like an army of trained men than a herd of wild beasts. The animals covered the road and the rest of the valley from edge to edge, the mass parting around shade-trees and haystacks and the witches' huts and barns like water in a rocky channel. To get around them, or let them pass, Shigius and Tek would have had to climb far into the surrounding hills.

In the midst of his gawking at the spectacle, the bee in Shigius' ear had fallen silent without him noticing at first. He suspected it had suffocated, and wondered what could drive a bee to such a foolish course of action. As far as he knew, people were the only animals that killed themselves on purpose.

Tek was staring aghast at the herd, unable to speak. But his question didn't really need to be asked. For the moment, Shigius had no thought that the man might be a fraud. He wanted to explain things as best he could, for his own benefit as much as anyone's.

"No, this isn't a thing that happens here. I've never seen

anything like it before, no more than you have."

Tek looked at once relieved and disappointed, relieved that something so nightmarish wasn't routine, but disappointed that Shigius understood it no better than he did.

"Darest we attempt to pass betwixt yon rats and lizards?"

"Darest ye?" Shigius snorted. "I daren't, for my part."

"So we needst must take to the hills. To which side?"

"Seaward. At least if we get lost we'll have the breeze to tell us which way's which. And, we'll have the breeze."

By this time, they'd reached the ford, but felt no need to use the rope-hold because they found the current weak and sluggish. Still, Shigius put his feet in with trepidation, since the water had gone nearly black with excrement from upstream. He'd never seen a river so soiled, unless it was with blood from a massacre.

The dankness of the air was beginning to cancel out the invigoration he'd been feeling, and even some of his beetle-strength. One sack of treasure felt heavy now where two had felt like nothing before. He got out of the river on the other side all muck to the knees, and added fatigue to the list of deadly things attempting to overtake him.

A footpath leading east presented itself between a field of seedling gourd plants and a fallow one. There was no cover at all, but Shigius wasn't concerned about being seen. If anyone was defending this valley, they had much bigger problems on their hands than a pair of wandering rogues.

Though the herd drew nearer by the moment, he hadn't heard the sound of a single animal, not the squeal of a tusker nor the bellow of a big draftlizard. There was something, though, a delicate hum, at first mistaken for a reprise from the dead bee in his ear. It sounded like a song, a chant, but a brain on firebeetle had a way of turning random sounds into music. That was one of the things he'd first loved about it, long ago. Or was it long ago? His doubts fluttered back, but the path of soft clay, the rumbling of ten thousand claws and hoofs, the stink in the air, all felt more real than anything he could remember.

He was already deep in confusion when he looked up from his feet to see the witch standing before him. She had appeared out of nowhere, or perhaps he'd been looking down and brooding for so long that she'd had time to walk up. With his sense of time curling up like the ends of an old wooden plank, Shigius had no idea which it was, but the creature standing in front of him surely looked like she'd come from the realm of tales and dreams. She wore a blue-grey robe with a hood that came to a point at the top, like the shape of the Roost, and flaring sleeves big enough to conceal all sorts of charlatan's gear. Her face was the oldest-looking face he'd ever seen. At first, he thought she was a haggard old fiend, which might have explained her missing nose.

But Shigius, of all people, knew what the fiend-rot looked like—he was always checking his own reflection for signs. It didn't look like this. Instead of a pocked scar or a festering wound, she had parchment skin stretched neatly around her skeletal nostrils. Her eyes seemed to float in empty sockets, dry and fleshless, the balls held in place only by tightly drawn lids. It was impossible to tell what color they were were because something made it impossible to look directly into them. Her mouth was just a downturned crack in the striated surface of her lower face, where a concave chin gave way to reptilian wattles that in turn disappeared into the shadows of her robe. Shigius was thankful he couldn't see more.

He'd seen a valley witch before when one set him to laboring on the journey north. He remembered her as a woman, old, strange, but not as old and strange as this. With that recollection, the droning sound he'd been hearing came clear as a chant, a chorus of frail voices singing in a familiar-sounding but unintelligible tongue, the sense of the words hanging just out of reach. Something twitched in his ear as he strained to understand. It seemed the bee was alive, after all.

"Set down those bags."

Her mouth hardly seemed to move but her voice was in his ear, as if the bee were speaking for her. He couldn't say what language she was using, but he understood it perfectly, better than Saspian, which had all but become his native tongue. Stranger still, he found it impossible to defy her, despite the tiny, fragile person she appeared to be. His treasures, even the precious cage of beetles, landed in the dirt with a thud. A moment later he heard Tek's do the same, but didn't see it. He could neither take his eyes off the witch nor look directly at her.

"We'll turn back," Shigius said, "we never meant to trespass. We'll head back north and find another way."

"Don't be foolish. Show me your hand."

He knew without being told that she meant his right hand, the one he'd cut on the shards of the vial. As soon as he opened it to her, the witch began to spit on it. Her spit came yellow, in a thin, precise stream, and burned like strong liquor in the wound. She didn't stop until she'd gotten between each finger and under the nails. Then, a huge green beetle crawled out of her mouth and went under her hood.

"It's clean now. I won't have to cut it off."

Even without the insect to obstruct it, her mouth didn't move much when she spoke. Her tone of voice, if indeed it was her voice, was matter-of-fact, neither joking nor threatening as she spoke of dismemberment.

"Is that why they kept after us?" Tek asked.

He spoke the same tongue as the witch now, without a hint of his usual quaintness. Like the witch's, Tek's voice seemed to ring in Shigius' ear, not the air, and his lips were moving, but not in time with his words.

"I hope it is," she answered.

Shigius thought he saw an opening.

"Milady," he began, "you are possessed of great power. Your eye sees more than a mortal eye sees, you command the creatures of the world, and it seems you could have killed us long ago, by snakebite or the gods only know what other means. Why not? Why let us live if we've brought this curse upon you?"

"I knew Rhll as a man. You think that was long ago, but to me it was not very long. My whole life, perhaps, but an instant compared to all that can be seen. I was a brewer, a healer, an apprentice, a simple country girl. That's what witches were in those days, and we were everywhere. You could find us in the lowlands and the places where people gathered. The Dragon didn't whisper to us then, not yet.

"I was first to see the fire, what it did to the people. I was first to hear the whispers. When I began to listen, when I began to see, I vowed to protect all life against the lich and his ilk, and human life above all other forms. Perhaps," she concluded, "that was my mistake."

"You bring the beasts to halt the wraiths," Tek observed, "but that will make more wraiths of them."

"My sisters call them with their song, my bees carry the song to their ears, and I mourn for each that will be lost. But I see no other way. The wraiths must stop here and go no farther. Beasts or men will die, so I call beasts."

A long silence followed. Shigius tried with all the strength of his reason to doubt that this woman was thousands of years old, that she commanded swarms of bees and had "sisters" that sang in the language of animals. But he could not. The truth of it was thicker all around him than that of everything else he'd ever thought he knew.

"You gape as if I've told you a secret. There are no secrets here. If these things aren't taught to every child, it's the work of men, not witches, that keeps them hidden."

"That's a pleasant surprise," said Shigius. As his opening came more sharply into view, he could feel sweat forming on his upper lip, soaking his raggedy mustache. "Too many people in this world have too much to hide."

"Indeed," the old witch said, and Shigius might have detected a wry note.

"In your benevolence," he continued, the sweat at his temples now, "I wonder if you would spare us one thing: our humble curing beetles. I admit I came here for treasure, but above all, I came for this medicine. It will come as a great relief to my people."

"What ails you? I can cure it at once," she said, the wryness now coming sharp and clear.

"Not for me, mind you," he said, his armpits turning to swamps, "I'm well. It's for my people, far to the south. I'm much like you, you see. I can't bear to see my people suffer."

"But I saw you take the beetle. Thrice you took it, once by fire and twice in your nose."

"That was only to prevent fatigue as we fled the wraiths. They would have ended us if we stopped to rest."

The lies were starting to burn his skin, despite its chilling coat of perspiration. He'd never found it so hard to lie to anyone before, but he'd perish in the struggle before giving up the truth. To be kept from lying was like being kept from breathing.

"Your beetles have touched the Dust, and must remain here. I cannot clean them as I cleaned you. But they are simple things, not hard to make again. Not like my bees."

Shigius could think of a lot of things to say to this. *How about a couple thousand fresh ones for the road, then, if it's so easy? How'd you like to come work for me in Za'ar?* When the cause was lost, it always came down to mockery. He knew now there'd be no changing her mind, and they were as good as dead without their beetles. How much worse could she make the situation than it already was? Yet something kept him from mocking her, something like fear. He'd never met a captor he was too scared to chide before.

"If that's all, milady," he said, making his first empty-handed step toward the hills to the east.

A spread of grey, bony fingers blocked his vision and his way.

"No. You go south."

"I'd rather you killed us here, by whatever means, than had us trampled to death."

"The beasts won't harm you. Walk between them. Go, and be gone."

He was still standing stiff with aversion to what she'd asked of him when Tek began to speak again.

"When there are no more animals, and all are turned to wraiths themselves, then what?"

It was a good question. For the first time Shigius was able to look directly into the hag's eyes, and he wished he hadn't as soon as he did. They were the most frightening and uncanny eyes he'd ever seen, light and dark parts in all the wrong places, centered around two rings as black as the blackest phase of lichfire, which seemed to point nowhere and bore into him all at once. But they carried all the old familiar signs of human fear. Fear, and sadness, too—a sadness much deeper than he was used to seeing in the heartless brutes that circled around him.

"I said, be gone!" the witch screamed. Her voice, though it

seemed not to come from her body, wavered on the edge of tears.

To drill her point home, the bee in his ear buzzed so loudly it doubled him over. He thought he'd been stung at first, but his pain and dizziness resulted from vibration alone. Not wishing to discover what more this little invader might do, Shigius lifted his feet, as if from a mire, and began what seemed like a brutally long trudge down the footpath, back to the Witchroad and into the face of the herd. The bee stopped its droning at once as soon as he started to move. But each step put him farther from his beetles, and each was heavier than the last.

When they reached the road, the herd was already upon them. In the front rank, a family of giant ground sloths were going along on all fours, setting the pace for the quicker animals behind. At a distance, there had seemed to be hardly any space between the files, but up close Shigius could see there was ample room for a man or two to walk between them.

Yet he stood as if paralyzed, his body's aversion to what it needed to do overpowering his mind's aversion to defying the witch's command. The buzzing started again, goading him forward, but instead he endured it, waiting stupidly for the herd to come to him as the droning wracked his brains. Tek had also stopped, and his look was one of even greater horror than Shigius felt, as if he'd truly never seen such creatures before.

The two parent sloths lumbered by as if they hadn't noticed so much as a shape or a blur in their path. Shigius had never been so close to giant sloths before and felt a new respect for the northmen that lived by hunting them. Yet they were nowhere near as alarming as the cave sqee that followed their young, a manlike biped twice the size of a man, with shapeless lumps where a man had joints and muscles. It was the kind of beast that was seen chained in a pit if it was seen at all, but this one walked with the dull docility of a peasant going about his daily chores, paying no mind to the men or beasts around it.

The droning in his ear grew stronger and more menacing, so he began to move to quell it, though still not trusting whatever sorcery was guarding them. The current of bestial movement produced its own hot wind, and walking into it felt like swimming against a stream. Shigius resisted an urge to grab Tek's hand, to pull him along and be pulled along, as if two could march with greater ease than one. The passing beasts ranged from great to small, mundane to strange. Most looked like natives of the outland forests and farms: camprats and hairy antelopes, red oxen, cartlizards, wooly goats.

After a while Shigius grew inured to them, startling only when the biggest and fiercest came into view. The gleaner walked tall as an obelisk, its huge, clawed arms looking tiny on its body, its teetering head like the prow of a ship made of teeth. Soon after came a pair of shovel-tuskers, not the largest of pachyderms but certainly the ugliest, with their namesake bottom teeth protruding at crotch height from bloody, painful-looking gums. When a wild draftlizard approached, a long-necked brute the size of a temple with legs like rumpled columns, Shigius was afraid that, even in its gentled state, its girth in passing might sweep them off their feet. But the wide part of its ribcage turned out to be much higher overhead then he'd imagined, and brought only a moment of welcome shade.

The day turned hot. As they went deeper into the herd, the dung on the road grew thicker and thicker until it was like a layer of pavement, canceling even the faintest hope of stepping around it. The stench was fiery, belaboring the lungs.

Shigius was starting to remember all the things firebeetle would make him forget about—drink, food, wellness, and rest—

the common concerns of a common humanity from which he was accustomed to absenting himself. If they ever made it through this herd, they'd be without weapons, rations, or a single skin of water for the road. Tek didn't even have shoes, and Shigius winced to watch the filth soaking into his bloody feet.

There was no end in sight, even as the road began to rise. Withdrawal was hitting at the worst possible moment, but every time he faltered, the tiny monster in his ear would start its tune again, torturing him into constant forward motion. A breath of fresh air would have been as welcome as a noseful of good flour. Almost.

Surely, he told himself, *the old hag has to run out of animals at some point.* But that only got him thinking about how many animals there were in the world, wild and tame, from the great herds of the East Saspian lizardfarm country to the packs of brutes ranging across the uncharted expanse of the Wilderland. That wasn't even to mention the parasites and scavengers, the multitudes of crawling things that turned up wherever others left their refuse.

The herd might have stretched all the way to Za'ar, for all he knew. Even from the crest of the hill he couldn't see the end of it. In truth, he couldn't see much at all with his view blocked by massive, lumbering forms in every direction. The downslope came as a welcome change for his aching legs but an ominous one, as it meant the power of the witch must reach beyond Witches Valley. The places south of there, which he'd been warned against so many times but couldn't recall in particular from the journey north, turned out to be completely overrun with marching animals and presented no other obstacles.

The shadows were long and the evening air had grown cool before they caught their first glimpse of open road ahead. The last of the herd was a sickle-tooth panther, a grizzled male with protruding ribs and swaths of mane lost to scarring. To Shigius, it still seemed unreal for a starving predator to walk by him without interest, but the foulness of the air and the soreness throughout his body had long before driven off any notion that he might be dreaming.

As soon as the panther was behind them, there was a tickling and a puff of air, followed by a hollow feeling in his ear. The bee was gone, and with it the chanting. He could hear two bees buzzing off toward the herd behind them.

They were left with a river of shit for a road and no chance of making Inirriu before they collapsed from exhaustion. There was no place to camp. But there were trees.

"Ever sleep in a tree before, Qabba Tek?"

Shigius awoke under a blue dawn with bark up his ass and the fiend in his belly raging like a half-slaughtered ox. His entire body itched with grime. It wasn't the worst bed in the world that he'd made on the fork of a huge walnut tree, but it wasn't a good one, either. The worst might have been the one Tek had chosen, a nearby branch where he'd spent the night sitting up against the trunk with dangling legs and most of his weight on his crotch. Shigius guessed he'd passed out from sheer exhaustion at first but not slept much past midnight. He was lucky himself to have made it nearly to sunrise, but his luck didn't add up to feeling rested.

Had he ever been so dirty before? He'd spent months in a dungeon and weeks in the bilge of a tramp galley, caught the pox from whores of every stripe in more ports than he could name, but he'd never felt such a filthy itch on every part of him. It was worst in the usual itching spots, but strong everywhere. If vermin were the cause, he must have caught them from the herd, since he hadn't shared close quarters with people in a long while.

More than likely, he'd developed a rash from the miasma of all that dung. He could picture the particles in the air chafing his skin. Yaay would have known what to do about it—Yaay with her oils and ointments and tinctures next to her flour-dabber and water-pipe and accounts tablet. He promised himself he wouldn't laugh at her the next time she told him he needed a chant and a deep soak.

His escalating thoughts of Yaay were interrupted by a loud and familiar snort. He looked over and knew at once that Qabba Tek had cracked a beetle. He was flicking the remains of its carapace off the end of his thumb.

"The what? How did you—" Shigius couldn't find the words to express his outrage and wonderment.

By the time he answered, Tek was already halfway down the tree, leaping from branch to branch with the spryness of a freshly glutted fiend.

"The beetle returneth in the night," he called up without looking back, "his kind hath taken board upon my person."

Just as he said this, Shigius felt the itch creeping up his neck and into his beard. Without finishing the thought, he caught the beetle and cracked it open. As its vile ichor drained down the back of his throat and into his dessicated nerves, the itching all over his body turned to pleasure. His limbs craved motion, and, with a joyous whoop, he joined Tek in descending the tree with apelike efficiency.

It was a miracle: the beetle had *returneth*. He was sure these were the very ones the witch had taken from them. He didn't think much about how it had happened, or why. Yaay talked about beetles flying to her, so maybe he'd finally become a sage like she claimed to be. He did know enough about beetles, after all. His only thought was to get his hands on a cage as soon as he could, before they flew off to the next wizard.

Although the road was buried in shit, and both hills and ocean were too far away to see, they could tell which way was south by the first rays of sun. They started for Inirriu, looking, Shigius hoped, like the two least interesting tramps in all the outland. Beneath the filthy rags they wore, their skin crawled with riches.

The dung thinned as they went, with patches of grass and even a paving stone showing itself here and there. The tracks grew more distinct, and Shigius marveled at the variety of hoof-, claw-, and pawprints and the straightness of each trail. He could see where individual beasts had joined the herd from places off the road, their tracks meeting the others at perfect angles. They looked like they'd been measured and laid by a carpenter, with compass and protractor.

But the witches, the herd, the wraiths, the uncanny things were all behind them now. A whiff of fresh air breached the stink. Shigius caught another beetle under his sweat-soaked collar and felt so happy he had to stop himself from bursting into song.

The plains gave way to a rolling hill country, the road veering westward to find the lower places. Here the last traces of spoor led away from the road and into the hills to the east. He realized the animals hadn't been following the Witchroad, but rather going north in a straight line, as if guided by a star. Certainly, the lack of a road would pose no obstacle to them, and their dung had done quite a job erasing all benefits of a road for carts and men.

Shigius let out another cry of delight when he saw the first farmstead. He knew better than to go bothering outland farmers to strike deals and build cages, but the neatly stacked hay and the smoke rising from a stone chimney reminded him of all the good things that awaited them in the world of men.

"Wherefore thy jubilance? Hast thou proof the shades no longer follow?"

Tek's look was as plain and grim as ever. Shigius had long since stopped thinking about the fiery horde. Surely a sorceress who commanded all the world's beasts could easily dispense with such dead, mindless things. He'd been thinking only of Za'ar, the pleasures that awaited, and the long road home.

"Proof? No, nothing like that," he conceded. "But if the wraiths were still pushing south, we'd be seeing more animals on the way to replace the ones they've turned. I think the hag must've buried the Dust and stopped them in their tracks."

Tek had nothing to say in response. As always, Shigius was unsure whether he didn't understand the words, didn't want to say what he thought, or simply had no thoughts. This man, wherever he came from, was going to make an excellent rogue.

The settlements grew denser on the outskirts of the first town called Inirriu, but Shigius wanted to reach the second Inirriu, the unwalled one with its open trade in sorcery. He pictured better prospects there for bargaining a few of his beetles into a cage for the rest of them, a pack of provisions, and, in the name of all the Gods of Men, a pair of shoes for Qabba Tek. Perhaps a couple of coursers, too, if the price was right. So he led at a brisk pace, even as they passed an outlaw tavern and several encampments of the kind of men they currently resembled.

Well past noon, within sight of the town's tall palisade, they saw two boys preparing to mend a fence by the side of the road. The fence belonged to an empty corral of split logs, attached to a little cabin of similar construction. The boys, in clothes as roughspun and brown as their home, were dragging a freshly cut young spruce to the spot where the old rails lay splintered on the ground. Shigius guessed it was the work of stock-thieves.

"Need a hand, lads?" he asked, thinking a bit of news might be worth a cup of sweat.

"We've nothing to give you, sir."

"That's good, because I want for nothing."

By this time, the boys had set down their ropes and were eyeing him suspiciously. He must have looked like a man who in fact wanted for everything.

"How'd this come about?" he asked, showing his ugly teeth in a friendly grin.

"Our buck broke the fence. We never seen nothing like it. Just walked right through it with the strength of a draftlizard. Our pa went up after him," the boy's head motioned toward the hills to the east, "but he's got nothing to ride, of course, so good luck catching him."

"Was he mad? Did he gallop off?"

"That's the fuck of it," said the other boy. They were close in age, but this one was the elder, greasy with pubescence and reveling in his own obscenity. "He weren't mad at all. Calm as can be, went off at a trot. But there weren't no stopping him, either."

"I think he got stung though," the younger boy put in. "Heard bees just before."

"When?"

"An hour ago, 'round midday."

They both felt it immediately. Qabba Tek's face dropped like a dying man's, and Shigius could feel his own doing the same. They clutched at their chests, their wrists, squeezing themselves foolishly as if they could stop it from pulsing through them. The boys, relieved to find their accosters were madmen, not robbers, went back to their labor as the men shook and sweated and stared at each other in the middle of the road.

They understood now why the beetles had returned. They felt

the thing they were becoming. The Dust of Rhll was in them, and the lichfire would follow wherever they might go.

And yet they would go home.

EPILOGUE

It was a new moon over the semicircular bay called Yeguadda, and the Mirsatic cuttlefish fleet had taken every available spot on the water. Garong was annoyed with himself for seeing beauty in the night scene, the beacons on the water like gently drifting stars. *Poetry and shit. Fucking memories.* He'd spent far too much time around the "men" who taught at the college.

The flux had been the worst thing he ever faced. Through much of it, he'd believed he was already dead, in some kind of hell that entailed ceaseless torture of the bowels and buttocks, the places he'd always imagined receiving eternal punishment whenever the concept arose in conversation. It all fit together neatly in a way the world never did otherwise: the things he had done, the things he was suffering, the endlessness of it.

But the pain subsided when his flow turned to clear water, the sign of recovery or imminent death. Coming out of his coma he could vaguely hear the others discussing this and decided he couldn't care less which it was. When he awoke, it was sunset over the cuttlefish station, and Yeguadda Bay was filling up with ships.

After a draft of weak ricewine and a few spoonfuls of thin gruel, Garong felt he might live. Sitting up in his pallet to gaze on the lights below, he noticed for the first time how much the shed stank, an aroma of salt and rot and smoke so thick he felt like it was trying to get into his ears. He began to fidget where he sat, restless to move, eager to get home.

"No chance of sailing out tonight?" he asked his pilot.

"Not now, not with a Salt Folk crew. You don't disturb a fisherman's patch. It's our law, and right now there's less of that bay that ain't in a fisherman's patch than I got ship."

Garong shook his head. He liked rules, except when they got in his way.

"It'll clear out before first light," the pilot assured him.

Garong really had nothing to worry about. It wasn't his fault he'd abandoned the mission. They couldn't blame him if anything had gone wrong in his absence. Or so he believed.

Besides, what he *had* done counted. He had gone to the Fistwreck and returned to the world of men. Because he was the first, his name would never be forgotten. Garong would be listed in the scrolls of history with the names of the great explorers and conquerors. That counted for something.

He had survived the greatest rite of manhood. He had been a soldier, led an expedition. He had seen the Witches Roost, and how many men could boast of that? He had done so much. So much of it counted.

Tutor Garong was almost pleased with himself.

THE END

PRONUNCIATION GUIDE

Aga	AH-guh
Asb Aq	AZZ-back
Azag	EH-zag
Capaz	kuh-PAZZ
Cim	tsim
Cucuthian, Cucuthi	kuh-KOOTH-ee-uhn, kuh-KOOTH-ee
Dhular, ,-i, -ite	doo-LAHR, doo-LAHR-ee, DOO-lahr-ite
Ennenia	en-EN-yuh
Garong	guh-RONG
Gihha	GWEE-ha
Herrin	HAIR-in
Hhule	HWOO-lay
Inirriu	in-EAR-ee-ew
Irrian	EAR-ee-un
Khlokhli	CLOAK-lee
Kyrik	KAI-rick ("Ky-" rhymes with "eye")
Lul	lool
Min Khune, Khunen	min-KOON, min-koon-EN
Mirsa, Mirsatic	MERE-sah, MERE-sat-ick
Naihard	NAY-ard
Nydhia, -n	NID-ee-uh, NID-ee-un
Oo'ogrin	ooh-WAH-grin
Orthox	OR-thocks
Qabba Tek	COBB-uh teck
Rhll	ruhl (with u somewhat swallowed)
Sdubb	ztub
Shadaghi	shuh-DAWG-ee
Shigius	SHIG-ee-us
Smatt	smat
Taz	tazz

Torkiz	tore-KEYS
Uthu, -an	OO-thoo, oo-THOO-un
Vixprin	VICKS-prin
Vydhmia	VID-me-uh
Yeguadda	yuh-GWAH-duh
Yharalon	YAIR-uh-lon
Yizian	YIZZ-ee-uhn
Za'ar	za-AHR
Zata	ZAH-tuh

www.ingramcontent.com/pod-product-compliance
Lightning Source LLC
Chambersburg PA
CBHW070527100726
47907CB00004B/1017